Childforever

OTHER BOOKS BY IAN McCULLOCH

Moon of Hunger (Penumbra, 1983)
The Efficiency of Killers (Penumbra, 1988)
Parables and Rain (Penumbra, 1993)

Childforever

A Novel
by Ian McCulloch

THE MERCURY PRESS

AUTHOR'S ACKNOWLEDGEMENTS

Much thanks to Ken and Ursula Stange, Denis Stokes, Dorothy Coffman and especially
Janet Calcaterra, who so willingly allowed themselves to be submitted to early drafts.
Also to Beverley Daurio at Mercury for her thoroughness and care in editing the
manuscript. Her dedication to the work was wonderfully gratifying. Finally, to Mabel
McWatch, my grandmother, and Alice McCulloch, my mother. The strength and
dignity with which you live your lives has always been my inspiration.

The publisher gratefully acknowledges the financial assistance of the Canada Council
and the Ontario Arts Council.

Cover design by Gordon Robertson
Edited by Beverley Daurio
Composition and page design by TASK

Printed and bound in Canada by Metropole Litho
Printed on acid-free paper
First Edition
1 2 3 4 5 00 99 98 97 96

Canadian Cataloguing in Publication Data

McCulloch, Ian
Childforever
ISBN 1-55128-035-3
I. Title.
PS8575.C83C45 1996   C813'.54   C96-931713-1
PR9199.3.M37C45 1996

Represented in Canada by the Literary Press Group
Distributed in Canada by General Distribution Services

The Mercury Press
137 Birmingham Street
Stratford, Ontario
Canada   N5A 2T1

In memory of W.C. "Mac" McCulloch,
who was everything a father should be
and more.

ONE

I woke to rain this morning, to rain drumming on the metal roof of my old car and running in torrents down the fogged windshield, flowing in sheets down the square side windows, making everything appear ambiguous and indistinct. The highway was a dark smudge off to the left, a black clot wavering on the close horizon of my opaque vision. I woke to rain and confusion and I started talking to the rear-view mirror. In retrospect, this seems to have happened to someone else and it helps to say it out loud.

When I looked in the mirror and saw those eyes, they were the only thing I had truly recognized in a long time. I'm not really talking to the mirror. I'm talking to the person behind those eyes, someone I remember from a while back. William Sawnet. Single. Happy. Will Sawnet. Small-time journalist in a small-time city.

When I think of him, I think of the way he looked above the "Bits and Business" column on page nine. Visible from the knot in his tie to the part in his tidy hair. A young man with a pleasant smile, slightly round face, neatly trimmed mustache, and dark-framed spectacles for that all-important intellectual demeanour— even though he'd switched to contacts years before. I can remember his orderly desk, his shined shoes, and even his favourite table at the Fish House Restaurant. He was an amiable man. A nice guy. Easy to talk to, and decent. Always the best choice for human interest stories.

He knew how to listen. Or he liked to think he knew how to listen, how to get a handle on any situation. He believed this strongly enough to fool the people to whom he was listening. To fool even himself. Now, I'm regaling him with the short sad history of the past couple of months. The Moon of Frogs. The Moon of Berries. The Moons of Sorrow and

Lies. One day, when Will Sawnet knows where he is again, it may all make sense to him.

Last night I became frantic with a compulsion that had me looking into the rear-view mirror every few seconds. Checking the side mirrors. Twisting my head to look into the blind spot, then into the darkness of the car directly behind me. From time to time I flicked on the small overhead lamp and the car became a bubble of light speeding along the black tarmac until my face, reflected in the windshield, became too wild with fright to bear. I drove on and on through the night, haunted by my headlights, cutting their relentless swath of straight-ahead light.

I am tired and confused and without any kind of clear destination. I need to see some precise instruction on a green billboard in fluorescent white letters like the glaring, ivory grin of reality. The answer written out in abbreviated highway language so I can catch it flying past at one hundred kilometres an hour. The quartz-halogen illumination of the right direction. *This way, Will Sawnet. This is the right way. This is your redemption.*

I want an arrow to point me towards rest, if only for one pristine moment. That single beautiful second when everything will keep its proper distance and even time will hesitate and allow my lungs their full measure of air. A moment to truly get my bearings. Or at least to come to some sure and sudden end. A closing that might speak of destiny, if that's not too naive an aspiration. Dreaming has entered my prosaic sleep; sometimes in fragments, strange images of birds and animals and unknown faces; sometimes in coherent episodes that seem lifted from another lifetime.

The night before I left on the journey west I had been sleeping fitfully, anxious to begin and full of trepidation for what lay ahead. I'd been reading a lot about native history and tradition. I've learned that dreams have their own treachery. In my life before, when I knew myself only as William Sawnet, dreams were vague and faded quickly when I woke. This was more. The images were articulate and precise and they shook me.

I was a captive. I stood beside a white stallion, surrounded by savage comic-book Indians armed with bows and arrows, their faces painted and their mouths set hard. My perspective kept changing in the dream, circling above as though I were a bird, or watching from a helicopter. Still, I could see details: the horse's huge eyes, the white shirt I wore, the gleaming metal tips of the arrows aimed at my chest. We seemed to be in a peculiar maze of hedges and small bushes. There was no speaking. No sound at all. Then I could hear the breathing of the horse, low and steady in the beginning, like a man sleeping in a quiet room. It began to build. A little faster, a little more forceful. Everyone stood frozen, listening to its rhythmic pulse. Faster. The hot breath blowing against my face. Whispering in my ear. Faster. Steady and powerful. Hot and urgent against my neck. Like an engine building. Winding up. Compelling. Run, it said to me. Run now while the wind is in my chest. There were only the flint eyes and the drumming of the horse's heart and then I made my lunge, grabbing the pale tossing mane and swinging myself up. Arrows cut the air around me, one sinking into my leg, the white horse kicking out then gathering the ground under its hooves and exploding up and over the hedge. We jumped barrier after barrier, dodging and weaving through the low brush, razor-edged metal like insects in the air around us. Fierce, painted warriors were everywhere in the blurred landscape.

Suddenly, the stallion missed a jump and we were tumbling to the earth, sprawling in the dust, both of us wounded and breathless. I saw myself stand up and brace against one of the green leafy barricades as the dark braves surrounded me, their bows drawn. When the taut strings snapped with release and the cruel shafts flew, I woke in the darkness of my room, cramped and sweating with terror, my hand clutching at my leg. I clawed at the tangled blankets and pulled myself out of bed, grunting and limping around. My foot was asleep, the painful electric tingling shooting up through my shin. I kicked at the air, groaning and grimacing, at the same time amused over the preposterous romantic vision of the dream and puzzled by its overwrought hostility and pain. Now a part of me longs for that kind of definitive finish. A courageous flourish, that is memorable if nothing else. That proves you were worthy of living. Instead, it seems I am always going back the way I have just come, closing the same tight circle.

Yesterday, the dropping sun suddenly became a bright affliction reflected into my weary eyes. I had been on the road over sixteen hours and I pulled into a roadside rest stop to relieve myself and wait for the sun to sink behind the horizon. It was a flat, cramped place of levelled gravel and mowed grass and frail little trees supported by twisted wire legs.

The park was deserted except for an older couple eating lunch at one of the dull brown picnic tables. They had covered the obscene graffiti carved into the wooden top with a plastic tablecloth that had thin pieces of elastic sewn across the corners to hook over the edge of the table so it wouldn't blow away. White tupperware containers were spread out on top and it was easy to imagine the little tubs holding a nice selection of meats and breads and condiments. I could see they were a couple who had reached an age when they had all their problems solved before they even came up. Emergency funds, extra medical insurance, and pre-purchased grave plots.

Their immaculate motorhome was parked nearby, and a diminutive black poodle with neatly trimmed fur and a red bow around each ear was yapping under the table. Just two old companions with their four-legged surrogate child seeing the country. I didn't look their way as I got out and headed to the outhouse marked MEN'S.

Maybe I hit my head when I walked into that stinking cubicle, slipped on some greasy spot on the putrid floor and smacked my skull on the black rim of the toilet. Perhaps, just as the stretched spring regained itself and slammed the thin door behind me, a bubble of blood burst in a cramped, defective vessel somewhere in my brain. Things changed in there. The past came roaring up out of the dark fetid vortex and set me spinning. Or maybe I'd been spinning all along, picking up speed until I reached a critical velocity. The universe tilted. Time, order, everything, shifted a few millimetres, shuffled a few degrees. When I opened the door, nothing was the same.

I stepped out into the sunlight like someone who'd been kidnapped, knocked unconscious and left on foreign soil. Another freed, confused hostage with unused, expired blocks of time spilling from his pockets. My head was reeling. The old man watched me over his tuna salad sandwich. The door banged closed behind me again, like a gunshot in that quiet mundane oasis. The effete dog took up its frantic barking. I felt dizzy and as though I were vibrating, every molecule oscillating, undecided between two different dimensions. It might simply have been because I hadn't eaten for at least two days. The only nourishment I'd had was warm pop.

I stumbled against the car and ran my hand along the edge to find the handle. I wrenched the door open and lost my grip. The door bounced back on its hinges and half closed on me as I bent to climb into the seat. I started the car and in my confusion turned the key twice so that the starter whined and gnashed its teeth. The old man stood up, watching, in the unabashed manner of old men. He said something to his wife and she looked my way. I looked back and I saw my own parents. I stared. It was them. Mona and Wilfred Sawnet, having lunch on the prairie in the shadow of their silver motorhome. They had come to meet me. I raised my hand to greet them and then I remembered that Wilf was dead. I whacked the car into gear and stepped on the accelerator, spraying gravel and dust on the twin outhouses as I wheeled around and headed for the highway. I slammed on the brakes just as I reached the asphalt, sliding halfway across the lane with the tires screeching.

I was lost. I couldn't remember which direction was the right one. I looked to the left and then to the right but none of it made any sense. A van swung around the front of the car, tires squealing and horn blaring in one long abusive blast. A woman stared at me with her hands over her mouth, and the driver shook his fist and mouthed obscenities. My hands gripped the steering wheel. Tightened on it. Shook it. Tried to wring direction from it. My leg was convulsing. I held the brake down like someone who had come to the edge of a cliff.

I looked in the side-view mirror. The old man, my dead father, was jogging towards the car with the little black poodle on a leash. It was yapping and yapping and running in circles, the tether wrapping around the man's bone-white legs so he had to stop and coax the dog to go the other way every few steps. With every passing second my trepidation grew. He was a familiar ghost and a stranger. He was coming for revenge. He was after an explanation of my betrayal and I had none. *What's wrong with you, son? William, why do you have to be that way?* I never had an answer. Not when I was growing up. Not now. I would only look at my feet and feel something below my stomach crack open and empty out. Feel my limbs drain and grow weak. Feel the chambers of my heart wither and feebly pump the thin residue of my blood. I cranked the wheel to the right out of sheer desperation, and sped away.

Rain in the morning. Rain and all this confusion cluttering up my head and making it ache. Rain the first time I saw her. A deluge is beating out its hollow tattoo on the roof of this feeble hunk of metal that I call a car, and the puzzles are like storms percolating inside my skull.

A crumpled mass of coloured paper lies on the passenger seat beside me. Once, it was a road map. The red tracing of my journey home. Everything laid out precisely: the highways, the secondary roads, the rail lines, the lakes and rivers. A black dot for every little town and all of them named in meticulous, immaculate lettering.

Last night in the dim interior of the car, the map had lied to me and refused to cooperate. I found where I had started from the day before. Moving my finger across the map I found the place I had left before that, the place I had fled and left behind. I've spent my whole life leaving places, travelling from town to town and base to base. My father was in the Air Force and we were like the other Service gypsies, always packing up and moving on, the house perpetually full of crates and cardboard boxes. Friends and neighbours dropping in to say, *So long, see ya 'round.* Then it would be the three of us together in the front seat of the car. Mona, Wilf, and William. Everything we owned in a moving van on the highway somewhere. Our lives reduced to road signs and streetlight hesitation and songs to pass the time. Our friends growing microscopic in the distance.

How did I end up here, at the centre of this confusion? Even a journey of a thousand bewildered miles starts with a single muddled step. I guess with me it was walking away from my father's open grave.

I thought Mona held up pretty well considering everything. I don't understand how you go on from waking up next to your partner of forty-four years and finding they're just not there any more. I thought she was just being Mona. Ever strong. Ever ready. Always sure of what to do. I was selling her short. Sometimes we can hide from our own weakness by magnifying the resilience of others.

She knew the moment she woke up. That was why she hadn't turned on the light. She made coffee and while the hot black liquid dripped and hissed into the pot she stood in the hallway outside their room and asked what he wanted for breakfast. She asked three times, waiting for an answer, her hands clenching and unclenching in front of her, shivering in her pink robe. He always set the thermostat in the morning. He ordered his breakfast, went to the bathroom, came out, checked the weather channel, and then set the thermostat for the day.

She waited a long time before she phoned for the ambulance. After she hung up, she sat at the kitchen table and waited for them, for the official word. She didn't want to see him, she told me. Every night they had kissed and said goodnight and lain together under the amiable darkness of the house they had waited so long to own.

At the wake, I walked around, solemn and important in my dark suit. People nodded at me. Men mumbled awkward tributes to my father.

Women held my hands and offered sympathetic looks. I met relatives and familial acquaintances that I hadn't seen in fifteen years. People slapped my back and hugged me and spouted the inane helpless things people spout on such occasions.

"He looks good, doesn't he?"

"He was a good man."

"He had a good life."

"You're a good son."

"It's good he didn't suffer."

"He loved you as if you were his own."

"Pardon me?" I was in the middle of nodding and smiling for the hundredth time. My hand clutched at the knot in my tie. A tiny, bent woman was looking up at me through moist, blue eyes.

It was Auntie Regina, my father's oldest sister. Grey and withered and somehow not of this world. She had always seemed ancient to me, angular and tight and constructed of something more rigid than bone, more impenetrable than flesh. When my father told stories about when they were growing up, I always visualized wizened, little Regina riding her bike off the dock at the cottage. Crooked, fossilized Regina punching out the bullies who picked on my father in grade two.

"Pardon me?" I repeated.

The recalcitrant curve of her spine made it hard for her to look up into my face. She reached a pallid, trembling hand to my cheek. It came slowly, wavering, like a snake mesmerizing its prey. When her cold fingers touched my skin I was afraid the vitality would be siphoned right out of me.

"He treated you like blood. Not everyone would do the same." She spoke in a slow, reassuring way, then coiled back into the hunched figure life had made of her.

"No, ma'am," I agreed, not knowing what the hell she was talking about and staring down at a dark mole on the back of her neck. I wanted her to go away. Mona came towards us, her face pale and her lips set tightly together. She took Regina's hand and led the old woman away.

"Regina. It won't do to have you on your feet so long."

The crowd parted as they approached, the dark stick-woman and my mother. Little short steps. The thick dark cane and then the feet. The thick dark cane and then the feet.

The night is a posse.

Lathered flanks and worn leather. Blood-toothed spurs and the wind slashing through the dark like wet rawhide. Heavy hooves pounding the shadowless earth, riding hard on the heels of the fleeing moon. The dry prairie is mute and seamless. Enigmatic gopher holes sigh like small, open mouths, drinking in a dream of invisibility. Grey swirls of ancient cow shit lie odourless and veiled. In daylight, they dot the rolling ground like the corrupt bodies of so many fallen stars. Above, the sequined sky is too crowded to be taken seriously, still winking out a private history of light.

It is a dimension of prosaic spectres, wind devils and dusty apparitions scraped from the dead flora, the white talc of bones turning in the earth for a million years, spinning somewhere in the deep black soil, in the yellow slaughterhouse wind. Through the green blades of the endless grass, decaying over and over into a blasted kinetic existence, a black history of blood is squeezed flat and nurtured by huge inky rollers: an ancient rendering of night worn thin and pierced with pinholes of light. A brittle whisper skims over the bristled earth, over a landscape compressed by its own inelegant mythology. A land of fossils and footprints. Of broken stone jungles and dead sea bottoms turned to dust and petrified memorabilia. A place of white skulls and grazing, where buffalo once ran for miles like a wild black river. Pursued, sometimes, by a people who had come across a white tendril of frozen time fleeing the frozen earth. Seeking a land big enough to hold their visions. They chased the frenzied buffalo. Driving them on. Leading them along a path of magic and deceit until the animals plummeted over the brink, falling through their own terror to the rocks below. Their heads cracking open with surprise. Their brains spread on a sudden sharp shift of history.

But The People walked their own precipice. They failed to see the signs. To read the strange medicine. To see the one they would come to call Trickster tying the long thick cord of their days to the tails of the plunging bison. When history zigged again they too were pulled over the edge.

Childforever flashes past all of this. He is a confused splinter of time skating over the prairie, a fragment of his own blasted past spinning through the aggregate night. A retreating sojourner. A travel-stained vagrant fleeing his own memories, he is a shadow gliding through the time of dreams as the prairie night flows around him. A flat and moonless dark that rolls across the bow of his travelling. A night buried in the past. As dead and lost as driven nails. There is a steady flow of sad music, a repertoire of maudlin songs, and he cannot help thinking of one lying in another darkness. Under a different sky. Sleeping in his abandoned bed and moving farther and farther away. Drifting deeper into the distance that will drown them. He leans forward to look up to the stars but there are no recognizable constellations. No road signs. Only the dark asphalt singing as tires roll over it, the notes echoless and swiftly buried in the wake of miles left behind. Lines and shadows and the rolling humps of prairie hills barely visible. They are like great whales breaching thick, slow waves in a sea that swallows all sound.

Somewhere, deep in the stretched womb of this night, in the heated wake of this fleeing, shadows begin to coalesce. A shape forms from mist and wanting and fragments of the broken past. Legs rise up out of the earth like stalks, a body blossoms out of the dark. A head appears in a shaft of moonlight, long snout sniffing the road. The scent is rich with fear and with blood. Coyote begins to follow.

TWO

I waited almost a week before I questioned my mother about what the old woman had said. Mona had enough to deal with but Aunt Regina's words wouldn't go away. At first, I thought Mona was trying to hurt me, to punish me for being so difficult and so inadequate in offering comfort. Perhaps, I reasoned, she was angry because the last decade or so had been marked by a deepening chill between my father and myself. We had been courteous and cordial but distant; we weren't a demonstrative family to begin with, and I could never shake the feeling that I failed to measure up to being the man my father expected.

"Oh, come on," I kept saying.

Mona insisted it was true.

"Who were my real parents, then?" I asked. She winced. I should have said "my biological parents," I suppose, but it was all a shock. I had no idea what the protocol was.

"No one knew anything about the man... who fathered you, except that he was white."

"White?"

She looked into my eyes and then away again. "Your mother...was an Indian— I mean a native Indian, not an Indian from India— but we don't know much else. The government had taken you away from her. She used to... imbibe. We were looking for a baby and you were so cute. Not Indian looking at all."

I looked at Mona. My mother. Or so I had believed for thirty years. She looked frightened and small, fingers trembling against her lips.

The year I was ten, for Hallowe'en I had wanted to be Chingachgook, the silent and sure sidekick on *Last of the Mohicans*. He was inscrutable, stoic, and brave, possessed of some secret knowledge about the world that even Hawkeye didn't have.

Mona had turned an old pair of Wilfred's work pants into fringed leggings and cut a loin cloth from some rough brown material that had once been curtains. She made a headband with three brightly coloured feathers and even sacrificed an old wig to make two long braids that she stapled on either side of the headpiece. I pulled on an old tan shirt that belonged to Wilf, and Mona used lipstick to put a couple of short red stripes across my cheeks. I played in the costume for the rest of the afternoon. When my father came home I jumped out from behind the chair in the living room.

"How," I said solemnly, holding up my right hand.

It was the one and only time he clouted me. He whacked me so hard the headdress spun off my head and hung down the side of my face. One of the staples caught in my real hair.

I stood stunned and blinking at him. He pointed a finger at me. "Don't play the idiot with me. Don't start that Indian crap in this house." He was beside himself with rage. "You wipe that garbage off your face and get to your room and stay there," he bellowed. Mona came rushing in and we almost collided as I hurried off to my bedroom, fighting back tears. I stayed in there the entire night, listening to the neighbourhood kids coming to the door and calling *Trick or treat.*

Later, my parents argued. My father banged his fist on the supper table. "What the hell is the matter with you, Mona? Painting him up like that." He said it with such vehemence that I was afraid for my mother.

"It's just a kid's game, Wilfred. For heaven's sake," she said. "No one knows."

"I know, goddamnit. I can see it..."

"SHHH!"

Hushed disagreement continued for some time, but I couldn't make out their words. I had always assumed, later, that the lipstick on my cheeks had set him off. Too much like wearing make-up. I rescued my headband from the garbage the next day when my father was at work and kept it hidden for weeks before I actually had the courage to put it on again. Chingachgook now had an even stronger pull on me, the mystery deepened by my father's reaction and by the bitterness I felt over missing Hallowe'en. I began to suspect that there was more to it than a couple of streaks of red lipstick.

I began to watch my father the way I imagined Chingackgook would watch an enemy. Often spying on him, hiding, with the stiff braids resting on my shoulders like a conspiracy. I studied Wilfred Sawnet and came to know his mannerisms and what a hard and serious man he was. He seemed to find no joy in anything and it puzzled me. He mowed the lawn in straight row after row. He washed the car, dried it with a shammy, waxed it and polished the chrome. Every day of the week had its own meal. Sunday was a roast and Monday was leftovers. Tuesday was meatloaf and Wednesday was macaroni casserole. Thursday was chicken and Friday was fish. Saturday, Wilf made hamburgers. In the summer he barbecued. He rose every working day at seven, showered and shaved with the house silent around him. At seven-thirty Mona got up and started his breakfast. He sat at the table and ate with his black tie knotted tightly around his throat, drank his coffee, put on his uniform jacket and left for work.

I wonder at it now, at his living the same week over and over all the time I was growing up. I would stand at the sink in the bathroom after he had gone and lay my hands on the cool white porcelain and smell his aftershave, a ghost in the air around me. My only answer, once I had grown bold enough with my watching, was to slip out the front door and into the woods across the street. I wore my headdress and romped through that cramped overgrown lot, a jumbled haven of crippled trees, brown needles, and dirt. I mumbled words in my own Mohican tongue, coarse, guttural phrases of terse intent. I smelled changes in the weather, put my ear to the ground and heard the approach of enemies. I talked with my brother the bear and made war on those who meant me harm.

My friends came along and we developed into a tribe of our own. We became Mohican Blood Brothers. I taught them the words to say and we sliced our palms with a shard of glass and grasped hands, one by one, mingling the essence of our lives. I grunted a made-up Mohican Blood Brothers phrase and we drifted back into the trees where we had constructed a rough fort. I gave each of them one of the garish feathers from my headdress and these we stored like holy sacraments near our crude outpost before going home for band-aids. While the thin cuts on our hands were still scabbed, we met every day and practised our invented language and stalked the woodlot for game and renegades. Then the bright feathers began to wither and got broken and the scratches on our palms became thin white scars. The weather became too cold for crouching in the woods and what was left of our feathers was lost under the first snowfall. We found other things to do.

"Your father had been transferred back east and we were set to move. Everyone assured us you would be much better off. When we went to pick you up they said your birth mother was dead. She had been drunk, walking along the highway and struck by a car. No one stopped. After that, we never heard anything, and we raised you as our son."

"Do you have papers?"

"No. We did, but Wilfred never showed them to me. He destroyed everything years ago. Your father never wanted anyone to know."

It was easy to picture him near the blackened metal drum in the back yard, even though the fire would have happened long before we settled here. Flames licking up over the rusted rim, his face set hard, as he burned away all evidence of my past.

One afternoon, a month or so after Wilf's death, I sat staring at the monitor at work, unable to write a single line. I had been relegated to the simplest local stories only the day before— until such time as I had my shit together— this was how the city editor had bluntly explained it to me. I looked at the blank, expectant screen for half an hour without typing a single word. Everyone buzzed around me, busy with their assignments, avoiding me as I sat frozen in my chair, overwhelmed by the very effort of being there. I turned off the monitor and walked out.

My apartment was suddenly a cold and alien place. When I slept there I had to leave the lights on and I avoided the black spaces of the blank windows. I was afraid of the face I might see floating behind them. I became aware of every odd noise and fearful of closed doors. I left my apartment and moved into the house to look after Mona. I had been spending most of my time there anyway.

For the first few weeks, living back in the house was great. I told my mother nothing of what had gone on at work and let her believe that I was on an extended leave. The managing editor phoned a couple of times and then the publisher. They were very understanding and offered to keep my position open for a few months. I thanked them for their kindness and said I probably wouldn't be back.

Mona and I sorted through Wilf's things, and reminisced, and I managed a few minor improvements and repairs around the place, little jobs I had put off because Wilf would have been looking over my shoulder the whole time. When I was finished he would only have offered advice on how it could be done better. I had questions I wanted to ask Mona but I never managed the courage to speak them.

Then things began to sour. Mona was more interested in looking after me than the other way around. She insisted on waking me at seven-thirty every morning. It was important, she said, to have a routine. Plenty of time to have a shower and eat the hot breakfast she had prepared and relax with a coffee while she told me about her friends and their families. About all the minor tragedies of the neighbourhood in their complete historical context. Plenty of time, even though I had nothing to do all day but run the trivial errands she had planned for me. Mona was determined to amend the moral decay that had come from my living alone for twelve years. I fixed the eavestrough while she attempted to repair my self-discipline. She set out my clothes, ironed my shirts, and picked up after me. No matter how many times I asked her not to bother, she still cleaned my room and straightened up in the study where I read and worked. She condemned my habits and my reading material, and even threw a few books into the trash. They were smutty, she said.

One night, as I lay in the dark of my freshly cleaned room, between neat just-laundered sheets, I saw an escape route, not just from Mona's solicitude, but from the morbid ennui that had descended over me since Wilf's death.

I would dig into the mystery of my roots. I became possessed by the energy of the idea. I lay in the darkness and tried to feel Indian, to find some ember in myself that I could hold against the dark rumour of my past.

That night the dreaming began in reality; it seemed like something much older, familiar and dredged from the deepest sanctuary of memory.

I am watching through the eyes of a child, intent upon the soft brown face of my mother. My own face is unknown, buried too deep in childhood to be recognizable. It is a stranger's face, without distortion, and clean in a way that only a child's face can be.

The boy is gazing up and his mother is bent over, holding his hands and spinning around him so that the sky is a blue whirling wheel and the ground a soft green blur. *Husha*, she is saying. *Husha. Husha.* They are turning around each other and the universe is turning around them. Faster and faster. *Husha*, she is singing. *Husha. Husha.* It is like a prayer. An invocation for continued mercy. A thanksgiving on a warm summer's day, in a pleasant back yard. She is dressed all in white. White blouse and soft white skirt. Her face is brown against the endless cyan sky. There is no sound but her singing. The boy is lost in the song, dizzy with the warm turning. He sees her face, her mouth, the moving lips, but her voice seems to float like feathered dandelion seeds in the palpable air, to emanate out of the green earth, out of the dark mystery of his mother's long hair. She turns and turns and everything turns with her. Behind her, he sees the tall grey house and, instantly, I know that house, its deep foreign closets, its solemn brown rooms and solid doors, its long green hallways and scarred linoleum. The sombre oval portraits. The heat of the fragrant kitchen. The grey happy shapes of the people who live there. I feel that house spinning like an awkward, tilting planet. Around and around through black space with its porch light still on. Still there. Waiting for me.

We all fall down, she sings merrily. *We all fall down.* Happily. And she is in slow descent towards the deep grass, lifting the boy so that it seems he has taken flight. He spreads his arms and levitates into the soft summer air, hovering above her as she lays her body underneath his small form. Then he falls to her chest and she rolls over and over again and they are both laughing until, breathlessly, she holds him close. He can hear her heart pounding, her quick gasping as she forces air into her compressed lungs, while he pulls his weight into her with his small arms. She has one hand against the side of his face, holding him down, and he feels his eyelashes brushing like insect kisses against her moist brown throat. The boy opens his hand and in it, shimmering and golden, there is a tiny gold cross on a chain.

I awoke with a sense of things splitting open, like some B-movie where a huge, ominous crack has appeared in the world, a deep black void that has snaked out of the past and altered everything. Mona and I had pushed the pieces together and covered it up as best we could, but it wasn't holding. I wondered about my true history, about this fragmented dream that possibly was the only memory I had of my mother, the only one in which she truly existed. The others had all been rumours given to me by someone else, hearsay of a woman I did not know and could not visualize. Her drinking, her failed love, our forced separation, even her pathetic death were all without corroboration. All ugliness, except for this. This dream of ghosts and lullabies.

I left the rest stop, barrelling east, driving wildly. I checked to see if I was being pursued, and found that the mirror had become twisted towards me so that I was looking into my own fear instead of the distance behind me. Maybe I'd turned it when the sun was reflecting so harshly off the glass, or accidentally in my clumsy attempt to get in the car. At any rate, the apprehension and dread I saw in those familiar eyes made me laugh out loud. "What the hell's wrong with you?" I asked. I eased off the gas pedal and my heart rate slowed down. I was sweating profusely and trembling. I tried to get my bearings from the passing scenery.

It all looked the same, the same rolling landscape, the same brown brittle fence and withered posts rising and falling along the roadside. The same poles and the unchanging black wires measuring off the fading blue sky. I was travelling in the same direction I had been going before I stopped, but couldn't escape the feeling that I was driving over the identical piece of road again and again. There were only my hands on the wheel, the prairie repeating itself in all the windows, the radio gnawing on the bones of a fading signal, and the dull morse code of painted yellow lines. I buried myself in the routine of driving.

I passed through a damp refuge of choked swamp split by two lanes, and suddenly the highway was littered with little red blisters of fur. Prairie dogs were everywhere. They dotted the pavement, scampering back and forth across the lanes. This way and that way, each seeming to ply his own vector of self-destruction, running along the highway like tardy commuters after a bus, standing up on tiptoe for a better look at the undercarriage of death. Many of them were feeding on the smashed remains of their tribe. The small bodies burst under the tires. I tried swerving to miss the first few, but it was hopeless. They were unavoidable, darting from the sides of the road, crippled and squirming on the hot pavement, twitching in death throes, perched like Romans along the asphalt edge.

Cars and trucks roared over them and they exploded in ballistic curiosity, flattened into what looked like the ragged, red footprints of some willful demigod dancing in a gory frenzy. A clumsy, brutal celebration for this short, dry season of death. I began, suddenly, to cry, a quiet weeping without sobbing or any real sound. Tears ran from my eyes as I drove, gripping the wheel and feeling each writhing brown body pop as it was crushed under my wheels. There was nothing I could do but hold on and look down the road and wait for it to be over.

The next thing I knew, I had pulled over on the side of the empty highway. The place names on the road map meant nothing to me, and I couldn't remember the last town I had been through. I had the idea that its name started with *Sp* and some sense of the syllables that made it up, but nothing on the map matched up with the vague shadow of sounds clattering around inside my head.

I checked the index and I ran my trembling finger the entire length of the route I thought I had taken, my tongue curling against my teeth in an effort to make the right noise. None of the names fit. I did it again and again. Each time it seemed less familiar. I ran my finger through the cities and black dots of towns and across the borders merging with other highways, and then I read place names I didn't remember seeing before. I began again, but when I went back to the point of origin, that name seemed somehow changed. I said *Spartan* out loud and it was as if I had never spoken it before in my life. Close, but counterfeit. Twisted or altered or mispronounced.

The more I tried to puzzle it out, the more enraged I became. The muscles of my forearm tightened as my finger jabbed at the map like a bird pecking at a squirming insect. I swore and cursed. Now I would settle for nothing less than the image of my own battered wreck parked somewhere along the careful diagram with a label saying *You are here*.

I tried to relax and clear my head. I started to fold the map, but I was slipping over the edge into hysteria. I slapped my hand into the creases to make it fold but it bunched hopelessly. I wrenched it open again and tried to follow the obvious lines, but it pinched up along some wrinkles and flared out against the windshield. It became the bird, large and panicked, fluttering and flapping huge delicate wings. I wrestled it and tore at it, squawking like a madman, and when one wing flopped up and beat against my face I bit it. Finally, I threw my weight on the map, smothering it against the seat and crumpling it into a ball under my body.

I sat up and rested my forehead against the steering wheel. A bit of the map was still clenched in my teeth, and I could taste salt where I had bitten my own lip. I spit the stained paper onto the floorboard between my feet.

A storm was just beginning in the dusky sky above me. Two huge rigs rolled past on the shrouded asphalt and their headlights poked weakly into the thin darkness where I sat, hunched and foolish. My little car rocked with their passing, heaving on its decrepit suspension in a slow metal trembling. I mumbled curses into the vinyl padding of the steering wheel, and let them drip slowly from my swollen lip.

A curse for the approaching darkness. A curse on my own absurd hands. A thousand curses on the heedless giants roaring past in the halogen-blasted night. Tormenting me. Rocking me. Wearing me down.

In the weak grey light of a rainy morning, the map looks small and pathetic. I pick up the twisted, torn mess, turn it slowly in my hands, and study the red and blue veins of its bloodless corpse. The colour-coded skin of its treachery. There is nothing there for me. I have been left without destinations. I roll the window down an inch and force the mangled map through the opening, out into the rain, out onto the road where the wind catches it and sends it rolling like a spooked rabbit, the entire country crumpled around itself and bouncing ass over tea kettle down the wet highway.

Coyote is travelling in the dark. It is windy and the clouds are like mountains running in front of the moon. The wind tugs at Coyote. Pulls at his ears. Squeezes his heart with a wild, rapid pulse. Then he sees the dancers. Swaying and swinging in the scattered light. Hears the rustle of their ceremonial clothes and he joins them. No one can dance like Coyote. He whirls and capers and leaps about. He wants to out-dance them all.

All night he dances. While the moon travels and the clouds circle, he dances. Till his tongue is hanging out and his legs are trembling. He is in a trance, staring at the ground, trying to keep pace with the celebrants. When he realizes the sun is finally up and he raises his weary head, he finds himself standing among a field of bullrushes.

A truck roaring past jolts the car and leaves it in a wet fog of spray thrown up from the churning wheels. I watch the truck's blurred image shrink into the distance, and reach for the key in the ignition. Time to move again. Now, though, it is only a matter of leaving.

THREE

The first time I saw her it was outside the Red Clay Cafe, a simple building with an angular painted facade and roofed front deck trimmed in red. The cafe was low and rectangular and made of nondescript cinder blocks. A wooden sign out front bore letters hand-painted in crimson. I had pulled in behind the wheel of my compact, ruined car and opened the door into the same cloud of thick dust that had pursued me for thirty miles. Rough, curving miles that twisted through endless bush.

It was a kind of road I had never been on before. A road that appeared to have found its own way, slithering through thick stands of bush, shouldering around sudden rock cuts, and slipping past chaotic swamps where black, bony trees fought to maintain their balance. The road dropped away impetuously, leapt up in a spine-numbing row of abrupt bulges, or turned back on itself in long viscous curves rutted with washboard. Huge logging trucks materialized out of nowhere, rumbling down the long hills towards me, their immense, cumbersome loads of limbless trees rocking menacingly as they roared past, the cloud of dust behind them rolling up like gritty surf and smothering my wheezing car; the road, for a few seconds, merely a stony rumour rattling under the wheels as my tormented red heap fishtailed and bounced and chattered its complaints.

It was a lost, forlorn road, thick with jeopardy and loose stones. Every so often there would be the rusting carcass of a battered old car overturned in the ditch, or half hidden where it had cut a swath up into the trees. I had just about given up on arriving anywhere alive again when I saw the weathered sign: RED CLAY CAFE 5 km. A little further on there was a second sign: RED CLAY CREE INDIAN RESERVATION, and underneath, Red Clay Indian Band.

Mona had remembered the name Elsie Whiteduck and that she was from somewhere in northern Alberta. I had driven to Edmonton, bought a map, headed up north, and picked this place at random. I studied the reserves and Métis colonies marked on the map. Red Clay seemed north enough, remote enough, a good place to find Indians. Red Clay. Red Man. White duck. What the hell, it was as good a place to start as any.

I didn't bother with official channels. I wasn't ready for that. I knew they didn't have the kind of information I wanted. There would be time enough for bureaucracies later.

Lying in my old bed in my old room I had tried to assess what I knew about Indians. I knew Tonto and the noble savage. I knew the stories about lazy drunks and I knew there were places called reservations where supposedly their every need was provided for, but it was all hearsay. I really didn't know much at all.

In my fantasies I would be guided by some secret element in my own blood. A genetic connection would start clicking away under my skin and I would know where to go. There would be visions and signs. I would walk in and only have to mention the name of my unknown mother. *Whiteduck,* they would say. *We're Whiteducks. You must be Elsie's boy.* Hug, hug. Kiss, kiss. Prodigal son. The fatted calf. Dancing around a huge bonfire. The secret ritual of initiation. The triumphant return to My People. The blood brother ceremony all over again.

I stepped out of the car in Red Clay and stood helpless for a moment, blind and choking on the road dust that swirled around me and clotted in my throat. I waved my hand, trying to clear the air in front of my face, then stumbled ahead a few feet, praying I wouldn't run into anything or be run over myself. When I looked up there were eight sets of eyes watching me. Young kids were perched all over the low porch in front of the cafe. I nodded to them and they looked right through me, passing a cigarette among themselves, blowing smoke rings and standing tough. A middle-aged woman shuffled out of the place. She was stout and dark-skinned and bulging through her tattered clothes. She teetered off the step while the young boys laughed and imitated her unsteady progress. She stopped only a few feet from me and bent over suddenly, hands on her knees as she hacked and gagged and spit into the dirt. A thick strand of saliva hung from her lip a second or two and she tried unsuccessfully to coax it to fall with her tongue before she wiped it away with her sleeve. She straightened up and stumbled off across the parking lot without giving any indication of having noticed me standing there. A little nauseated, I walked past the bubble of sputum left by the ragged woman and, avoiding the eyes of the boys gathered on the porch, entered the cafe.

I'm not sure what makes a cafe a cafe, but this place certainly wasn't what came to mind. It was more convenience store than restaurant. There were three or four tables with folding chairs scattered around and a counter with short metal stools in front of it, but most of the inside space was taken up by rows of shelves holding everything from toilet paper to breakfast cereal. Two old men sat together at one of the small tables, drinking coffee and smoking roll-your-owns. A young woman stood behind the counter under a white back-lit sign, with the ubiquitous Coca-Cola logo dead center, that served for a menu.

"You want somethin'."

She didn't smile. I hadn't really expected she would. I was dirty and dust-covered and a total stranger. I smiled at her.

"Hi. My name is Sawnet. William Sawnet. I'm looking for my mother..."

"You lost your mommy?" The voice came from behind me, followed by laughing. Even the old men were chuckling. I glanced over my shoulder and saw that the young boys had followed me inside off the front porch. I turned back to the girl behind the counter, my face flushed with heat. It had been foolish, trying to lay out my entire mission in a few words and hoping she could solve my problems with a few words of her own. I looked into her eyes, trying to think of what to say next, pleading for patience. She must have seen something there because she looked past me and spoke a few harsh words I didn't understand to shoo the giggling boys back outside. She met my gaze again.

"You need some help?"

I sat down on one of the small stools. "I'm looking for someone. I'm looking for someone who might have known someone." It was the first real step on this journey and it frightened me. Five days ago, leaving my parents' home, I had been excited. It had seemed like an adventure then, as if the answers to my questions were just around the next corner. The idea of writing a book about it had given it some distance. The concept of it as merely a project had allowed for a cavalier attitude. The possibility of real answers frightened me.

"I'm looking for the Whiteduck family."

She looked at me suspiciously, "I thought you said somethin' about your mother?"

"My mother's name was Elsie Whiteduck."

The girl behind the counter looked at me again, at my eyes and my so-fair skin, and then away out the dusty window and down the long dirt road I had just come up.

"Sorry," she said, "I don't know no Whiteducks."

The door slammed and a couple of young men walked up and stood behind me, staring up at the sparse, bright menu.

"What'ch you got for soup today?" one asked, and the girl stepped to the side and out of conversation with me.

I swivelled the stool around, grimacing at its high metal screech.

One of the young men put his hands up over his ears. "Cheezus..." he said. It sounded strange, brutal and somehow more of a curse then I'd ever thought it could be, as though there was another syllable twisting there inside the word like a hooked worm. The young man's long black hair was tied back with a blue headband that looked to be torn from a t-shirt, and he wore cheap drugstore sunglasses, the lenses scratched and marked with fingerprints. He met my gaze with a wry smile.

"Sorry," I said.

He looked at his friend then back at me, shrugging. He was wearing a striped sleeveless shirt and the muscles in his shoulders rippled under his shadowed skin.

"Don't apologize man. It was just the fuckin' chair."

His companion guffawed and shook the mop of hair on top of his head. I got to my feet and stepped between the two young men. My light skin flushed again as I brushed past them. When I looked back they were contemplating the menu and I felt like an imposter in front of them. The lives of the people in the cafe flowed around me as though I wasn't there and the whole endeavour began to seem fraudulent.

"Hey, you."

One of the old men was calling out to me, finger raised, beckoning. I smiled and walked over to the table.

"Hi," I extended my hand. "I'm Wil..."

"Better roll your windows up. Rainin' like hell out there."

I turned towards the screen door. A thick curtain of rain could be seen moving up the road. The wide dirt ribbon was darkening to a deep brown and the sky had turned black and mean overhead. I hurried out through the spring-loaded door and leapt from the porch. I was about halfway across the gravel parking lot when the downpour hit, drenching me. I struggled at the handle then, cursing, slipped in behind the wheel and began to work frantically to crank up the window. I had to push out against the glass to get it to roll up properly. Lightning flashed across the windshield and I reached over the seat to find my jacket. Thunder rolled deep and long above the little settlement and the air trembled. I struggled to get my jacket on in the cramped car, then began to rub at the fogged windshield with the palm of my hand.

Now I saw the horse from my dream, huge and white, shimmering in the wet as it pounded up the gravel road tossing its head and blowing steam as the cloudburst cooled the early summer air. My jaw went slack as I stared into the mirror for a few seconds watching as a vision galloped past my car. A young woman was riding it bareback, clinging to the reins and crouched low over the muscular back. She was soaked through, the brown skin of her arms glistening, and her white t-shirt clinging. I could see the dark circles of her nipples and the way her wet jeans had tightened around her thighs. I ached staring at her naked feet dangling down, brown and elegant and splashed with mud. She reined the horse in hard and as it stopped and half turned, I saw a boy hurtle from the deck in front of the store, his arms extended like wings, and run with shoulders hunched against the rain. She sat gripping the bridle with one hand as the horse danced in place underneath her, and she reached out her free arm in slow motion. The boy stretched to seize her slender wrist as she pulled back with the momentum of his leap, his small body vaulting up through the silver curtain of rain onto the horse's back behind her. The animal stamped the wet earth as it turned twice and sat back on its haunches, frozen a moment, stalled energy rippling under its skin.

I stared at the boy, the woman, and the horse teetering on the brink of that charged second. Focussing on the details, the boy's hands clenched together over the woman's breasts, her long wet hair as she shook it back out of her face, the flared nostrils of the wild-eyed horse. Then the animal exploded forward and they passed right in front of my car, leaping over a low concrete divider and racing off down the road under the pouring rain.

It was like waking from the dream all over again. I looked around, twisting back and forth in the seat, my mouth wide open. The boys on the porch were huddled together, oblivious. One held out a disposable lighter and another had his hands cupped around a cigarette. They hadn't even noticed. I looked around. There was no one else. Only the puddled, muddy lot, the long treacherous road, and the dark raging sky.

A dreamrider had galloped bareback into this rutted dirt-packed parking lot and plucked a young boy from the earth. A brown, supple vision, slick and shiny as birth, had dashed past my wreck of an automobile on a slightly dingy horse. I felt as though she had pulled the eyes out of my head on long elastic bands and then let them snap back against my brain. I was in love with her for that. Before I knew her name. Before I had ever heard her speak, I loved the sweet blue bolt of excitement she left.

I sat for a while playing that reverie over and over in my head. I wanted her face etched into my memory. I wanted to be able to see her on that horse any time I felt like it. She was already too blurry. Suddenly, through the rain-soaked window I saw another face coming towards me, and I jumped on the brakes even though the engine wasn't running.

The face floated sideways a few inches away from the windshield, then righted itself and drifted around to the side window. I watched a hand come up and tap on the glass. I pretended to be adjusting the radio. I had only caught a glimpse of the man, but I still hoped he might dematerialize if I ignored him long enough.

His hair was shoulder-length and incredibly unkempt. It clustered together in black spiky crests that protruded everywhere, as if his head had started to explode and then come to a sudden stop. The rain was having only a minimal effect on strands so matted and filthy that most of the moisture simply ran off. A long piece of orange surveyor's ribbon was tied around his head and was apparently purely decorative. Below that bright fluorescent strip was one blood-shot eye and one dead one. The lightless orb lolled in a milky cloud, the iris nothing more than a dark shadow behind a veil. His face was pitted and marked with patches of thin stubble and dirt. His lips were dry and cracked. He tapped again, much harder. I looked up and smiled as though just noticing him and rolled the window down.

"Hey, you got a smoke?" His breath was harsh and chemical.

"Sure." I managed an even bigger smile and reached for the pack of cigarettes on the dash. I handed him the half-empty package. "Keep it," I offered nonchalantly. "I've got a carton in the back." His head turned slowly, in a shaky and tender manner, as though it might drop off at any second. He had to lean in slightly so that his good eye could take in the jumbled mess my belongings had become over the past week. He was soaked, though he didn't seem to notice, and water dripped from the tight clumps of wet hair onto my leg. I leaned over towards the passenger side and started playing with the radio again. With some effort he pulled himself back out of the car window and focussed his good eye on me.

"Thanks, I'd do the same for any whiteman." He laughed. I laughed harder. I wanted to tell him I wasn't really a whiteman, but he probably wouldn't believe me.

He pointed to himself, his finger tapping against his chest. "I used to be pretty important on this place, you know. Used to be a Special Constable." I nodded and tried to look impressed. I wanted the cloudburst to start up again and drive him away. I wanted someone he knew to come by and call to him. I wanted lightning to strike and fry him to a black crisp.

"Hey, show me your license."

I reached for my wallet and this doubled him over with laughter. He weaved back and forth, bent and spastic, one hand anchoring him to the car door. I looked at his dirty fingernails and smiled through my disgust. His laughing decayed into a fit of coughing until he was hacking deeply and spitting out a thick wet froth on the muddy ground. Finally in the midst of his paroxysm, his hand let go of the car. I turned the ignition, slapped the gearshift to drive, and, spraying mud, wheeled out onto the slippery road.

I had passed a dead horse before I realized I had turned the wrong way and was heading deeper into the reserve. This horse was long past being dead, nothing but white and yellow bone stretched out in the short wet grass. It lay on its side in the ditch like part of a diorama in a museum, undisturbed, and not a fragment missing. The long neck extended, each perfect vertebra in its proper place, the elegant fleshless head like an arrow pointing to the green sign that announced arrival onto the reserve proper. I stopped to carefully read its message. "WELCOME TO THE RED CLAY BAND RESERVE." There were five huge bullet holes in the centre of the sign, ominous bits of punctuation full of the threatening grey sky. I decided to drive on anyway, and have a look around.

The wide gravel road swung past the little settlement of houses that was the village of Red Clay, and meandered on between dark tangled mysteries on either side, heading north into the lumber and oil fields and lands of rich labour. I turned right and drove onto a narrower twisting road.

There was a fenced-in compound on the left. It was a six foot high, solid-looking chain-link affair with half-a-dozen tidy little mobile homes clustered inside. They were all nicely painted with plants hanging outside and little asphalt sidewalks joining them together and leading out through the padlocked gate. I didn't know it then, but this chaste enclave was the preserve of the transitory teaching staff sent by the government. On the right, a little further on and at the crest of a small hill, was the yellow, concrete-block school house.

Rougher roads led off from the main one towards an assortment of houses and muddy lanes. The roads ran in loops. The main loop joined back to the main road. Off of it were smaller loops. Off of these ran even shorter loops that skirted two or three houses then arced back to the secondary arc. Few roads were dead ends and the design seemed to be centred around not having to back up. I drove around a few times following different circular paths, looking at the rail fences and miserable dogs and various living arrangements.

I would pass a bungalow with bright aluminum siding and sheets hanging in the picture window for curtains and adjacent to it would be a log cabin with square shuttered windows and a dilapidated outhouse. The next one down would be a tar-papered shack with sheets of plastic stapled over the windows to keep out the wind. Behind one or two I could see animal skins stretched to dry.

It went on in that haphazard manner. There wasn't the sense of order and planning I was used to, having grown up mostly in the precise sameness of Armed Service subdivisions, better known as PMQs in typical military fashion. Private Married Quarters, where all efforts are directed towards uniformity and equality, dependent upon rank, of course.

Here, people had used whatever was available for shelter. Except for the occasional modern bungalow, most of the places were more like cottages or cabins. Some were little more than hovels built out of scraps of plywood and mud. A few had rough rail fences around them, and some even had enough property to keep a horse or two.

I had just begun to believe the place was deserted when I saw an old man walking on the road ahead of me. He was strolling in the middle of the right lane carrying two rabbits in one hand and a small shotgun in the other. I pulled to the left to ease by him, but as I approached he began to angle into the centre of the road. I honked the horn as politely as possible but he didn't seem to notice. I edged over even more towards the left ditch and he held his course in the middle of the muddy lane. Just as I was about to pass him, he cut right in front of the car, as if this had been his plan all along. I hit the horn and cranked the wheel to dodge past as he half turned, throwing up his hands. One drab, bloodied rabbit was sent spinning high into the air, end over end like an acrobat. I managed to avoid running him down, but my outside wheels slipped over the edge of the road and I slid helplessly down the muddy bank, my foot senselessly jamming the brake to the floor. As I came to rest at the bottom of the steep ditch, the dead rabbit landed with a thump on the hood.

I was fuming as I got out of the car. "Jesus! Didn't you hear me coming?"

The old man stood there, his baggy brown pants tucked into the yellow rims of his black rubber boots. His red plaid bush jacket was held together with a safety pin and he wore a bedraggled beige sweater underneath. The other rabbit dangled from his hand, blood dripping slowly from its mouth. "Eh?" he said.

I spoke slowly, hissing through my teeth. "Didn't you hear the horn?"

He raised his arms out at his sides and shrugged. I took notice of the dead rabbit, with its bloody obliterated head, and the old shotgun with its long black barrel. I remembered the sign at the outskirts with the huge holes blasted through it. I calmed down. The old man pointed at me with the barrel of the gun. He had it gripped in his left hand at about the middle, nowhere near the trigger, but it made me nervous. I inched back towards the open car door.

"I didn't know you were a stranger," he said, sputtering with his own anger. "I thought it was just some damn kids tryin' to scare me. We don't get tourists out here. Everybody on this place knows where old Henry lives. They know I cross the goddamn road here all the goddamn time and they don't try to squash me with their goddamn cars." Throughout his explanation he made jabbing motions towards me with the barrel of the gun. I held my hands up in surrender. It was an argument for which I had no counter. I was in a place where I probably didn't belong and I wasn't sure of the rules.

"Look, I'm sorry. I was afraid I might have hurt you. That's all."

The anger faded from his face immediately. His arms dropped back down to his sides and he cradled the gun so that it fell over his arm with the butt hooked into his armpit and the business end pointed at the ground. He nodded towards the car.

"Can I get my rabbit back?"

I smiled, "You all right?"

"Hey, fine. Scared me pretty good." He smiled back.

We both looked at my car with its forlorn hood ornament. I picked up the dead animal by its long hind feet and struggled up the bank to hand it back to the old man.

I tried to drive out of the ditch but it was hopeless. The tires spun on the wet clayish soil and I only slid farther down the bank. The old man watched, holding his rabbits, the little shotgun cradled in his arms.

I got out and locked the door. The old man turned and started to leave. I had to shout to get him to stop.

"Do you have a phone?" I asked.

He nodded and jerked his head to the side. "Yeah, sure. Come on."

When Rabbit saw Coyote he knew it was already too late. He sat very still. Very calm. Coyote trotted up and stood right over him. "Waiting for me," he said in a cocky manner.

"No," said Rabbit. "For my father. He told me to wait here till he signalled it was safe over in the clover field."

Coyote was curious. "Couldn't you go on your own?"

"No," Rabbit chuckled. "I'm too young. Too small yet, eh."

"Too small?" Coyote said in surprise.

"Yes, too small. Don't tease. We are big in our tribe of rabbits. Like your tribe must be."

"I'm not..." Coyote stopped himself. He licked his lips over the young rabbit's naivete. "Is your father close by? I would like to meet him and offer some gifts."

Rabbit jumped up and down a bit. "That would be fine. I'll take you to him."

"No, no," said Coyote. "I have to prepare myself. I'll wait here." Rabbit nodded and raced off. "Anxious youngster," thought Coyote as he crouched down to hide in the grass. He snickered over his cunning. He waited a long time. When he left, his growling stomach reminded him that sometimes things are exactly what they seem.

I drive and drive. Only stopping for fuel. Not even eating. I am possessed by the compulsion to put distance behind me. It is as if I am hoping that at some point the odometer will click over and I will know where I am going. This travelling will have purpose. Or at least a fresh start. The way an entire carload of people will watch when the numbers have almost gone completely around and the mileage is about to shift back to a neat line of zeros.

I feel an emptiness but it is not a longing for food. From time to time I look at the billboards advertising meal stops just ahead. Home cooking. Best burgers for miles. But I drive past. The miles are what I am after. I only want the road.

I find myself tiring more and more quickly each day. Surrendering more easily. The highway sings its lullabies, the scenery repeats itself in an incantation for sleep, and whole sections of asphalt drop away behind me without any memory or recollection. Even without sleeping, the dreams are there, waiting in the folds of my clothing, or like a stranger in the back seat. A hitchhiker who sits directly behind you so you can't find their face in the mirror. Talking distractedly into the back of your neck.

It is a persistent infection. Driving is a temporary and ineffectual diversion. I can only resist so long and then I must pull over and rest my eyes. The dreaming is there immediately. Forcing in under my eyelids. Pushing its phantoms and regrets into my sleep.

FOUR

I jogged a bit to catch up with him. It was surprising how fast the old guy could walk in those clumsy rubber boots. As we made our way down the muddy road, faces peered out of windows, watching us. Curtains moved and even the lazy forlorn dogs lifted their heads from the damp earth to watch us pass by.

"Quiet here," I remarked in a leading sort of way. I found myself already breathing hard.

"Sometimes."

"Nice rabbits."

He glanced at me and said, "Good for stew."

We walked on, my shoes sliding and making wet sounds, his rubber boots thubbing away with each step in loose percussion.

I felt like part of a small pathetic parade, the hunter and the stuck motorist marching through the village to the music of their footwear, homeward bound with their limp trophies. It seemed to take a long time to reach his little square house, a plain plywood shack, painted white, the grain of the wood showing through the single inept coat. It had a lean-to style roof and a small front step. He pressed his thumb down on the simple metal latch, pushed the door open and stepped inside.

I followed him in. The dark single room smelled of fried bacon and wood smoke and mildew. There was one window in the front wall and an old wooden table in the middle of the floor. A low brown dresser with a cracked mirror was pushed against the back wall in one corner and beside it sat a single bed. In the other corner was a woodstove with its black pipe going straight up through the roof. There were no inside walls, just the framing with nails driven here and there into the studs and various things hanging from them: a cast-iron frying pan, wash basin, several shirts and other articles of clothing, a fishing rod, big-bore rifle and picture of a haloed, praying Jesus. I took another step inside and tripped over something wet and corpulent on the murky floor in front of me.

The old man tossed the bloodied rabbits on the table and cursed. "Damn them fellahs. Watch out there." He reached down and pulled up the huge bloated corpse of a beaver by its flat, leathery tail. He carried it out and set it on the front step. He looked at me apologetically. "I'll bet that damn Danny Elkhorn left that here. He hunts with me sometimes and I teach him trappin' in the winter. Summertime comes I never hardly see him. Young guys like to hunt but they don't wanna do the work of skinnin'. Just want to fool around, you know?"

He shook his head sadly from side to side for emphasis. I nodded as if I understood, then pointed to the simple black wall phone beside the door.

"Mind if I use this?"

He stepped back in past me and pulled a string hanging in the middle of the shack. A bare forty-watt bulb shone dully. "Sure, go ahead," he said.

I started to reach for the handset, then realized I had no idea whom to call. The old man had taken the rabbits back outside and was tying the back legs of one together with a piece of string. The second rabbit had already been trussed up and was hanging upside down from a nail driven into a tree standing in the yard. Three large dogs were slowly beginning to amble closer. I stuck my head out of the door. "Excuse me. Do you have a phone book?"

He slid the point of a long-bladed knife into the groin of the hanging rabbit and slit it down to where the ribs met. "Nope," he said. He used one crooked finger to spill the guts out of the dead rabbit and onto the ground between his rubber boots. "Burned last winter."

"Oh." I was staring at the red and black gleaming mess steaming on the grass. The dogs were crouched at the edge of the small yard, waiting patiently. He shrugged, the blood-stained knife pointing up towards the lacklustre sky. "Can't read and I got nobody to telephone anyway." He offered his warm, broad smile again and I gritted my teeth in return.

Obviously, the operator was my only hope. I picked up the hand set and dialled zero. The phone was as dead as the rabbits.

"Phone's dead," I shouted out the door as I whacked the plunger a couple of times with my fingers. Nothing. The old man appeared in the doorway, straddling the threshold and leaning through to jab the air with his bloody knife.

"You know," he said thoughtfully. "Them government guys said they was goin' disconnect me. But they never come and got their phone so I thought they forgot. Telephone lady was the only one that ever called me anyway. To say I owed money. I told her, I says, 'I never use that damn thing.' It's them young bastards, you know." He was waving the knife the other way now, indicating the general direction of the reserve. I was nodding agreement with everything he said, holding onto the useless handset.

"They broke in here when I wasn't home and phoned all kind of places. Long distance. Them young bastards. Can't skin a beaver but they can dial long distance. Ahhh." The sound came from deep down in his throat and he was forced to spit after he'd made it. He ran the sleeve of his bush jacket across his chin, then poked at the phone with his knife. "I never liked that damn thing anyway. First time it rang I almost jumped outta my skin. I never asked for no phone. They just come here one day and said 'Today you get a phone.' Damn thing."

Suddenly he started to laugh. Short, deep, little ha ha's like he was trying to catch his breath. His whole face wrinkled back into its comfortable smile, "Not like Ida Mae, though, that crazy old lady. She's old. She's really old. Maybe a hundred years, I think. She remembers a lot of the old ways but she don't know nothin' about telephones. One day I'm going out huntin' and I see Ida Mae throwin' rocks at her house. 'Ida Mae' I say, 'why you throwin' rocks at your house?'" The old man stepped over the threshold into the meagre shack and tossed his knife onto the table. He pantomimed taking pebbles from the palm of his left hand and throwing them with his right. He spoke in a high shaky voice, the way Ida Mae spoke, I guess. "'Matchi Manitou is in my house.' Only she said it in Indian. She don't speak any whiteman language." He said it again, barely able to contain his laughter, throwing imaginary stones like Ida Mae. "'Matchi Manitou is in my house.'" He looked at me standing there tightlipped, holding onto the shiny black appendage of the wall phone as though I was tethered to it.

"Matchi Manitou is like a demon. Like the devil, you know, in the Bible," he explained, then carried on with the story, acting out each event. "'How do you know, Ida Mae?' I says. 'Listen,' she says. We listen. At first I don't hear nothin' and I think maybe Ida Mae's gettin' too old. Then I hear it. The phone starts to ring. 'Listen,' she says. 'There he goes,' and she starts looking for more rocks. I laugh and laugh. 'Ida Mae,' I says, 'that's just your telephone machine. Someone's calling you.' This scared her. 'Who?' she says. 'Who's callin' me?' So I go into her house and pick up the phone and it's her daughter Rose, callin' to see how Ida Mae's doin'. She was pretty worried because her mother didn't answer the phone all those times. But nobody ever showed Ida Mae how a phone machine works. She don't usually like whiteman's stuff but now she likes talkin' on the phone. She's got seven daughters, you know."

I nodded, my lips tightening into a strained smile. It was apparent that he was disappointed I missed most of the humour in his story. I hung up the phone as the old man retrieved his knife and went back outside to the rabbits. I stood for a minute or two in the doorway of that tiny place crowded with the old man's things, staring at the picture of Jesus and wondering what to do. I felt more lost now than when I had started. More separate from everything and without direction. I hadn't realized there would be so many places to look. I moved to sit down on one of the wooden chairs and rested my head on the table. I hadn't slept well in over a week, perhaps longer. Not since I had been struck by the idea to find out more about my real mother.

I must have dozed for a while. I dreamed of the back yard again, and the brown woman in the white dress spinning me through the blue sky. I dreamed of falling into her embrace. It was brief and happy and distant. I woke to the steady, rhythmic drumming of the old man chopping kindling, the dry wood tearing along its grain and splitting away with a high hollow sound. I watched him for a while before he realized I was awake, the flat slabs steady between his fingers, his other hand swinging the axe, the shiny silver edge slicing into the wood a hair's-breadth from his hand. Over and over, as a neat pile of thin strips piled up next to the stove.

A large pot sat on top of the cast-iron stove, and he was stacking the small sticks on some bits of paper and an empty cereal box. I raised my head and groaned at the stiffness in my neck.

"You must be pretty tired," he said in a soft, kind way, as though he knew my dilemma. He pointed to the large stock-pot sitting on top of the stove. "Pretty good stew..." It was an invitation.

I ran my hands over my face. "I should get going. Thanks anyway..." He stood up and walked over, extending his right hand.

"Henry Cardinal," he said shyly.

I responded warmly, touched by his kindness. "William Sawnet. It's been nice meeting you, Mr. Cardinal."

He waved his hand, brushing aside my formality. "Call me Henry," he said bashfully, then went back to stacking the kindling for the fire. For a few awkward minutes I sat there quietly watching him work, as he arranged the wood, then took a box of wooden matches out of his pocket. He struck one on the stove and held the flame to the paper crumpled underneath the neat mound of dry wood. We both watched the fire for a few seconds and then he closed the cast-iron door on the crackling, spitting wood.

I sat there, contemplating my next step, unsure of what I should do, as he moved the stew so it was over the heat and pulled a large ladle from where it hung by a nail on the wall. "I made this up a coupla days ago, but didn't have no meat then. I'll fry some of that rabbit and throw it in. What'ch you doin' around here anyway?" he asked, staring into the pot. His directness surprised me.

"Looking for information about my mother. Elsie Whiteduck."

Henry took the heavy black frying pan down from its nail and placed it on the stove. He opened up his half-fridge and pulled out a waxed-paper square of lard. Using the skinning knife, he flipped a corner of lard into the pan, then tossed in the diced rabbit. I sat at his kitchen table, pale and weary. He raised his chin towards me. "You Indian."

I couldn't look him in the eye. I felt as though I were lying. The meat began to sizzle in the skillet. "Half. Part. Something."

"Your dad. He was a whiteman?"

I nodded back, looking down at my pale arm. I couldn't think of what other choices there might be. I stood up and rummaged for my cigarettes. Henry busied himself with his cooking and opened the loading door on the stove to toss in a couple more pieces of wood. The little shack was beginning to heat up.

My smokes were still in the car. I studied Henry's back as I sat at the table again. I began to tell him my story. "My mother was living in Edmonton when they took me away. I was only three years old, and I have no real memories of it." The dream flashed through my head. The blue sky. The green yard. The gold chain clutched in my hand. "I was adopted by my parents... I mean, they weren't my parents, then, they were just Wilfred and Mona Sawnet. Wilf was in the service, stationed near Edmonton. After I was adopted they were transferred back east and I grew up thinking they were my real parents." That felt traitorous. "I mean, my biological parents." Henry was flipping the rabbit chunks, not looking my way but listening intently. "I only found out recently about the adoption. After my dad... Wilf... died. Family skeleton kind of came rattling out of the closet at the funeral, if you know what I mean." I snorted and made a breathy attempt at laughter. Henry raised his eyebrows. "When you're in your mid-thirties and you find out you're adopted it's a bit of a shock."

The old man didn't comment. He didn't grunt or shrug or move his head. He dumped the meat from the frying pan into the stew pot. The little shack was filling up with the heat from the fire and the smell of cooking stew and other mysterious things that were coming to life with the flames in the small wood heater. It was intoxicating. I sat watching him watch the pot. It was quiet and strange, and as I looked around the dense interior of the shack I began to feel out of place again. I didn't belong. It seemed hopeless now with so little to go on. I had believed I would find Elsie alive somewhere, that a mysterious energy would draw us together, as though some remnant of that mythical summer day would be a magnetic, undeniable force pulling us towards one another. I had given up everything to try and find this missing piece of myself. Now I felt more fragmented than ever. I had an irresistible urge to escape, to return to the safety of my ignorance.

"Listen, Henry. I have to get myself a pack of cigarettes from the car before it gets too dark. I'll be right back." I decided to walk back and see if there was someone around who could pull my car out of the ditch and get me back on the road. I wanted to leave. No matter how dangerous the road was, I wanted to be on my way. Henry half turned and waved, to say okay without making eye contact.

"See ya," I said trying to sound like I'd be right back, pulling the door open to leave. The old man muttered something, but the tiny refrigerator kicked in, whirring like a helicopter winding up and pushing its busy white noise into every corner of the cabin. "Yeah. See ya, Henry. Thanks."

I closed the door behind me, stepping out into the cool dusk and stretching. It was late, but as far north as I was the sun was in the sky much longer in the day. I stood in Henry's little yard a few moments taking in the small houses gathered under the deepening shadows. They looked worn and unruly. Not like the neat anemic bungalows and trimmed yards in the subdivisions where I had grown up. I studied the odd mixture of crude log cabins and tar-paper shacks and split-level houses with gleaming white siding. The yards were patches of dirt and twisted clumps of long yellow grass from last year. Some had doghouses, some just had dogs. Most had the hulks of cars or decrepit washing machines speckled with rust or some other such wreckage littered around. There was barking and kids yelling and gruff voices shouting somewhere in the distance. A screen door slammed shut and farther off a chainsaw started up with its wicked, toothed whining. Over everything the pale round ghost of the moon showed its face.

It was strange to me. I tried to imagine growing up in such a place. It seemed dangerous and rough, a kind of living I had never even suspected existed. There were no corner stores, no restaurants or burger joints, no handy gas stations or garages. No movie theatres, no hospitals, no taxi stands or barber shops or shopping plazas. It was isolated and insular and moment to moment.

I paused at the edge of the road. Henry lived right on a curve at the top of a little hill and I could hear a car approaching on the loose gravel. I decided to wait till it passed. I wanted to make my way to my own car seen by as few people as possible. I wanted to slip into the night away from this place and back to streetlights and neon and territory I was more familiar with. I hoped that maybe the ground had dried out enough that

I could just drive out of the ditch and escape down the long, afflicted road to the first motel on the highway, a place with neatly made beds and the same landscape painting in every room. A television hooked up to a satellite dish bringing in dozens of stations so I could flick through the world for a few happy hours. A clean, antiseptic bathroom with the reassuring paper strip around the toilet seat and running water and miniature personal bars of soap.

The car rolled by, and as it travelled down the road its headlights shone across my mired vehicle. My jaw dropped open. All the doors were agape and the hood was up. Figures were moving around, pulling things out of the car. "Hey," I yelled. "Hey."

They looked my way, frozen, thin and luminous against the night for a second, then swallowed again by the darkness as the car continued past. They hurriedly stuffed things into their jackets and then took off. One paused a moment to aim a malicious kick at the side of the car, the heavy thud echoing across the hushed reserve.

"Sonovabitch!" I started to run after them, but that was utterly senseless. They disappeared like shadows across the unlit yards, darting between the silent houses. I ran down to the car but it was too difficult to see what was missing in the murky, jumbled mess. I leaned in and pulled the knob for the interior light. Nothing happened. I moved to the front of the car and squinted down at the dirty, indistinct engine. There was only a black space where the battery had been. I slammed the hood, locked the car and ran back to Henry's place, leaping up onto the low step and bursting through the door just as he was setting a plate down on the table. He jumped back and the plate fell spinning from his hand. I looked around frantically, then snatched the receiver up from the wall phone. The heavy plate clattered on the floor but didn't break.

"Henry! What's the number for the police?"

Henry stood staring at me. "Police?"

"Never mind." I put the dead handset to my ear, started to dial zero. "Sonovabitch! This phone doesn't work." I held the useless instrument out towards the old man. He could only nod in agreement. "Henry. Where is a phone I can use?"

"Phone?" He stood dumfounded.

"Henry, I need to phone the goddamn police. Some kids just ransacked my car. They stole my battery. That's a new goddamn battery."

Henry was beginning to understand. "Don't phone the police. We'll get it back."

"What?" It was my turn to be bewildered. "Listen. Everything I own was in that goddamn car. My money... everything. I quit my job. Sold my stuff. Paid cash for that wreck and came out here to find out about my mother. That battery's not even two weeks old, Henry." I sat down heavily at the table, beaten.

Henry sat down opposite me, the scarred wooden chair creaking under him. "Don't worry. It's just kids. We'll find your battery in the mornin'. Jesus." He crossed himself. "Jesus Christ, you scared the shit outta me. You gotta stop scarin' me."

I peered into his weathered face. His deep brown eyes. I pleaded with him, "Henry, I need that car."

"Don't worry. Believe me, the police won't come out here till morning anyway. They'll just think it's one drunk Indian stealin' from another."

I didn't know how to argue against this. It was completely foreign and I couldn't think of anything to say. I was on the verge of tears. "This whole damn business has been a bust. You know that?" I looked away from him down to the dusty floor of the humble cabin. "I should have stayed where I was, who I was." I didn't want to be mollified by Henry's soothing manner. I wanted to be decisive and feel in control again. I reached for the crude door handle. "I'm goin', Henry. I'm goddamn goin'. I'll hitchhike or I'll walk if I have to. I'll talk to the cops personally. They'll help me. They'll see who I am. They'll see I'm not..." Henry looked away.

He shuffled his hands around on the table. Brushing at crumbs that weren't there. "You know I been thinkin'. Maybe I knew an Elsie Whiteduck."

"What?"

"She didn't live on the reserve, though. I think she lived in town."

"What?"

"I think maybe she was a cousin. Second cousin, maybe."

"You knew her?" I had to sit down. The cabin was lifting, turning in the approaching night. *Husha,* I heard. *Husha. Husha.*

"I think maybe I mighta known someone named Elsie. Don't know if it was Whiteduck. I can't remember too good. I don't think she lived on the reserve. I think she lived in town. I don't know, I got a lot of cousins."

He sat looking at his hands and I sat watching him. The little old man I'd almost run over. Could he really be a long-lost relative? Maybe something had been guiding me down that road after all. Bringing us together. My dreams. The vision of the white horse.

"I have a dream about her..."

Henry's head snapped up. "Eh? A dream?"

I felt embarrassed talking about the dream of my mother. "Yeah. It's nothing spectacular. She doesn't speak to me from the dead or anything. Can't even really make out her face that well. It just seems... happy, I guess. Pleasant. I'm only a little boy and we're playing in some back yard. Not a yard like around here, though. A green, clean yard with a painted fence and mowed grass. And I'm holding this gold cross that shines in the sun. I think she must have given..." Unexpectedly, the thought of a gift from my unknown mother sealed my throat.

Henry pushed back from the table, his chair scraping across the bare wood floor. With the old man in his tiny crooked house I replayed the dream over and over in my head in an endless loop. He moved stiffly to the squatting woodstove and threw in another piece of wood. Then he pulled down an old flat tin from one of the haphazard shelves nailed to the wall and brought it back to the table. He set it in front of me as he settled heavily back into his chair. It was a tin that had once held Regal brand cookies and there was a picture of King Edward centred on the top in an oval frame with a lion rampant on either side. The rest of the tin was covered in pictures of Buckingham Palace and the Union Jack and other such stoic icons of the monarchy.

I pulled the lid off. It was filled with a jumbled mess of old mementos. Henry pointed across the table with one crooked brown finger. "I had that stuff for a long time." I nodded and began to gingerly sort through it. There were ancient lighters and huge copper-coloured bullets. Keys and the bent wire frames from an old pair of glasses. Little plastic playthings that must have come out of cereal boxes, a jack-knife with a handle of yellow bone and the blade worn down from sharpening, a brown leather billfold and a few odd medals and ribbons and some foreign coins. I lifted one from the box and turned it in my fingers, it was Dutch and dated nineteen-thirty-nine.

Henry had been watching me intently. "Where did you get this, Henry? Were you overseas?" I knew enough from listening to my father that overseas meant the war to his generation.

"Some are from my brother Luke, and some from my Uncle Jacob from the first war. He didn't live too long, cause he had that yellow gas in his lungs. My brother Luke was a sniper in the second war. He came back but he was never the same. He would drink and talk about shootin' soldiers and then drink more."

I set the coin gently back into the box and as I did I spotted the crucifix, lying among the bullets and plastic souvenirs and foreign currency of the dead. Tangled in the middle of Henry's memories, it caught the light of the dull bulb and shone as if it had just dropped from the sunlight in my dream.

Henry knew I had seen it. I wanted to ask if it was hers, if he remembered more than he was telling. But I was afraid. I didn't want him to say that he didn't remember. I didn't want him to tell me that it belonged to someone else or that it was his. I wanted it to be hers.

The old man rubbed his face. "I remember a long time ago a dream my mother had." Darkness filled all the windows now. The fire snapped and spit in its cast-iron cave and through a tiny crack an orange spirit escaped the flames and danced on the shadowed wall. I could smell the heat and the smoke and the ghosts of thousands of other such fires. The cluttered walls seemed to huddle in closer and the night beyond them grew deep and huge.

"I was only a young lad then. My dad had us all out at the winter hunting grounds up north. Maybe thirty miles from here. Nothin' but bush then. He and his brother were workin' their trap-line and mother and auntie were cookin' meals and takin' care of camp and helpin' with the furs."

I settled back in the chair with the cross laid out on the table in front of me, listening to the old man.

"One day we took our toboggans and our dogs and went fishin' at this lake a few miles from the cabin. We had a lot fun but didn't catch too many fish. When we get back we find out a wolverine got into the camp. Wolverine is mean. What he can't eat he tears apart. Then he pisses on everything. Wah! What a smell. I still remember that. Almost all our food is gone. Then the weather turned bad. It snowed and snowed and the huntin' was no good. The wolverine, he hung around but he was very sneaky. He steals the bait from the traps and eats anything that gets caught. My dad and my uncle went out every day to try and shoot him but he was sly. My uncle kept saying that he must really be one of the little people disguised as a wolverine.

"Pretty soon we were starting to get very hungry. The two men decided to go out after a moose and left the women and us kids. That day the weather went mild and that night an ice storm blew in. Storms scared my mother bad. And she was more scared because the men were out on the trail, camped somewhere. I woke in the dark. My mother was at the fire whisperin' an Indian prayer. The wind was blowin' hard and howlin'. I heard a clatterin' sound and I was scared because I thought it was

Geen-go–hongay scratchin' at the door. That is what Indian people call the wolverine. I thought he would come in and eat us all.

"My brother heard me whimperin' and whispered in my ear, 'Do you hear that? That's Paguck, the flyin' bone-man. He's caught in a tree out there. Hear his bones rattlin' in the wind?' Then the wind howled again. 'Listen,' my brother said. 'Paguck is cryin' for help. Go pull him out of the tree and he'll give us good luck.' I almost started cryin'. Then my mother turned and threw a piece of wood she was holdin' at my brother. It just missed the top of his head and he laid down fast like he was sleepin'. 'Hush,' my mother said, 'don't be stupid. It's only ice on the branches.' But then I heard her start prayin' a little faster and saw her drop somethin' into the fire. I knew it was tobacco when I smelled the smoke."

Henry got up and took a pouch down from the shelf. He opened it, pulled out a simple pipe and stuffed the bowl with tobacco as though telling the story had reminded him of it. It was quiet. I tried to see out into the night but the black windows showed only my own reflection. An eerie feeling crept over me and I glanced at the door to see if it could be locked. There was only a small hook dangling on the door frame. Henry had his pipe going and the shack was redolent with the sweet, luxuriant smoke.

"My father, he rolled cigarettes all his life. First thing in the mornin' he would roll one for himself, but he was a real Christian man. He was sent away when he was young to a school run by the church and taught not to follow heathen ways. But my mother, she still lived by the old ways a lot. She was scared to forget about Indian spirits, 'specially in the bush, so she prayed to everybody. She was always sneakin' father's tobacco and throwin' a little in the fire or in the water before we went out in the boat or if we caught fish. My father would get very mad." Henry contemplated the happy memory and puffed deeply on his pipe a second or two, enjoying the past. The exhaled smoke rose toward the ceiling and his eyes were shining. He mumbled something softly that I could not quite hear or understand.

"When we woke up the next mornin' a crust of ice covered everythin'. The trees all looked like glass and the snow was smooth and shinin'. All we had for breakfast was thin, thin soup made from the boiled fish bones. Our mothers did not even eat. We were all very, very hungry and everybody was scared. My mother looked at us all lookin' so sad.

"'I had a dream last night about dancers,' she said. 'Funny dancers. They had masks that were like the faces of birds and their headdresses were decorated with partridge feathers. They danced crouched over in little circles. They would stand very still and then there would be fast fast drummin' and the dancers would turn in little circles and wave their arms over their heads. I have never seen dancers like that.'

"We were sorta cheered up by her story but not too much. A little later she went outside to pass water. Suddenly she came runnin' back in and grabbed the axe from beside her sleepin' place. She kept it there, she said, to split wood at night to stoke the fire but I think it was in case of Geen-go-hongay. 'The little drummers.' she said. 'The little drummers.' And she ran back outside, leavin' the door open. We all ran out behind her, and my aunt was askin' 'What's wrong witch you? What's the matter?'

"My mother held up her hand. 'Listen,' she said. We stood quiet and looked at each other because we could hear nothin'. Then there was a sound. A far off little thumpin' sound. Like drums. She stood in the snow, raised the hatchet, and smacked through the crust with the head turned sideways. She dropped the hatchet and began diggin' with her hands. She reached in and pulled out a partridge, trapped under the crust of snow after it dug in to sleep. Dead from the hit with the hatchet. Seven more times she pulled partridges from where they were trapped by the ice."

I don't remember the night too clearly after that. The stew was hot and filling and had a soporific effect. Henry pulled a sleeping bag and some blankets out of an old trunk and made up a bed on the floor for me. I remember lying in the dark, amazed by the star-filled sky out the window, and listening to Henry lying in his bed quietly praying in Cree, the syllables sounding short and soft and musical. Then I slept till morning.

Coyote walked for a time as a Wolverine. People trusted Wolverine. Even those that feared him knew that Wolverine was honest and forthright. He was independent and pragmatic but he was not cruel. This gave Coyote the opportunity to play many pranks. He fooled everyone, and even slept with those who loved Wolverine, because that was his nature and he saw it as the best kind of prank. Soon the entire world feared and despised Wolverine. Everyone avoided him and he became bitter and defensive. Finally, Wolverine tracked Coyote down and berated him for the damage he had done and for the false picture he had painted. "I like to try different things," was Coyote's excuse. "I like to see what it's like to be different beings."

"Putting on my coat and walking in my footsteps doesn't make you a Wolverine. You know nothing of me."

Coyote threw back his head and laughed. "I know my magic is stronger. I know I am smarter and faster. I know I've made a fool of you."

"Yes," said Wolverine. "But you know nothing of my pride. That I would rather walk alone than explain myself or beg forgiveness from those who now hate me. That I hold my independence dear and will do whatever it takes to protect it. That is the lesson I have for you, Coyote."

Coyote shrugged and turned to run away. He was bored. He had no desire to be lectured to by an inferior being with no sense of humour. Just then he felt Wolverine's fierce teeth sink into his ass. He cried out and kicked and clawed till there was nothing left but Wolverine's head. He gnawed the flesh from the skull and at the last bite saw, to his amazement, the eyes turn to stones and fall back inside the grinning skull. With every movement he heard them rattling around inside the drum of bone that had been Wolverine's head. It took many years for the skull to break away, and no matter what shape Coyote took, the noise followed him and warned everyone of his true identity so that they would not even give him the time of day. Coyote travelled for years in the loneliness of Wolverine, and pondered often the tenacity he had so misjudged. He never took that shape again.

Driving. Away from the past and its dreams. I drive till I spot an out-of-the-way gas station that doesn't appear to be too busy. I pull in at the pumps and clamber out to borrow the washroom key. A withered, bent old man who runs the garage comes hobbling through the doorway to pump gas. I tell him to fill the tank and ask about the restroom. He points to a key hanging from a hook on the wall. The key is chained to a board that is ridiculously long.

The bathroom is tiny and stained. Old senseless messages show through the thin green paint and new ones are already beginning to accumulate. Hostile, terse incantations. I stare into the mirror over the sink without recognizing myself. I linger for a while, the face staring back at me blotched by dead spots on the mirror, pale and framed by long dark hair that hangs twisted and dishevelled. There is no plug for the brown-rimmed sink and the taps are spring-loaded to turn themselves off, so I have to hold the cold on with one hand and splash water up onto my face with the other. I use my wet fingers to smooth out my hair as best I can. I have no desire to stay in that ill-lit claustrophobic place too long. The face in the mirror frightens me.

I open the door and blink against the earnest morning sun. Everything seems altered again. I'm unsure how long I have been in the small bathroom. Time outside the car reels by in unknown increments. The sky has become an intense blue and the day grows warmer with each minute. I have no sense of the clock. I walk around the corner of the building and see my car sitting alone by the pumps. I return to the squat station and hang the key from its long crude handle back on its hook by the door.

"Gonna be a beaut." The voice comes out of nowhere. I look around the storefront, peering through the doorway into the darkness of the service bay. "Sun's hot already." The old man sits on a stool behind the counter in front of the huge picture window. His clothes are all light brown and his skin is grey and marked with dots of darker pigment. He seems part of the woodwork, and makes me think of a little spotted frog clinging to the trunk of a tree, camouflaged. Behind him are shelves of cigarettes and pine-tree air fresheners and cheap clip-on sunglasses. There is a hand-written sign over his head that says, *NO Personal Checks.* He hops off the stool and walks, pivoting on his bad leg to the cash register to ring in the gas. It comes to $9.35.

"Round as I could make it," he says. His voice is high and soft. His mouth offers a bemused twitch as I fish five two-dollar bills out of my pocket.

"Squaw money."

I freeze, unsure if I heard him correctly, "What?"

"Squaw money," he says again. "We used to call that squaw money."

I watch as his crooked hand reaches out to scoop up the pile of brown bills. He is beaming. "You could always get a squaw for two dollars."

I stare into his face. Contemplate his wet, guileless eyes. There is nothing else to do. I hate him, then and there. Hate him for everything I've gone through, for every turn my life has taken. The hatred rises up out of my stomach and burns like acid through the veins in my arms and pools into the tight fists my hands have become. But he is old and twisted and frail and my hands stay at my sides. He senses something and shuffles backward from the counter. I dig out another two dollar bill and toss it on the counter.

"Can I get a coke?"

He slides open the upright cooler, pulls out a can and pushes it across the glass countertop. I pick it up and leave without waiting for my change. He doesn't follow me out.

I turn left at the highway simply because I don't want to go back the way I have just come. I have no idea of where I am going. I keep thinking about that old man. Seeing him in some small-town hotel, buying wine for an Indian woman and plying her with a couple of bucks. Then the two of them under the prairie night in an empty lot not far from the bar, his suspenders pulled off his crooked shoulders, his pants pulled down, her legs spreading as he pushes her skirt up over her hips. The contorted hump of his spine rising and falling like the back of some maimed mongrel dog. The woman mumbling underneath him incoherently. His quiet frail grunting, one grey hand fluttering up over the woman's dark face as her head rocks from side to side. The face becomes Agnes' and suddenly I am weeping. Without a sound, the tears stream down my face until I can hardly see.

A car horn screams at me. I've drifted into the wrong lane. I wrench the car over to the shoulder and slam on the brakes, sliding to a stop on the loose gravel. More horns, and someone cursing me as they drive past. Then the sobbing starts. I collapse against the steering wheel, repeating her name over and over. I can't escape the past. It is there waiting for me to catch up. I have nowhere to run. No hope of sanctuary. I am utterly lost.

FIVE

I woke that next morning stiff and sore, surprised to find myself lying on Henry's floor on top of the old cloth sleeping bag with a wool blanket covering me. I was still fully dressed, and my clothes were damp and coiled tightly around my body. I sat up pulling at my shirt, feeling grubby, rubbing my hands over my face.

"Want some coffee?"

The old man was sitting at the end of the table. I felt self-conscious and foolish as I rolled out of the makeshift bed and stood up shakily, surveying the one-room cabin to get my bearings. "Bathroom," I mumbled and staggered towards the door. I struggled with it a few seconds before realizing it was still locked. I flicked the little hook up out of the eye and stepped outside.

The sun was low and blindingly bright. I held my hand up to shield my eyes and stepped off the low porch. Three indistinct women were standing out on the road, silently watching me. I nodded hello, blinking at their wavering shadowy forms, embarrassed as I tried to nonchalantly make my way towards the outhouse around back of the old man's place. I was in the middle of some fond memories about running water and flush toilets when I stopped dead, stunned and staring down into the stinking hole. What had that shape been, beside the women? Tucking myself back in, I ran out front.

My car was there. My red, rusted, and dusty heap was parked right in front of the old man's property. I hurried over and looked in the driver's-side window, holding my hand up against the glass to shade out the morning sun. The keys were there, dangling from the ignition. I looked around. The three women were still watching but they had moved across the road. "This is mine," I told them, running my hands over the roof of the car. "This is my car." They pretended not to notice me.

I ran my hand along the right fender and found the dimple where the boy's foot had buckled the metal, then climbed inside and began to check my belongings stored in the back seat. Most of it was actually still there although it had been tossed around a bit. The carton of cigarettes was gone, and so were the cassette tapes, but everything else seemed to have been deemed unworthy of theft. An empty wine bottle was sitting on the front seat, and for some reason the green, tubular shape caused a wave of panic to wash over me. I ran my hand along under the dashboard until I felt the little nook where I'd stashed the billfold with my savings. It was safe. I pulled it out, deciding it was best to keep it with me. I reached for the keys and turned the engine over. It started. I locked up, doublechecked the doors and headed for the outhouse a much happier man.

Henry wasn't surprised to learn that my car had been returned.

"I was up early this mornin' and walked over to Danny Elkhorn's. You left your keys on the table last night so I took them with me. I went by your car and the battery was sittin' in the ditch up the road a ways.

Too heavy to run with. I got Danny and he put it back, hooked up them wires, and then pulled your vehicle out. He's got a truck with a winch and towed your car right here. Danny was kinda hung over, but he didn't mind. Likes to show off that winch whenever he can. Danny thinks he knows who did it, too. He might get your things back."

I waved this off, feeling magnanimous. "Tell him not to worry. Just tapes and cigarettes. No big deal."

"Anyway, he'll give them a good kick in the ass."

I could see that Henry wanted to make things all right for me and I was touched. I tried to give him some money for all his trouble but he declined the offer.

"If you go into town, bring back a case for Danny, that's all."

I questioned Henry over breakfast about memories of my mother or the woman he felt might possibly be my mother. He let me have the gold crucifix and I wore it around my neck. I couldn't stop playing with it, turning it in my fingers and squeezing it into the palm of my hand until it hurt. I felt it was the first tangible evidence of my true existence. Henry couldn't add much to what he had said the night before, but I was willing to give him time. I began to feel comfortable as I moved around the shack, heating some water on the stove for washing, stoking the fire. I went out to the car and retrieved my suitcase and pulled out my shaving kit and a towel. Henry excused himself and went outside to deal with the beaver that had been left the day before. I washed and shaved and changed into some clean clothes. I felt like a new man. A rediscovered man.

I emerged from the cabin clean, well fed, and totally refreshed. Henry was smoking his pipe in the back yard. He had the beaver pelt stretched on a frame already and was sitting on a rough wooden bench enjoying the morning sun.

"I'm going to town, Henry. You need anything?"

He shook his head, pulled the pipe from his mouth, and pointed at a low pile of stacked firewood at the edge of his small yard.

"Gonna need wood soon," he said almost to himself. "Young men don't bring wood any more. Used to be someone always took care of the old people. Now it's not the same."

"What about... Mr. Elkhorn?"

"Pah. Danny only wants to work for money. He wants things like a whiteman. Big truck. Big TV. All that stuff."

He sat smoking his pipe in his baggy work pants held up by suspenders and the plaid shirt that was like a second skin. A man who had worked hard all his life to look after himself, but was old and alone and finding it harder to be self-sufficient.

Three ravens sat together near the top of a tall birch tree, squawking in their broken tongue, and lusting over the remains of the skinned beaver.

"I'll be back, Henry."

It felt good to have my car again. I drove slowly back out through the reserve, past the spot where I had almost run over Henry and then driven into the ditch.

I passed a wagon loaded with young children, just as it was turning onto the laneway that branched off towards the school. It ambled along through the lambent morning, pulled by a plodding, swaybacked, chestnut horse barely able to keep its head up. The man driving held the reins loosely, relaxed and completely oblivious to the shouting, frolicking kids behind him. I revelled in the scene a while. The disinterested horse, the sedate driver, the happy children, the dilapidated wagon that rolled along on old car wheels with the hubs painted a vivid red.

I turned onto the main road and started up the hill towards the Red Clay Cafe with its same crowd of young boys clustered on the porch. One stood suddenly as I was passing and swung his fist hard into the face of another who fell sideways down the short steps, clutching at the handrail. The others pointed and laughed. I twisted around, peering over the headrest, startled by the casual violence. When I turned my attention to the road again, a young woman was standing at the edge of the ditch, wearing sunglasses and hitchhiking. I pulled over, and she opened the door and plopped into the passenger seat.

"Going to town?" I asked.

She nodded.

It was the woman I had seen in the rain the day before.

"You're the woman with the horse," I blurted out.

She looked at me over top of her sunglasses.

"I mean you're the one riding the horse. Yesterday. In the rain. In front of the cafe."

"You're the one staying at Henry Cardinal's?" she said, shrugging her shoulders.

She wore tight faded jeans and a simple white t-shirt under a denim jacket. Her long black hair was braided and fell to the middle of her back. Her skin was a soft smooth brown. She looked over at me and smiled. I couldn't help but smile back.

"Are you going to town?" she asked.

I felt myself flush. "Yeah. Yeah, I am." I stepped on the gas but the car was in neutral. "Car's in neutral," I stammered. I slid the indicator to drive and headed off down the road.

Neither one of us said anything. I was edgy and trying to think of something witty to dispel any impression of me as a total idiot. I wanted to keep my eyes on the road but couldn't help glancing her way every now and then. She seemed content to watch the scenery go by. Finally, the only offering I had to break the silence was my name.

"I'm William."

She didn't turn her head. She just kept looking out the side window. "Agnes," she said. I mouthed the name to myself. Agnes. It was too much. Such a hard simple name for someone so pretty. Agnes. It was like a stone in my mouth. I had expected something more musical. Something like Laughing Wind or Star Flower or even Linda.

"William isn't much of a name." She kept looking out the side window, intent on the forest line. I was taken aback. Was it a coincidence or had she read my thoughts in some way?

"What's wrong with William?"

"Too stuffy. Too businessman. William," she said in a low voice, pulling herself up as straight as she could and throwing her shoulders back. She pursed her lips into a tight pout. "Hello. My name is William. William B. Tightass."

"Hey," I was hurt. "I didn't make fun of your name."

"Of course not. No one named William would be so impolite. You wanted to, though." She waited for an answer. I couldn't meet her eyes. I kept looking at the road ahead and there was only the harsh whisper of the gravel road beneath us.

She turned back to her window and the thick green blur of the passing forest, "You remind me of the boys in college. 'Agnes?'" she said it with mock surprise. "'Agnes? That's no name for a sweetheart like you.'" There was an edge of bitterness in her voice. "You white boys are all the same."

"I'm not really white," I told her, feeling slightly affronted. "I'm here looking for my mother."

"I heard the sad story."

At this point I felt it best to keep my mouth closed. The sullen road stammered on underneath the car wheels and pitched back and forth and rose and fell in petulant, low hills. Agnes maintained her vigil at the passenger window and I stole looks from time to time, studying the curve of her breasts, the colour of her folded arms, the dark, controlled plait of shining hair. I wanted to say something to make her feel better and to demonstrate that I wasn't the same as those others. Something to push the chill out of the small car and get her to talk to me again. "So what would you call me?"

"Billy," she said without a breath of thought. As though it had always been meant to be.

"Billy was what they called me when I was a child."

She turned from the window and even through the green lenses of her sunglasses, I felt her eyes peering into mine. "I still see a child in you." She said this softly, and I knew it wasn't meant to be an insult. "That will be my Indian name for you. Childforever. Billy Childforever."

We drove on in silence, but this time it was more amiable. We weren't strangers any more. I repeated the name to myself. Billy Childforever. She might have been half-joking when she said it — I couldn't tell — but she hadn't meant to hurt me and I liked the name. I wanted it to belong to me.

She guided me into town, which began along the highway as one long truck stop of gas stations and restaurants and a few rough homesteads. As we drove on, the houses became more refined and numerous until they finally evolved into side-streets and fenced yards. Then stores began to pop up and the speed limit dropped as the two-lane turned into the main street. I let her off next to a bland storefront with a sign indicating it served as the Ministry of Social Services. She thanked me for the ride.

"Are you going to be long?" I asked.

"It's always long in there," she said dryly.

Coyote wandered and danced through many years this way. He fooled and was fooled many times, and he loved a good joke even if it was on him. He would have been happy to live this way forever, but one night the prank-playing came to an end and a great change came to Coyote's life. Coyote had come to sleep beneath Grandfather Oak, who had stood tall and steadfast for as long as he could remember. It was said that the great tree's roots ran down to the very centre of Mother Earth. Coyote always came in the fall when the weather turned clear and warm, with days that seemed left over from the Moon of Berries. He liked to crawl under the ancient one's yellow cloak and open his medicine bag and curl into the last dreams of summer. On this occasion, as he slept, the visions came even more vividly than usual. In his dream he saw himself sleeping, coiled nose to tail and in fact, dreaming. The sky was filled with stars overhead. Suddenly a constellation began to pull itself together. Its points of light growing brighter and converging as the space between them grew solid and took on form. It metamorphosed into the brilliant shape of a huge bird and began to fall out of the sky with terrific speed. Lightning flared from its belly and cracked the sky ahead of it and thunder rolled deep and long across the world. Coyote knew it was Binay-Sih, the Thunderbird. He watched his other self tremble in the sleeping world. The bird dove straight down upon him out of the dreaming sky, eyes like flame, wings like tongues of fire, talons sharp and open. SleepingCoyote stared at himself still sleeping in his dream. He wanted Dream-Coyote to wake and run, to shake off the vision of the giant bird burning down out of the heavens. But DreamCoyote didn't wake, and Thunderbird flew past, straight through the counterfeit earth as though it were mist, and his claws fell on SleepingCoyote and snatched him up and pulled him through into his own dream.

The highway hypnotizes you. The lines flashing past. The steady hum of the tires. The endless, leaden road. It is always there. Waiting for you. I think about driving to the end of the highway. Staying on as far as it goes, till it runs down and touches the Atlantic. Or I could turn south. Next stop, Tierra del Fuego. If the money holds out.

Then I begin to think about dying. About crashing. Death zipping by every few minutes or so. Headed the other way, or maybe headed my way. Sunglasses on, bony arm out the window, and the stereo playing loud. Death behind the wheel of his import with a gunsight for a hood ornament. Every approaching car seems ominous. This could be the one. Bang.

What would it be like? The suppressed mystery of sudden impact. The old heap exploding in a cloud of rust and blood and fire. There is a glint in the distance, sunlight off a windshield or a chrome bumper. It disappears as the highway rises up between us. My hands begin to sweat, gripping the steering wheel. What if thinking about it could make it happen? What if I've set something in motion with my thoughts? The car surfaces again under its bright gleam, bigger now. An ominous blotch of blue rushing towards me. Then it dips back into the road again. It's like walking down the sidewalk and you see someone coming your way and you think to yourself, I don't want to run into that person. Just as that thought enters your brain your eyes meet theirs and you can tell that they are thinking the same thing. You look directly at each other and start evasive action, but each time one moves the other seems drawn to them.

The two of you are trying so hard that it becomes an absurd minuet until finally you either both have to come to a complete stop or you end up walking into each other.

There is one more small hill and then the road is level. I adjust my grip on the wheel and I've pulled myself forward to stare out through the windshield. I am waiting for him to come over the crest and bear down on me.

I had to cover fatal accidents as a reporter. The number of dead and injured, the damage to the vehicles. That seems so ludicrous now. Two killed in weekend accident, damage to the car estimated at ten thousand dollars. Lives have ended, now on to the property losses.

I was never on the scene, though. I wrote the stories based on police reports and pictures the staff photographer took. I never saw anyone dead on the pavement. Never looked upon mutilated corpses still oozing their sanguine surprise. Only photos of bodies covered by plastic yellow sheets or the injured on stretchers. Only names read dryly over the telephone. Just the facts, and a colour picture on page one.

I am almost to the hill now, and the other car still hasn't come into view. I expect to meet it somewhere along this flat straight stretch and to watch him grow bigger as he approaches, taking up more and more of his lane, the car expanding as it closes in, bulging like an over-inflated balloon. Its colour beginning to change. Blue pulsing dark to almost black then softening, growing lighter till it matches the clear summer sky, then deepening again, changing to brown, then magenta, then crimson. Glowing from inside, becoming like a hot rushing coal till finally its own speed fans it into flame and it is a solid mass of fire spread across both lanes and surging forward to swallow me whole. My own old heap rocketing towards its destiny. Thirsting for the junk pile. The slow delicious sleep of soothing rust. Even if I was to take my foot off the accelerator, my car's speed wouldn't decrease. It would no longer be a matter of internal combustion, just molecules rushing to collide. Things compelled by a time and space we know nothing about. Maybe we are all innocent bystanders turning in the darkness, fooled by our illusion of light.

Still no sign of the other car. Of hellfire on wheels. Of death's dark sedan. I have to laugh. Nervously, but with relief. My shirt is damp and perspiration has beaded along my forehead. There probably was no car. I've been staring at this grey ribbon for far too long. Sleeping next to it and dreaming of it. Dreaming even while I'm on it. Lost at one hundred kilometres an hour and driving deeper into confusion.

Maybe he is waiting just over the crest. I'll reach it relaxed and believing everything is all right, and then as I top the hill he'll be there, huge and unavoidable. I'll have a second of realization and then I'll be gone. Is that the way it is? One second here with the sunshine and the radio and the yellow prairie a blur going by and then nothing. Not even darkness. Nothing.

The crest looms, seconds away. I'm trembling and clutching at the wheel. There are those eyes again in the mirror. Help me, I know you. You are sure and happy. I remember you. If anything happens. Take me back.

The road lurches up, lifts over the small rise so that more and more of the countryside comes into view. I can see down the road but not directly ahead where it drops on the other side. My stomach folds over the way it does on a roller coaster and my ears fill with a rush of air as I try to take in every little sound, my eyes growing wider and wider, my body stiffening. Then, as I plunge over the crest, a cloud crosses the sun and a shadow falls over the car. In a panic I crank the wheel hard to the right and cringe at the dirt and stones running underneath and deflecting off the frame. I mow down a few small bushes bouncing down a slight embankment, the car fishtailing as I try to find the pavement again, my foot reflexively jamming on the brakes hard, pushing the pedal to the floor. A barbed-wire fence slices through the horizon in front of me, and turning the wheel frantically I steer the car parallel to it, finally coming to rest up against one withered post.

I open the door and slowly crawl out. Nothing can be seen on the highway in either direction. It is a puzzle. This dirty hunk of metal is pressed against the wire like a child at the zoo. The placid highway looks like it has always been here. But it hasn't. It was built by human hands and since then many humans have passed this way. Maybe on this low hill, on this relatively flat landscape, some have died. Maybe even before there was a highway, humans ended their days here. Who would know?

All day on the radio there has been news of a catastrophic plane crash on a mountain top in Peru. A hundred lives gone in the same moment, and I can't escape the image of so much coming to an end at one bleak set of co-ordinates. Disintegrating in a flash of exploded fuel. Bones and luggage mixing like puzzle pieces stirred in the box.

I watch the still prairie waver in the heat and puzzle over how each heart in the brief seconds of the crash must stop beating. Some specific thing has to end each particular life. That is why there is so much destruction, why everything blasts apart into such small pieces. It is not just the tremendous impact or the aviation fuel, it is too much time being jammed into too small a space. I lean against the car and in my head I hear a hundred lives compressing into the same detonated second.

SIX

It didn't take me long to do what I had to do. I bought another carton of cigarettes, a couple of t-shirts, some pocket books and a case of beer for Danny Elkhorn. It felt good buying the beer. Not because of any gratitude I felt to him, but because I thought it would make Henry glad to see that I was a man who paid his debts. Next I found the laundromat. Looking at the sullen, clanking machines I decided I could do laundry later in the week. I drove back to where I had dropped Agnes off, parked the car so that I could keep an eye on the building's front door, and settled back in the seat with one of my new books.

I waited for over an hour, but she didn't come back out. It seemed unlikely that I had missed her, since I'd been watching the door so intently that I'd only managed to get through a page and a half of the novel. I got out of the car and walked up the street, then strolled back down, peering into the stores as if I was window shopping. In front of the Ministry building, I slowed down and studied the inside.

It was a typical government office. People dressed very business-like moving around busily or at their desks talking on the phone, the room divided by ubiquitous fabric-covered curved partitions. A lot of ordinary people standing around, sitting in rows, lined up in front of the receptionist. Waiting.

I could see no sign of her. Perhaps she had never gone in there, or she'd found the lines too long and decided to try again later. I returned to the car disappointed. I had wanted to see her again, buy her lunch, drive her back to the reservation. Most of all I wanted to hear that name again. Childforever.

I started the car, then turned it off. I was in town. I might as well go for a beer. I made sure everything was locked and headed for the Grande Level Tavern.

It was dark and noisy inside, which is not all that surprising for a hotel bar early in the afternoon. I pushed through the double doors and stood for a second adjusting to the murky interior. It was familiar. Long bar against one wall, pool tables near the back, small round tables covered in red terry cloth scattered around. Across the room from the bar, against the opposite wall, was a low riser that passed for the stage, and in front of it an open area on the scuffed, hardwood floor for those who might be inclined to dance. There was even a band setting up.

The clientele seemed equally routine. Baseball caps and cowboy hats. Solid middle-aged guys carrying basketball-sized paunches inside dirty shirts and young men bent over the pool tables with sleeves rolled. Shiny boots and hard moustaches and Patsy Cline on the juke box. Except for the electronic cash register, it could have been any year since 1957.

She was sitting practically dead centre in the place, on the edge of the dance floor. Two full beer bottles rested on the table in front of her. I walked over and sat down. She didn't look up right away. She kept turning her glass on the table, slowly, with one hand.

"You must have been quick in that place?" I said.

She turned her head, surprised. "It's you." She didn't smile.

"Yeah, it's me, Childforever."

"That was just teasing, William." She still wasn't smiling.

"Oh," I said, and then I was stuck. Some guy on stage was setting up equipment, repeating, "Check. Check," into the microphones. It felt as if the entire bar had its eyes on us.

A pair of cowboy boots appeared in the periphery of my vision as I sat absorbed with the cigarette burns in the tablecloth. The bartender was a tall, slim giant. From my perspective, his slicked-back gleaming black hair seemed to be brushing the rack of coloured lights pointed at the stage.

"What'll it be?" he asked.

"Uh," I felt small and confused, my head tilted back like a child staring up at his father. "Uh, I'd like..."

"Nothing," Agnes answered for me. The bartender shrugged and ambled away. I pushed my chair back from the table and started to get up. Agnes reach out and pushed one of the full beers towards me. "Here," she said dryly, "I don't drink."

I plopped back down in the chair. "If you don't drink why did you come in here?"

"Habit," she said dryly. "And it's the best place to catch a ride back."

"Why did you order the beer?"

She looked at me to see if I was being serious. "I didn't, Childforever, some of these nice gentlemen did. They're looking for a little dark meat this afternoon."

Stunned silence again. I took a long drink of beer as I looked around the bar. Most of the men met my gaze with a sly smile or a conspiratorial wink. One old man in the corner by himself raised his glass of draft in a salute. I nodded.

"Listen," I said, studying the smooth brown symmetry of her arm. "Do you think we might talk about the weather or something pleasant?"

Agnes had a sip of her pop. "We don't have to talk at all."

"Jesus. You know, when I wrote for the paper back home I had a few tough interviews. Asking questions when someone had just had a family member die or talking to people who weren't all that happy about being in the paper. I even got shoved a few times, and had one old fellah take a swing at me. But nothing was ever this tough, and I'm just trying to be friendly."

"Hey, whiteman, everybody in this place has been trying to be friendly with me since I walked in."

"I told you I'm not a whiteman." I was starting to get angry.

She was almost shouting, and the bar patrons were watching intently. "I know what you told me. But every time I look at you, I see a whiteman."

I pushed my chair back violently so that it scraped sharply on the wooden floor. The beer I had been drinking tipped over onto the table. I pointed my finger, and then someone took hold of my collar and jerked. It was the dark-faced gargantuan bartender.

"This guy givin' you trouble, Aggie?"

"Fuck off, Norman. We're just talking." Agnes had snatched up the tipped bottle before too much had spilled.

The bartender sat me back down in my chair and leaned over close to Agnes. "Any more trouble, Agnes, and I'm throwin' botha youse outta here."

I pulled my chair back in close to the wet table. "Man," I said, "I think you've pissed off everybody in this joint."

She softened at that. "Sorry," she said and then looked right into me with her deep hazel eyes. "So, how's the weather?"

We did talk about the weather for a while, about my trip, and what it was like where I'd grown up. About my job at the newspaper and my things being stolen. Agnes asked about my wife and how she felt about the whole affair.

"Never married," I said. "Came close a couple of times, but they gave up on me. Time went by and I got used to being alone. Selfish, you know. Even my parents gave up nagging me for grandchildren. In my father's eyes it was just another indication that I'd never grown up. Accepted responsibility. That sort of thing. Never quite made it to manhood." I raised my eyebrows then picked at the label on my beer bottle. "You?" I asked, holding my breath.

"Came close," she said. After a few seconds we turned to less personal matters. Easy conversation in the dim, subdued bar. I drank the two beers bought by strangers and one I paid for myself. I studied her face and her hair, the way her hands held the perspiring glass and brought it to her lips. The way her throat moved when she swallowed. The way she looked shyly at the table when I made her laugh her low, husky laugh.

I ordered another beer from Norman.

"Do you think you'll find your mother?" she asked suddenly.

I looked at Agnes as I handed a five to the waitress who had just come on shift. I waited for her to put the change on the table before I answered. "I don't know. I don't know much about her. Except that she's supposed to be dead." We stared into our individual drinks. "Maybe she's alive. Maybe she doesn't want to be found. I don't know what's true and what's not. If I can find out about my past, that will be enough, you know. I mean if I can learn a little about my heritage kind of thing." I felt uncomfortable talking about it. It was hard not to sound corny or trite.

Agnes nodded her head as I spoke but didn't look up from her glass. "I would want my son to find me."

I wasn't sure what she meant. "Do you have any children Agnes?"

She tilted the glass towards her mouth and started to say something but the band started up, loud and abrasive, as if they all had picked a different song for the opener. It was a kind of musical implosion. Guitar, bass, drums and electric piano all on separate vectors, and after a minute or two splicing together a barely recognizable rendition of "Whisky River."

We drank and traded shy smiles as the band blared, unencumbered by musical tradition. The lead singer and the rhythm guitar player each had music stands in front of them and every so often reached out to frantically flip a page in a large black binder. The drummer and bass player either had better memories or were just winging it. They ended the first set with a medley of drum solos that included the obvious "Wipeout" and the somewhat more obscure "In-a-Gadda-Da-Vida."

By this time I had finished a couple of more beers and was leaning over to talk loudly into Agnes' ear. I was commenting on the quality of the music I think, when I lost my train of thought. It was the scent of her, the way her hair curved around her small ear, the shadows that played along the nape of her neck. I stopped talking, lost in those shadows.

She turned and looked at me as the drummer mashed out the last few beats of his ten-minute tirade. It was dead quiet as we stared into each other's eyes. I was dizzy from the alcohol and lack of food, and my peripheral vision was blurred so that it seemed the entire bar was spinning around the red centre of our damp table top.

"You all right?" she said.

The lights came up and I sat back heavily in the chair, blinking. The bar came into focus. The same crowd of sullen men sat around drinking.

"Yeah. I'm okay. I forgot what I was going to say. You want another drink?"

I ordered another round for us and we sat sedately, avoiding each other's eyes. The bar was too bright and the murmur of low voices too serious. There were no distractions. No camouflage for my eyes. I wanted to steal looks while she watched the band. I wanted an excuse to lean in close and smell her neck and her hair. To feel the electric charge of being close to her.

She offered no indication of it being a mutual attraction and regarded me in a bemused way. I was beginning to lose my nerve in the well-lit afternoon doldrums before the second half of the band's matinee. I finished my beer quickly and raised the empty bottle towards the bar. Norman nodded glumly and turned to open the cooler. I was working hard to convince myself that some time during the next musical interlude I would steal a kiss.

"I'm going to get going."

"Huh?" I said.

"I'm heading back. I was hoping to catch someone but it doesn't look like she's gonna show."

It was as if she had read my mind again. I looked around the bar to see if the band was getting ready to start their second set.

"Let me finish this beer and I'll drive you back," I said, trying to act casual.

She looked at me dubiously. "You've had a lot to drink..."

She left it open so that I could fill in the blank myself.

"I'm okay," I said, shrugging and turning my palms up. "What's the problem?"

She mulled it over. The band walked across the tiny dance floor and stepped up onto the low stage.

"All right," she said, half-sighing, as though she felt she was making a mistake. A shiver of relief went through me as I took a sip of beer.

There was high-pitched squealing as the lead singer approached the microphone. He backed away and made some adjustments to his guitar and then stepped to the front of the stage again, turning a few pages in the black binder on the music stand in front of him.

"Howdy, folks," his voice boomed through the bar. It was obvious that he had been doing a little drinking between sets.

"We're going to start off the second half of our show with something a little slow. A little number by The King." He nodded to his rhythm guitar player and they broke into their rendering of "Love Me Tender" with the beefy lead singer doing his best Elvis impression.

I leaned in close to Agnes. "Want to dance?"

She turned away, shaking her head.

"Come on," I shouted at her. "If we're going to listen to this we might as well have some fun."

"You really are drunk," she retorted, her face full of light.

"Yeah, but that's when I do my best dancing."

I looked up at the band, and the lead singer was scowling down at me. It wasn't part of his Elvis impersonation. He'd caught me a few times during the previous set laughing at their mistakes and shaking my head. Now my loud overtures to Agnes in the middle of his big romantic number were obviously getting on his nerves.

"Come on, Agnes," I pleaded. "One dance and then we're out of here, before he starts doing Wayne Newton."

She laughed and didn't resist when I took her hand and pulled her onto the dance floor. I had just gotten my arms around her and begun to sway in close to her body when the band stuttered to a halt. I looked up at the stage to see them huddled in an impromptu conference. I didn't want Agnes to sit back down, so I stood watching with my arm around her shoulders.

"Folks," the lead singer was grinning wickedly. "We've decided to do a special number for the dancers here."

I looked at Agnes and we both started chuckling.

"One, two, three..."

Agnes told me later it was a popular song on the local radio station recorded by a northern singer-slash-songwriter. The full title is "Squaws Along the Yukon are Good Enough for Me." By the time they hit the first chorus I was charging the stage.

The band leader had some experience in these situations and I didn't get too close before I was kicked in the face. His cowboy boot shot out snake-like and I remember distinctly how the heel looked a fraction of a second before it smacked into my right eye. This caused me to veer sharply to the side of the stage where I crashed into the bass player's legs. He fell heavily on top of me. The lead singer then planted a second kick in my lower ribs. I couldn't see a thing. I could barely breathe. I tried to pull my legs up into a fetal position but someone had taken hold of the left one and was tugging furiously.

Agnes was shouting at the bass player to get off me. He rolled to the side and as he did, shoved down on my head so my face bounced off the plywood riser. Once he was clear, the lead singer kicked me in the chest. He pulled back for another boot and I lay there stunned, the wind knocked out of me, watching the brown leather missile float back and cock into position.

There was a moment's hesitation as he lined up on my clouded head and then I saw the pointed toe screaming towards my face in hazy slow motion. The scuffed brown boot bore down slowly, gracefully, full of great violence like some diving bird of prey. I was pondering whether or not it would flatten my nose when Norman the bartender appeared and jerked the lead singer off the stage. The sole of the boot barely grazed my cheek.

Agnes pulled me to my feet. "Come on. Let's get out of here."

The entire bar was involved in the melee now. Everywhere people were wrestling and punching. Chairs flew about the room and glass was shattering around us. Agnes led me by the hand, pulling me through the storm of bodies and debris. I heard the door opening and then I was dragged outside.

Light exploded in our faces. I couldn't believe how bright it was. I had forgotten that it was still the middle of the afternoon. I stumbled around with my arm thrown over my aching face, blind with pain and the stabbing glare of the sun, clinging to Agnes' hand.

"Jesus! I can't see a thing," I blurted out.

"Come on." Agnes tugged and we started running. I stumbled slightly as we stepped off of the curb and started headlong across the street. My eyes were beginning to adjust and I could see the pavement as we ran, and then, too late, the side of the car. I bounced off and sat down heavily on the hard road.

"Shit," Agnes said. She opened the back door and helped me to crawl onto the seat. Her hands probed the pockets of my jeans for the car keys. I felt kind of giddy. I heard the front door close and the car start up and then we were headed out of town.

I lay on the back seat watching the blurred tops of things go by. Trees splayed against the blue sky, a few buildings, a church steeple, power poles. At a stoplight an older man with a beard pulled up on the right riding a bicycle. He looked down sadly at me and then the light changed and we pulled away from him. I felt small and weak lying there, my body quivering with the movements of the car. I looked up at Agnes, serious in her driving but calm. She had saved me. I slowly raised my arm and laid it over my throbbing face, covering my eyes, unworthy and ashamed.

I remained like that with my face hidden, letting the car rock me, the pain pulsing inside like another organ. Agnes was quiet in the front seat. She didn't try to make conversation or ask how I was or berate me for being such a fool. I lost all sense of time ruminating over the bizarre chain of events back at the hotel. I had never even seen a bar brawl before then. I didn't snap back to the present until gravel flew under the car. We were on the long torturous road that led to the reserve.

I gripped the back of the front seat to pull myself up, and the hurt washed over me from the top of my head to my feet.

"Do you want me to drive now?" I asked.

"I can handle it," she replied into the mirror. "This road needs someone with two eyes."

I shifted to see myself. The right side of my face was swollen grotesquely and my right eye half closed. Dried blood ran out of both nostrils and was caked around my mouth. Nausea undulated out of the pit of my beer-filled stomach and bloated my cheeks.

"Pull over," I croaked between tight, distended lips.

"What?" She shot a quick look over her shoulder.

"Pull over." I put my hand over my mouth, reaching for the door handle with the other.

The car had barely come to a halt when I tumbled out into the dust cloud. I struggled to my feet and Agnes was there helping me up and guiding me to the green blur of the woods. I bent spasmodically at the waist and vomited forcefully onto the ground. Bile filled my mouth and pushed through my throbbing nose, burning my nostrils and bringing on another surge of retching.

Through the stupor of my misery I sensed her at my side, her hand gently rubbing my back. I choked and sputtered through the last few evil tremors and allowed her to lead me away and lay me down in some tall grass. I looked up at the cloudless sky but it started to spin so I closed my eyes again. Something roared by on the road, throwing dust and stones and honking its horn. Then she was over me again, dabbing at my face with a wet cloth and cleaning away the blood.

"Does it sting?" she asked.

"No," I said. My face was senseless now. Stinging was out of the question.

"It's pop I found in the car. Really takes the blood off, though."

I ran my tongue along my teeth to check that they were all in place.

"Here. Sit up."

She helped me pull myself up and handed me the can. I swirled the dark liquid in my mouth and spat on the dry ground. The liquid was warm and thick and soothing. I looked up at her like a little boy who's fallen out of a tree.

"Well," she said wryly, studying her watch, "not even six-thirty and you're drunk, been beat up, kicked out of the hotel and puked on my shoes. Maybe there's some Indian in you after all."

I sat in the front seat the remainder of the way back to Red Clay, my head resting against the grimy window as the car rattled and shivered along the twisting road. I didn't talk and Agnes made no attempts to draw me into conversation.

We drove past the cafe and past the first turn onto the reservation. She eased off the accelerator till she was only doing a few kilometres an hour and then the trees closed in overhead so that it became a kind of tunnel.

A figure stumbled out from the trees, the man who had bummed a cigarette from me the day before. His hair stood out from his head just as wildly and his clothes were dirty and covered in leaves and dead grass. He stepped back as we approached and leaned against a tree to steady himself as the car passed by. Agnes stared straight ahead and did not even glance at the spectre of the man with the twisted hair. He glared at us at first and then when he saw Agnes his mouth dropped open.

"Hey," he shouted hoarsely. "HEY. Agnes. Agnes." He shouted something in Cree. She did not slow down or even glance in the mirror.

"Who the hell is that guy?"

"They call him Ditchhair." She didn't offer any more and I didn't ask her. Not about the strange man on the road, not about where she was taking me. I had already put her through enough and she had pulled me out each time I was in trouble. The very least that I owed her was my trust.

We drove for a long time under the overhanging trees down the narrow dirt road. She went slowly, sunlight barely filtering in, lost among the dense shadows and tangled dead shapes. I slumped down low, my head resting against the back of the seat and rolling back and forth with the movement of the car. The trees opened up and we drove into a large cleared area of low rolling hills. The car climbed and then dropped down like a small ship on a turbulent sea. My head lolled and bounced on the seat and I felt frail and insubstantial.

She rounded a curve and passed through another short archway of snarled branches and a house appeared, a charming little bungalow with white siding bright and shining in the late afternoon sun. It was so new there were no curtains on the windows and the manufacturer's stickers were still on the glass.

The road ended a few yards from the front of the house. There was still evidence of recent work: a palette with a few bricks sitting on it, the tracks of trucks and some heavy machinery and dirt piled about here and there.

Agnes turned off the car. "This is where my ko koom lives. My grandmother."

"Ko koom," I tried to repeat. I made a slight grimace that I had meant to be a more congenial expression. I wasn't exactly in the mood to meet the family but I didn't want to hurt her feelings, either. "I don't know if I really want to meet anyone in this condition."

"You look fine. Well, not too bad. Come on. I'll tell them what a hero you were."

I shook my head. "First impressions are important," I said, trying not to sound disagreeable, my numb lips pressing together like two obese men in a bus seat.

She got out of the car and headed toward the house. "Suit yourself, William Sawnet," she called over her shoulder.

I fumbled with the door handle and slowly pulled myself out into a semi-erect position. I bent back into the car and adjusted the rear-view mirror so that I could study my abused face. My right eye had swollen almost completely shut and the bruise had grown dark and angry. I flattened my hair down and straightened my shirt and tried to wipe the dust off my pants. When I looked around, Agnes was gone.

The house stood mutely in the clearing, the front door tightly closed. I thought I saw someone standing at the window waving but, with the angle of the sun and the reflection of the trees, it was hard to distinguish. I took a few hesitant steps up the dirt path that led to the front entrance and glanced up at the big front window again. Once more I saw only shadows and the reflected sky. I stalled, fussing with my clothes and hoping the door would swing open and Agnes would be standing there with her arm around her grandmother beckoning me to come in. The door stayed closed. It was strange and still. I took a deep breath and walked up to the door.

The thought popped into my head that maybe her grandmother had got a look at me through the window and an argument had taken place. Maybe she had sent Agnes to her room, or forbidden her to see me. Perhaps I was supposed to just go away. For all I knew her father or brother or uncle or husband was making his way to the door now, looking for a baseball bat or loading a gun.

I raised my hand and knocked lightly, leaning towards the door and listening to hear if someone shouted, "Come in!" or "Get lost!" or anything. Nothing but silence. I knocked a second time, more forcefully, my palms sweating and my empty stomach churning. I reached into my pants pockets. No keys. Agnes had my keys. It was either meet the family or walk.

Maybe I'm supposed to saunter right in, I thought to myself. After all, it was a culture that had lived for centuries in tents. Agnes' grandmother had probably lived in a tent. You can't knock on a tent, I reasoned. I turned the knob and slowly began to open the door. It was deathly quiet. No conversation, no TV, no radio, not even the sound of the birds singing outside.

I peeked around the open door. It was empty. Completely empty. No furniture. No pictures on the wall. Nothing. I stepped inside, holding the door open.

"Hello." I said it softly as though in a church.

There was no answer. "Hello. Agnes?" I spoke her name so that the people there would not see me as a complete stranger, but there were no people there. Only the shadowed, pristine walls and the unfinished plywood floors.

"What are you doing?"

I couldn't help an involuntary jump. It was Agnes, standing behind me on the dirt path leading up to the house.

"I'm looking for you," I said, exasperated but relieved to find her.

"We're waiting for you out back."

"Out back?"

"Yes," it was her turn to sound piqued. "Didn't you see me go around this house?"

I shrugged. "I'm not seeing so well."

She took my hand. "Well, come on. Granny is impatient to meet you."

I hesitated. "Could I go in and clean up a bit first?"

She dropped my hand. "Not really. There's no running water."

I turned and took in the lovely little bungalow. "Huh?" was all I could manage.

"No running water, and no electricity down at this end of the reserve yet either."

I stood for a minute, confused and unsure of what to do or say. "How do you..." I didn't even know what I was going to ask.

She didn't meet my eyes. "We manage. The way we always have." She took a step back and I sensed disappointment, "Look, it doesn't matter. I told them what happened. They won't care how you look or what you're wearing. It's not important."

I pleaded with her. "Agnes. I'll just whip back to Henry's and straighten up. It'll only take a minute. Please. I want to make a good impression. Please." I reached out to take hold of her arms but she backed away.

"Fine. Go change, William Sawnet." She stepped back so I could walk past, handing me my car keys.

I started for the car. "One minute. That's all." She nodded.

I jogged to the car, holding my right arm tightly across my aching ribs, and pulled myself gingerly in behind the steering wheel. When I looked up, all there was to see was the white house sitting naked in the clearing. The setting sun seemed perched on the low black horizon of the shingled roof. Now that I knew how void the place was, it seemed I had never seen a more desolate house. An open forty-five-gallon drum sat at one corner to catch rain water running out of the plastic downspout. It seemed like a lot of trouble to go through, building a house just to fill a rain barrel.

I reached into the back seat and snatched up one of the new plastic-wrapped t-shirts I had purchased a hundred years ago that afternoon. I ripped away the cellophane, checked for pins, and got out of the car. I walked to the rain barrel, unbuttoning my shirt. I stuck my head into the cool dark water, then straightened up, pushing my hair back, and let the water run down over my shoulders and along my spine. I cupped my hands and splashed water onto my face three or four times.

I used my old shirt for a towel, sniffed into my armpits despite the pain of raising my arms over my head, and put on the clean t-shirt. Taking a deep breath, I followed the path around behind the house.

Coyote tried to shake off his surprise, as though it were drops of rain caught on his fur. "Thunderbird," he said. "Why have you brought me here?"

"It is Gitchie Manitou who has brought you into the dreaming, Coyote, not I. You are here because a great transformation is coming to the world, a time of strife and sadness for many. We are all in danger. We all need to be strong. You have wandered and played as a child all this time, Coyote, and now it is the season for a more implacable vision. Stay beneath this sacred tree, and dig a pit to lie in. Fast and wait for your manitou to come. It is important you do nothing but wait, and don't let the fear of what you do not know control you."

Coyote felt himself falling as though from a great height. When he looked down he saw his own sleeping shape stretched out beneath him. He stared wide-eyed as he hurtled towards the dreaming one. The giant tree, the ground, the DreamCoyote rushing up to meet him. He crashed down through the bright orange branches in a shower of dry leaves and dead limbs until, with a jolt, he woke with Grandfather Oak laughing and trembling above him, and shaking down a rain of acorns.

I sit on the hood for a while, my car resting against the barbed-wire fence like an old cow, the two of us watching shadows drift across the yellow grassland. A few cars pass. In the quiet of the afternoon, in the middle of nowhere, you can hear them coming from a long way off. The earnest humming of tires, the whoosh of air shoved aside as they pass, the fading buzz as the growing distance falls in behind them. I don't even look. I watch the prairie shimmer in the heat. Arid and still. Patient under the searing eye of the sun.

It is soothing to sit here. Stopped, as if by the road itself. As if these few acres of asphalt and fenced emptiness have been waiting for me all this time. Waiting to seep in through my eyes. To be touched and remembered. As though I've been driving around with this chunk of time in the trunk and a half-remembered address.

"Are you in need of some help?"

It is a woman's voice. I wasn't even aware of the vehicle approaching. "P-P-Pardon me?" I stutter.

"Need help?" she shortens the question but it is still pleasant enough.

I jump off the hood, my legs twitching as circulation returns.

"You've been here a-time," she says. She is middle-aged and heavy, wearing a baseball cap with a Cat logo and gold laurels on the brim, her elbow stuck out the rolled down window of a Toyota wagon. A man sits next to her behind the wheel. He is red-faced and round and dressed all in green. "We saw you on our way in to do groceries."

The little fat man nudges her sharply, "Quit jabbering, woman. Does he want some goddamn help or what?"

She twists towards him and lashes out with a half-closed fist. I can see a tissue poking out between her fingers as the blow smacks into the man's shoulder. "Of course he wants some fuckin' help, Adrian. Do you think he stopped here to get a tan?" She turns back to me, smiling demurely. "You want help don't you, dear?" she says softly.

It seems best to nod.

The car lurches forward, angling sharply out across the pavement, then shudders to a stop. I stand at the edge of the road hunched over, peering at the place where it was a second before. I am having trouble following this staccato sequence of events. There is a brief grinding of gears and then the little wagon backs down towards my car. It stops short again a few metres away and the driver's side door springs open. The little fat man pulls himself out.

He is grizzled and dirty and his belly is distended to amazing proportions, yet somehow the rest of his body doesn't seem flabby. He waddles to the back of the car like a troll coming out from under a bridge, ranting and waving his hands around. I step back out of his way.

"I wanted to take the pick-up, but oh no, we have to take this little Japanese piece-of-crap. You always want to take this goddamn riceburner. Jesus, I hate this fucking car." He wrenches the hatchback open, rummaging around in the back for a few seconds before whipping a length of rope out and shaking it at the passenger side of the car. "I have chains in the goddamn pick-up. I wouldn't have to use this son-of-a-bitchin' useless rope." He is almost in a froth and I inch back further.

"Sweetie," the woman in the car says, beckoning to me. "Come over here, sweetie. You can't help, believe me. That old foul-mouthed cocksucker has to do everything himself."

I go and stand by her passenger window.

"Where are you from, dear?" The old man has thrown himself down violently behind the car and is busy tying the rope onto his axle.

I look at her. "Maybe I should..."

"Let him do it. I'm Marguerite and that old bastard is my husband, Adrian. Now, who are you?"

"My name is..." I am undecided a second or two. "Wil... Billy... William."

Adrian bounces up out of the dust and begins playing the length of rope out towards my car. He is cursing less vehemently.

Marguerite takes my hand. "I think you've had a little too much sun, William. You look like a William. Where are you headed?"

I smile pleasantly, blinking into the sun. "I think I'm going east." She lets go of my hand and I let it drop and go back to watching the muttering, grubby leprechaun tying a rope to the undercarriage of the car. The world is spinning and picking up speed. Marguerite opens her door. It nudges against me and I see her sandalled foot, her thick, waxen calves with their heavy blue veins. Her hands are on my shoulders, guiding me into the passenger seat. I am dreaming again.

SEVEN

I'm not sure what I expected to find when I followed Agnes behind the empty bungalow. I think I was prepared for the kind of rustic, one-room dwelling that Henry called home. Or a log cabin. Or an old trailer. What I saw, set back from the house a little ways, near the edge of the woods was a tepee. Actually, two tepees.

I paused a second or two with my mouth hanging open, then I walked towards the large cone-like structures, taking it all in. The white horse was there with another, darker horse, a mare with a startling ivory-coloured face, as if the front of the skull was exposed. The animals were grazing contentedly, tails swishing back and forth. There was no fence but they were both hobbled, each with a rawhide strap around its front legs.

No one seemed to notice my approach except a small girl who sat in front of the tepees playing with a frying pan and a plastic shovel. She watched me walking towards her along the narrow path but said nothing. I kept hoping Agnes would appear but guessed she had given up on me. I considered clearing my throat or dragging my feet or making some other polite noise when I got close enough, but became distracted by the tents.

They really were tepees. Triangular canvas shapes held up by long, rough poles, apparently freshly cut that year. I could see where several large sheets of tough material had been carefully sewn together. Each tepee had one whole side completely rolled back, opened to face the other. In between, a fire pit with a tripod set over it supported a hanging cook pot.

The tops of people's heads were visible, bobbing around in between, but no one seemed aware of my presence. Agnes was talking in an animated manner with someone in the tepee on the left. A middle-aged woman was busy near the fire and a small boy played with another woman in the back of the second shelter.

I felt out of place, not knowing the rules of etiquette involved, afraid of offending before I even got started. I stopped, hoping someone would notice me, and the little girl let out a long shrill scream before running back into the tent to huddle beside the boy and woman.

I was possessed by a similar urge to turn and run. Everyone was staring. "Hi," I said. My bruised and swollen face began to pulse.

"You decided to come after all, Childforever." Everyone turned and looked at Agnes.

"I didn't want to disappoint you." They all swivelled back to me. My eye throbbed.

"This is William, everyone. Rosemary, stop that silliness." She spoke a few sharp words in Cree to the little girl and then turned back to me. "The one I was telling you about."

The old lady said something I didn't understand. "Pardon me?"

"She said to thank you for helping me," Agnes translated as she took my hand and led me into the sheltered space between the tepees. I mumbled that it was nothing and blushed deeply. An elderly man I hadn't observed before met my eyes and looked away again.

We stood together near the cooking pot and, as the aroma reached me, I realized how hungry I was. Agnes directed my attention away from the bubbling pot and to the tiny, elderly woman who had spoken.

"I told ko koom how brave you were," Agnes said by way of an introduction.

The old woman wore a faded, plain dress and a tattered dark jacket with the top three snaps done up. The zipper appeared to be missing. A few wisps of down protruded from a hole in one elbow of the coat. She sat up straight on the hard wooden chair to greet me, her hands neatly folded in her lap. The two heavy-set women moved to either side, shyly waiting to be introduced.

"Hello, Mrs. Cokum," I blurted out stupidly.

Everyone laughed and Agnes jabbed her elbow into my ribs. She glared up at me through her long dark eyelashes.

"Ko koom. It means grandmother," she hissed, through clenched teeth.

"Oh. Right. Sorry." The old woman sat quietly, studying me with an amused expression. "My, uh, my name is William Sawnet." I wasn't sure if I should shake her hand and I didn't want to commit another faux pas so I stood nodding, eyes darting back and forth.

Agnes pulled me around to face the other two women.

"These are my aunts. This is Eleanor Yellowhorn and this is Daisy Cardinal." Daisy appeared to be a little older and bulkier than Eleanor, who had a round, happy face that constantly beamed at me. Agnes pointed towards the children. "The little girl is Rosemary, the little boy is Wylie. They're Eleanor's kids. This is Uncle David. He lives here with ko koom." Uncle David was a stooped old man with thick black-framed glasses and an old green hunting cap stained by years of sweat. Agnes pointed to a bassinet in the corner. "The baby girl over there is Emily. She's Daisy's granddaughter, but her mother is away in Youth Detention, so Daisy's takin' care of her."

"Oh," I said as she whirled me back around, then went over to talk to her grandmother. They spoke quietly in Cree and I stood with my hands in my pockets. Eleanor and Daisy watched me curiously. The kids stared unabashedly. I felt compelled to whistle but didn't want to try with my deformed mouth.

"Childforever."

It took me a minute to realize Agnes meant me.

"You want to eat, Childforever."

"That would be great," I said. I was ravenous. Prepared for anything. Raccoon stew. Dog soup. "What are we having?" I asked.

"Spaghetti," answered Aunt Daisy.

It was a pleasant, congenial meal. The two aunts saw to my every need. Refilling my plate, handing me buttered slices of bannock, topping off my coffee mug. Most of the extras came out of two large metal coolers shoved off to one side. The aunts efficiently looked after everybody, old uncle, the grandmother, the children, without complaint or a harsh word. I felt like an extra burden but every time I started to move one of them would rush to sit me back down and provide what I wanted. They refilled my plate twice, but I had to decline a fourth helping. They still wouldn't accept that I was full and kept checking from time to time to see if I might like something else. Even Agnes wasn't allowed to help, and the women kept coaxing her to sit closer to me. Uncle David appeared to be hard of hearing and half-blind. He would wander away into the darkness out of the stark circle of illumination from the lanterns that were hissing loudly. Then Eleanor or Daisy would put their plate down and go to guide him back into the light.

It was strange there with the lanterns throwing their loud, elemental brightness and the cook fire sputtering low, flaring with the occasional gust of evening breeze, then dying down to embers again. The two aunts were busy and sure as they went quietly about their duties, their mammoth shadows projected against the white canvas, the old woman knitting silently behind us, and the children playing in the space between the tepees. Huge yellowish moths bounced against the lantern glass while stars appeared in the black wedge of space above their heads.

The darkness deepened. The empty house disappeared forlornly behind the curtain of night and Daisy woke Uncle David from where he'd nodded off in an old armchair near the back of his tent. I watched, entranced by smoke and a full stomach and the gentle hour as they gathered up a few articles and the children. Then, as Rosemary stood gently cradling the baby in her small arms and Wylie held Uncle David's ancient hand, the aunts rolled the canvas back around so that there was only a small overlapping doorway and the tepee was sealed away for the night.

Ko koom said something and Agnes went to her and helped her to stand up. Eleanor came over and handed the old woman a cane, then took her free arm. The old lady spoke to Agnes and nodded at me.

"Good night, ko koom," Agnes said.

"Good night," I muttered shyly as everyone shuffled away. Except for the sickly light of the flashlight sweeping back and forth, they were swallowed by the darkness.

"Where are they going?" I asked.

Agnes had begun to roll the canvas around to seal up the tepee we had eaten in.

"They are all going to stay with Daisy at her house. Except Eleanor, who is going to her own place."

She had tied the canvas back in place, and I was shut up in total darkness.

"Do they need a ride?" I asked loudly out of my temporary blindness.

"No, no. Ko koom likes to walk and it's the only exercise Uncle David gets." She came in through the low doorway with a lantern and the tent became a cone of light. "There's a path through the woods that's much shorter than the road."

"They're going to walk through the woods?" I said, incredulous.

Agnes didn't bother to answer. She set the lantern down.

"Well, I hope we didn't drive them away," I continued, blinking against the white, hissing glare.

"Naw. Granny won't admit it but she likes to watch Daisy's TV set.

The aunts come over every night and make supper for ko koom and Uncle David. It's out of love... and respect for elders," she added almost as an afterthought.

"It's nice," I muttered, watching her throw down a big sleeping bag and open it out to its full width. She then began to spread some blankets on top to make a bed. When she was done, she stretched out across it and twisted the control knob on the lantern so it faltered and went out.

It was quiet and black as pitch inside the tepee. I sat without saying a word, waiting for my eyes to adjust to the darkness.

"Are you sleeping over there, Childforever?"

Her voice was different in the darkness. For a second I thought maybe there was someone else there with us, that it was all some sort of a prank. Her voice was deeper and sounded charged, somehow. Not nervous, but suffused with the night.

It was hard to find my own voice. "I wasn't sure what you wanted," I managed to mumble after what seemed like too long a time. Long enough, I was sure, for her to melt away in the darkness or for this night to end abruptly.

"I really named you well." Her hand was suddenly on mine, though I hadn't heard her move. She gently tugged me towards her. I reached out with my other hand to prevent us from colliding headlong. My fingers found her chin and she kissed my fingertips as they fell across her lips. My hand fell to her shoulder and I pulled it away as though burned when I touched her naked skin. She sighed and I reached out again and this time found her breast. I kneaded it gently and felt the erect nipple. I bent to take it in my mouth but she had begun to pull my shirt up over my head. I stopped and she jerked the t-shirt off and flung it away. I undid my jeans, pulled them down as far as I could, then had to teeter over to one side so that I could straighten out my legs and work my clothes off the rest of the way. I got as far as my ankles, pants, underwear, socks, everything bunched together on top of my feet. She kissed my forehead and face, her arms wrapping around my head and pulling me towards her breasts.

I left my pants alone and kissed and sucked at her nipples, her chest, her throat, her chin, till our lips met. We kissed long and hard but finally my back and left side began to ache from holding the awkward position.

"Wait," I said, breathlessly.

She moved away from me.

"Don't go." It was a shout. Desperate pleading.

"I'm right here." There was playful mirth in her voice. Her foot came up to rest against my chest. I took her foot in my hands. I kissed her heel, the delicate arch, her little toes.

"It's these goddamn pants," I grumbled with my lips tickling the bottom of her foot. "Just one second." I gently put her foot down and began to tear wildly at the bunched denim wound tightly around my ankles, cursing and clawing. Suddenly a flashlight clicked on and the beam struck me fully in the face. I blinked against the light and held one hand up in front of my face. The light played down over my chest and stomach then paused for a few seconds on my impatient erection. Finally, it was directed at my restrained feet.

There was enough light bouncing around to see her now. A lithe shadow behind the flashlight.

"Agnes?"

She laughed, throwing her head back and for a second I saw her again, wet and graceful on the back of the white horse.

"Who were you hoping for... ko koom?"

She chuckled and I watched the way her breasts moved and quivered. I studied her long legs and the subtle perfect curve of her hips, the wild abandon of her hair, and the deep, lush shadow between her legs.

"Get me a knife," I said, only half in jest. It had been a long time since I'd been to bed with a woman.

She became earnest and turned her face to look at me. The beam of the flashlight played up along my body again and I knew she was studying my face. I knew what she was seeing, though I couldn't define it myself. Lust and love and ardent wonder. I heard the passion in my own voice.

I would have cut the jeans away, I think. Looking at her standing there naked and full of a voluptuous glee, I might even have considered amputating my feet to get to her.

She walked over and turned the light on my bindings again.

"No need to get drastic," she said, but there was a nervous need in her voice now. She laid the light down and carefully tugged off my socks, then the pants, one leg after the other, and finally, my underwear. The anticipation grew as I watched her remove my clothes, as though she was tending a wound, taking care of me again.

I pulled myself up into a kneeling position and snatched away the flashlight, tossing it across the tent so that it spun light around us before it crashed among some pots and pans and went out. I clutched her hard against me and we fell back through the darkness and onto the makeshift bed.

It was a kind of love-making I'd never experienced before. Natural and elemental. She seemed to rise like the earth out of the darkness underneath me. There were no words. We met and explored each other with mouths, hands, feet, consumed by the night, devouring each other. There was only our shattered breath in the sheltered night. We burned against each other, igniting the oscillating dark, then slumped into the shadows, until, after a time, we searched for each other again with lips and fingers in the telepathic space.

When I woke in the morning she was gone. I lay curled under one corner of the scattered blankets, chilled and happy. The leafy shadows of trees swayed along the sunlit canvas and there was the smell of old smoke and cooking and sweat. I rested there for a time, remembering the night.

I expected Agnes to return in a few minutes. I thought maybe she had gone out to use the washroom or something. After twenty minutes of reminiscing about her body it began to dawn on me that perhaps she wasn't going to come back.

I looked around to see if she had left a note of some kind, but all I could find were my neatly folded clothes. She had straightened up a bit. The flashlight was back near the head of our makeshift bed, and I chuckled at the cracked lens and my melodramatic desperation of the night before.

I stood up, throwing the blankets off, and stretched towards the apex of the tepee where the crude support poles intersected and were tied together. I felt untamed and utterly guileless, naked at the centre of the ancient structure, my skin tingling with the heat of a full night of sex. I closed my eyes, letting all the sense memories of her body moving under me and over me rush through my brain. I felt myself growing stiff and eager again and I started to turn in a coarse, circular dance, whooping and smacking my open hand against my pursed lips.

A slight noise made me open my eyes. There was Aunt Daisy with her head poking in through the door flap. She remained fixed there a few seconds, her head stuck through the canvas at an odd angle, her mouth gaping. Then she disappeared, as if by magic. I heard a few voices in hushed, energetic conference outside. I waited without moving, trying to discern what was being said, but they were speaking in Cree. Someone kept saying the same thing in disbelief. I decided it would be best to get dressed and get the hell out of there.

I bent to scoop up my clothes and heard the flap being pushed open again. I whirled around and held the bundle of clothes over my now withered penis.

Aunt Eleanor poked her head tentatively through the opening.

She studied me for a second or two.

"Agnes here?" she asked.

I shook my head. "No. No, she's not."

"Oh."

Aunt Eleanor vanished back outside and I heard the women laughing. I dressed hurriedly and searched around for a brush or comb I could use to smooth my hair down. I couldn't find one and, sighing heavily with my hair ruffled and standing out in wild clumps from my head, I ducked out through the tent flap.

Everyone was there. Ko koom. The aunts. Uncle David, already nodding in the other tepee, which had been opened up and tied back again. The kids were off playing in the field and the baby was lying in the scarred crib, nursing on a bottle. Everyone looked away politely except for the old woman who watched me and smiled. I nodded to her and said something inane about what a lovely morning it was. She nodded back in a dignified and regal way. Agnes was nowhere to be seen.

"Well, I should get going," I offered to no one in particular. Studying the sky like a sailor, I started towards the path, immediately kicking over a metal tea pot. Thankfully, it was empty, but it bounced noisily ahead of me. I picked it up and replaced it, mumbling numerous apologies, then hurried off down the path, my face burning. It was a long, long walk and I had to resist the urge to run all the way.

By the time I had driven out of the dark laneway with its overhanging trees and broken limbs that scraped along the side of the car, I had become aware of the aches and pains from the injuries inflicted in the bar fight. I checked my eye in the mirror and saw that I had a first-class shiner. Everything else was just bruises and muscle aches.

I was puzzled over Agnes' disappearance but the glow of our lovemaking dispelled any anxiety I should have had. My tingling contusions, flashes of erotic memory, the preposterous exchange with the aunts, all filled me with a cavalier sense of freedom. On that gravel road with everything I owned in the car, battered and with the scent of sex clinging to me, I was a freebooter. A rogue. A halfbreed nomad.

The day shone around me, open and intense, and in the naked morning light the reserve seemed like a happy, virtuous place. Even the bleached white bones of the long-dead horse resting in the ditch seemed quaint and peaceful, somehow. I drove absent-mindedly along the gravel roads, pulling the habitual plume of dust behind me like a pennant.

I pulled in at Henry's place feeling guilty for having been away so long and not letting him know that I was still around. I got out of the car and bounded cheerfully across the small yard and up the steps. I started to swing the door open but had only moved it a few inches when it thumped into something solid and heavy. There was a low moan from inside.

"Henry?" Panic rose up out of my stomach and I shoved hard, throwing my weight against the door. There was the sound of a body sliding across the bare wooden floor as I squeezed in through the opening.

A young boy who looked to be about ten or so was sitting up behind the door holding his head and groaning. He seemed vaguely familiar to me.

"William," Henry was sitting cross-legged on his small bed, smoking his pipe and wearing boxer shorts and the long-sleeved undershirt that served as his nightclothes. Three other young boys were stretched out on the rough floor. Two were sitting up, looking at me curiously, and the third remained sleeping, curled in a semi-fetal position near the wood-stove.

"I thought maybe you'd gone home."

Henry seemed oblivious to the young boys rousing themselves from his floor. The one behind the door was standing now, rubbing his right arm and shaking his head. I turned towards the other two, who were awake but had their attention focussed on the floor. I did a double take back to the one I had shoved aside forcing my way in, and studied him. He wouldn't meet my gaze. He was the boy I'd seen on the horse with Agnes. The other two were now trying to motivate their snoring comrade.

"Jamie. Wake up, Jamie."

The one called Jamie rolled onto his back, his arms flopping out like dead disconnected things. He moaned and opened his bleary, bloodshot eyes.

"Goddamn. What's wrong with you?" His voice was a dry, cracked croaking.

The nudger kept nudging. "Come on, Jamie. Way meis tei koshoow."

Jamie's eyes tried to focus. He turned his head to take me in and I suddenly felt much older and much taller. He let his head loll back to a comfortable position and closed his eyes.

"You a worker?"

It took me a second to realize he was talking to me. "A worker?"

"You know," he said impatiently, "social worker."

"Nope, not me," I answered, amused.

He opened his eyes and sat up. He seemed a year or two older than the other three who, by now, had slipped out through the open door and were standing in the yard, spitting and kicking at the ground.

He pulled himself to his feet and stood in front of me. Something slipped from his pocket and clattered onto the floor. It was a cassette tape, a homemade compilation I'd put together for the trip. We looked at the tape, the song titles in my neat handwriting, then at each other. He bent slowly and with an arthritic tenderness picked up the plastic case and slid it back into his pocket without a word. "Well, what are you doing here then, whiteman?"

His manner wasn't particularly hostile, but I didn't feel as big as I had looking down at him on the floor.

"I'm looking for... someone."

He smirked, then shrugged and went out through the open door to join his friends.

I looked at Henry, who had gotten himself dressed during my encounter with the drowsy Jamie. "Who were those boys?" I asked.

He seemed preoccupied, and busied himself straightening the cabin up. "They come here to sleep sometimes. When they don't want to go home."

I noticed a brown paper bag on the floor where Jamie had been sitting, and meaning to help, I bent to pick it up. I had thought it was empty, but when I lifted it I could feel a weight shifting inside. I opened the rumpled bag and there was a baby food jar with no lid sitting upright on the bottom. Inside was a white mucousy substance. I held the bag under my nose and inhaled. The odour was sharp and chemical and its thick tendrils dug into my brain.

"Shit. It's glue." I was angry at their stupidity.

Henry looked at the bag but wouldn't meet my eyes. "I don't allow that in my house," he said defensively. "They don't do that in here."

I could see he was anxious and out of sorts having to defend himself. I was touched that he felt it necessary to do so and reached out to put my hand on his shoulder.

"It's okay, Henry," I told him. "It's not your fault."

He walked towards the open door and stood with his hand on the latch looking out into the front yard where the small circle of boys had been only moments before.

"Kids, you know. They do crazy things. All kinda crazy things. They don't go in the bush. They don't wanna do nothin'. They sniff glue, sniff gas. Drunk all the time. Drunk in school, even. I don't know what to do. I give them a place to sleep so they don't get hurt."

"It's okay, Henry," I said again, regretting the way I had reacted. I didn't know what else to say.

"That boy Jamie. He's my niece's boy. He's been sent away three times now. Soon he's gonna be old enough for prison. The last time he was only back two weeks when he broke into the school with a rifle. Cops everywhere. Guns all over the place. Jamie stayed in there all night, sayin' he's gonna shoot somebody. Sayin' he'd shoot himself. Finally he gives up. They go in there and he's got a .22 and a box of shotgun shells. He knew better. I know he knew better. The cops think he's just a stupid Indian kid. I think he liked where he was better than bein' home."

Henry remained fixed on the vacant yard, then closed the door and turned around. He pointed at my face. "So, what happened to you?"

We had coffee and a hearty breakfast. Eggs and sausage and fresh bannock. I was amazed by my appetite. I told Henry about the fight in the hotel and he had a good laugh. I told him I'd help him get some wood and this made him very happy. He suggested we start immediately, afraid

I might change my mind, I suppose, so after breakfast I emptied out my vehicle and stored the stuff in Henry's cabin. As I was slamming the trunk down for the last time, a bedraggled orange pick-up bounced to a halt next to my car. A tall man, maybe five years younger than myself, wearing a big black cowboy hat, got out. He was barrel-chested, his torso thick and round, and he wore his belt low underneath his protruding belly. His arms were thin and angular, composed of tight sinew and knobby bone. He kept his hair long and pulled back in a loose ponytail. He was chewing on a toothpick.

"Hey," he said.

"Hello," I answered.

He walked around the back of his truck and spit his toothpick into the rusted-out box. He looked my car up and down and stood uncomfortably close to me.

"You the guy that belongs to this piece of junk?" His smile was broad and cold.

"Yes." I retreated involuntarily.

"You're lucky those kids didn't set it on fire." He guffawed harshly and clasped my shoulder in his big hand.

I relaxed a bit. "You must be Danny Elkhorn. I've got something for you." I was glad for an excuse to put more space between us. I opened the trunk again and lifted out the case of beer I'd picked up in town the day before. "Thanks for the help," I said, offering the beer.

He stood with his arms akimbo. "No problem. Just throw it in the truck, wouldja? I got to talk to Henry." He walked down into the cabin without looking back.

I put the beer in the truck's box. There was no tailgate so I pushed the case up close to the cab. I decided to wait outside and sat on the hood, daydreaming about Agnes. After a few minutes I heard the door slam and Danny Elkhorn was headed back towards his truck. He stopped halfway and regarded me over the back of the dented pick-up.

"I'm glad you're helpin' Henry with his wood. I've got business to do today." He opened the door, then paused. "Don't believe everything that old man tells you. He thinks he's related to everyone." He climbed in behind the wheel, then pulled himself back out. He pointed his finger at me, "You're Henry's guest and that's fine for now, but some bullshit about a little Indian blood don't mean you belong here." He got in his truck and drove off, pulling an angry cloud of dust.

We spent the rest of the day cutting wood at the end of a dirt road a few miles north of the rez. Henry taught me to run the chainsaw and pointed out the trees he wanted. Mostly deadfall that was hung up or standing defunct and dry.

It was a lot more work than I had bargained on, but it was thrilling with the buzzing saw jumping and bucking in my hands, the grey trees crashing down out of the sky with limbs snapping and bark flying. I cut and cut, only stopping to fill the saw with gas and chain oil, while Henry knocked off limbs with his axe and smoked his pipe and offered advice on where to cut.

Under his direction, the trees dropped with amazing accuracy. It was something I'd never even considered, the idea of making a tree fall precisely where you wanted. I always thought you just cut till gravity stepped in, then jumped back and yelled "Timber." I yelled timber every time, which made Henry shake his head. There was no one to warn with only the two of us there. He'd probably never heard so much hollering in all his wood-cutting life, but by the fifth or sixth tree, he was bellowing right along with me.

We cut all morning. It was slow at first because I kept hanging trees up due to my inexperience and some poorly angled cuts made despite Henry's patient guidance. Henry never showed any signs of frustration. Not even those times when I cut too deeply and ended up with the guide bar pinched in the trunk. We would simply work to free the saw or the tree, pushing and pulling and, as a last resort, cutting down the entangling tree. Most of the time these were green, living maples.

"That'll be good for next year," Henry would say, slapping my shoulders.

When the third tank of gas ran dry he suggested we eat lunch. We found a couple of stumps close together and sat down. My ears were full of the irate buzz of the chainsaw and my arms were trembling from the vibration, but I felt fine. I couldn't remember feeling so good, so full of something I couldn't describe. Henry turned the top of his old thermos and the air was full of the fragrance of fresh coffee. Everything was new and rich. The trees, the birds, the sky. Even my twitching, tired arms.

Henry handed me a plastic cup of coffee and then the bag that held sandwiches. We sat quietly munching our food and sipping coffee and studying the woods around us. There was too much in the world for there to be any talking. Words were weak and insufficient things. We chewed and drank and listened and it was one of those times when you knew you were where you should be. On that stump, under those trees with the blue plastic cup at your lips. There was nowhere else.

Finally, Henry slapped his hands together and pulled the saw in close. He produced a triangular file from his jacket pocket and began to sharpen the curved metal teeth.

I sat and watched, sipping coffee and listening to the rasping of the file drawing across the dark teeth. One by one the small edges began to shine.

"Do you remember any more about her?" The question I asked surprised even me.

Henry didn't look up. He ran his thumb and forefinger over the toothed chain, clearing away sawdust. His head tilted to one side, the unlit pipe clenched between his teeth.

"No," he said simply.

I waited, thinking he was just gathering his thoughts, but he only went back to sharpening the saw. I continued drinking, feeling strangely foolish for having broken the spell. There was a tension between us now. Looking back, it was a surprising connection that existed between me and that old man. Without saying a thing, he made me feel every shift of sentiment passing behind his deep brown eyes.

I don't remember how many times during our wood-cutting expeditions I would be working with the saw, absorbed totally in the noise of the gnashing teeth and the heat and smell of the exhaust, when suddenly I would feel the need to find Henry with my eyes. He would be gazing up into a tree at a climbing porcupine or a woodpecker pounding holes into some rotten trunk and pulling out insects. He would never say anything to me. The lesson was in seeing, in observation. He told me in one way or another when to look, but he never once told me what to look for.

One morning he pulled me out of bed before dawn. I was surprised at such an early start. He had hot oatmeal waiting in a bowl on the table and stood by impatiently while I stuffed it into my mouth. We made it out to the woodlot just as a weak greenish light began to spread in the sky. I zipped my jacket up tightly under my chin to fend off the morning chill and jerked the starter cord on the reluctant saw a few times. I yawned and shook my head, watching the mist drift between the trees. The thrill of manual labour in the great outdoors was wearing thin. Halfway through the first cut I was sure I felt Henry's hand pulling at my shoulder.

"What?" I shouted, hitting the kill switch in annoyance and turning around. Henry was more than fifty feet away, standing next to the car. I was about to ask if something was wrong when I heard it.

It was a sound I recognized, though I'm not sure from where. Movies or television maybe. Wolves howling, somewhere in the distance. It was very different hearing them there in the woods, melancholy voices stretching across the forlorn silence that comes before dawn. It was a mournful, disconnected song that rose from the earth, through the dark shadows of the trees. It fell from behind the cryptic sky to resonate against my bones. The hair stood up on the nape of my neck. In the half-light of the bush around me, I expected to see the glint of feral eyes. The gleam of curved fangs.

Henry showed none of this discomfort. He stood, eyes closed, listening intently, but he sensed my nervousness. He said, "After a hunt, Maheegun always sings of his thankfulness."

It was helpful to know that their stomachs were full, though the uneasiness would not go away.

"That's how you say 'wolf'? Ma-hee-gun," I repeated. I thought talking might help dispel some of my uneasiness.

Henry's face wrinkled into wry amusement. "You call him a wolf but his name has always been Maheegun."

"Exactly what are they giving thanks for?"

Henry gave me a look one reserves for simple children. "For everything." He bent and began to gather some small twigs together.

"What are you doing, Henry?" I asked.

"We should give thanks, too, William. We oughtta remember who we are."

He placed a few strips of birch bark and the tinder he had gathered on a flat piece of ground, and pulled them into a rough pyramid shape. I stood watching, still holding onto the chainsaw.

"William, put the saw down and gather some firewood for me."

I balanced the awkward machine on a large stump and began to collect dead limbs displaced by falling trees. Henry had taught me a few days before that the dry grey branches recently knocked down were the best for burning. I accumulated an armful and took them to where Henry was setting a match to the tinder, then broke the limbs into shorter pieces. In a few seconds there was a vigorous fire going.

He squatted next to the flames and reached into his pocket for his pouch of tobacco. I noticed he had left his pipe resting on the hood of the car and started over to retrieve it.

"William. Where you goin'?"

"I was just going to get your pipe."

Henry turned to look at me, "Don't need it. Come here."

I squatted down beside him, perplexed. He reached over and put a small wad of tobacco in my hand, then reached out over the burning sticks. Rubbing his forefinger and thumb together he allowed the fragrant mulch to fall into the flames, a few strands at a time. As it burned he said a few words in Cree. Then he looked at me and indicated I should do the same.

"I don't know the words."

"Don't matter. As you offer the tobacco, feel thanks... here." He touched his hand to his chest. I felt foolish imitating his actions with the tobacco.

We were crouched near the flames. The thin brown filaments began to curl and burn as the pungent waves washed against our faces. I blinked and peered through the smoke at Henry for some indication of what to do next. His eyes were closed, his head bent towards the fire as he pulled a cupped hand up in front of his face, over his thick silver hair and down the nape of his neck. The smoke coiled and undulated behind his gesture and wreathed him in a slow, white bouquet. I did the same, made the same cleansing motions like someone lifting water from a basin, like an anointing. And yet it felt artificial to me. I was too busy with the process, wrapped up in each separate element. I concentrated on holding my hand exactly the way Henry held his, trying to pantomime his actions and make the smoke spiral towards my body in precisely the same manner. I parrotted sounds that had no meaning to me. For the old man it was a very natural process and there was an aura of reverence in the way the draft of his hand pulled the smoke around him. I only found myself feeling more apart from everything, remote and irrelevant, trying to decipher the exact nature of what was supposed to be happening.

When I glanced over again, Henry had produced a folded bit of hide from inside his jacket. He carefully laid back the flaps of soft deerskin and exposed a large, grey, white-tipped feather.

"What's that?" I asked, curious.

Henry carefully lifted the feather and held it up to the sky. "This was given to me a long time ago as a sign of honour. People here cared about such things, once." He passed the feather slowly back and forth through the smoke.

He shook his head sadly. "Now people drive around with eagle feathers hangin' from their rear-view mirrors. You can buy them at pow wows like t-shirts. A lot of people think you just hang it on a wall. Like a decoration. Or a picture. But that's not the way." He stared into me and held my eyes in a way he had never done before. His voice became earnest and emotional.

"You must honour it the way it honours you. You must remember that it comes from the eagle. You must take it out from time to time and show it the sky."

The old man gently laid the feather back down and folded the hide envelope around it before sliding it back inside his coat. I was feeling giddy, like someone who starts to giggle in church and is fighting for composure. I couldn't help thinking about what it would look like from the outside, the two of us tossing tobacco on the flames and waving a feather around. I imagined what Wilf's reaction would have been.

Henry poked at the fire with a branch, his uncanny intuition working again. "My mother gave me this feather. I was a boy, about fourteen, I think. Luke was away fightin' the Germans. He'd been away at residential school before that. They beat you there if you talked your language, you know, or if you talked about spirits or such. He didn't want to learn the old ways any more. He wanted to live in the city. Drive a car. He loved to go to movie shows and he would tell us about them when he came home. They filled him up with their magic and when he talked it was as if these stories had happened to him."

Henry sat on the ground staring into the fire, holding his strong, weathered hands out in front of him for warmth. They trembled slightly over the flames.

"My father kept me home to help on the trap-line. I wanted to be like Luke. To travel and see the big buildin's he told us about and have adventures. But..." He paused and sighed heavily. "... my sisters, Ellen and Molly, and my little brother, David, had died the winter before from influenza. Two summers before, the second oldest, Simon, he drowned in the lake durin' a storm. Luke and I were the only ones left. It was a very bad time." Henry seemed to contemplate this as he prodded the fire, threw more pieces into the flames.

"Back then, a lot of people lived in tents in the summertime. Big canvas tents and tepees. Some people still like that." He glanced at me and I blushed, though he had no way of knowing about Agnes and me. "My mother and I were sitting inside one mornin' and she told me she needed my help. She was worried that she was goin' to lose Luke in the war. She offered tobacco and sang a song. She still mourned for her dead children. I remember I was feelin' a little shy for some reason. Kinda embarrassed, you know? I was startin' to become like Luke, I think, and my father believed only in Christian ways. Then she handed me this feather and told me it had been in the family a long, long time. It had been given to her by her grandfather who was a powerful shaman. She told me to lift the feather up to the sun and sing the song, too. I had to do it because she was my mother. The sun was very bright. I could see it shinin' through the canvas." He turned to me, his brown, open face marked by the bittersweet pain of these memories. "I felt foolish. I thought it was a heathen thing to do and I wondered what Father Stokes would say when I told him about it in confession. I wondered what my penance would be. It was a bad thing to get on the wrong side of Father Stokes. Still, she was my mother, and so I started to lift the feather, but suddenly it became very heavy. My arm was like a piece of wood. I blinked against the sunlight. 'Lift the feather,' my mother said. I couldn't. I was sweatin' like... someone who had chopped wood all mornin'. I tried and tried and my arm shook but I could not lift it. It was as if my arm were tied to the ground. Then my mother began to sing the song. I started to chant, too. I was afraid. The feather seemed to lift on its own. I sang louder and my arm raised higher. The tepee disappeared and the feather pulled me up. Pulled me into the sky. When I looked down I saw my mother hugging Luke. He was home from the war. He looked sad and I knew his heart was heavy, but I knew he would come back. Then, like that, I was back with my mother and I told her what I saw. She was very happy."

I was mesmerized. My head throbbed and my stomach tightened into fluttering knots. Everything I had been wanted to analyse the story I had just heard, to shatter it into logical fragments. If it had been told to me somewhere else from anyone other than Henry I would have been amused and thought of it as an exaggeration and I would have said things like "power of suggestion" or "psychosomatic." A few days before, I had known only an old man living a simple life in a crude, backward place. Like so much before I had only known the surface. There was something deep and ancient and mysterious residing in Henry. A wisdom that easily pierced the centre of my being.

I stood slowly and the circulation returned to my legs. I had been squatting the entire time without realizing it. "Henry, why did you bring the feather today?" I was turning in place and lifting my feet one after the other in a strange little blood dance.

"Because of a dream I had."

I stopped my slow jig and stared at the old man as he kicked sand onto the sputtering fire.

"When?"

"Last night." He turned and walked back to the car to retrieve his pipe.

I wanted to know more. Were my dreams so strong now that they were creeping into other people's heads? Henry sat in the car to smoke his pipe.

"You mean I appeared in a dream to you and said, 'Henry, bring that nice eagle feather with you tomorrow?'" My tone was more mocking then I intended it to be.

He exhaled a lengthy blue sigh of smoke. "Not every dream has to be a dream of your future, William. I dreamt of my mother last night. When I woke this mornin' I had a feelin' I should bring the feather. When my mother gave it to me I was someone who was lost."

It was obvious he didn't want to answer any more questions and that perhaps he was perturbed at my obtuseness. He wouldn't even look my way. I ambled back to the saw and began felling trees and cutting them up with single-minded purpose. We hardly spoke the rest of the day. Henry sat in the car ignoring me.

Coyote dug his pit between two huge roots as big as trees themselves. When he lay with his head against one he could hear deep into the earth and feel the pulse coming up through it out of the centre of everything. Up through the trunk of the Grandfather Oak and into the sky.

At first Coyote did as he was told. He didn't eat or drink. He only lay in the pit and watched the sky and slept. But after a couple of days he began to get bored. Things were too quiet around him. As if everyone were waiting with him. Holding their breath, almost. The silence was oppressive and Geesis, though bright and unhindered by clouds, seemed to drag his feet across the day. The things that Binay-Sih had told him all seemed ridiculous now. What was time to Coyote? What was the world? He had been in this land even before the great ice had come. He had seen mountains ground to dust and oceans drain off the prairie. He had watched The People cross over from a distant land and followed them as they drifted south. He had played in their dreams and walked among them in his disguises. Thunderbird, first-born of Mother Earth, protector of all, had always taken his responsibilities a little too seriously.

The third night he sat up and tried to talk to the Moon. Tibiki-Geesis. He called out her name. Teeee-beeee-keeee-Geeeesis. Teeeee-beeeee-keeeeee-Geeeesis, he howled out again and again, trying to tease her, but she hid her face in Grandfather Oak's outstretched arms and ignored him.

The next day when he woke, dreamless and alone, he tried changing shapes to see if that would ease the waiting. He tried being a rabbit but he couldn't see out of the pit and every shadow made him jump. He felt too panicky as Wa-Booz.

He tried being a frog but, as O-Ma-Ka-Ki he was too tempted to eat the bugs and worms in the earth around him. He tried being a wolf, but that was too much like himself, only more cramped. He tried becoming Shi-Gak, the skunk, but couldn't stand his own smell. Finally he tried being Ei lei lo. This was better. There were more parts to play with. He decided he would be a person for a while.

I wake from a dream about Agnes and for a few seconds think I am at Henry's, but I am in a real bed in a small room with faded, simple wallpaper, an old scratched dresser with a square mirror, and a few cardboard boxes stuffed into the corners. The bed is neatly made with fresh linen and a homemade quilt.

I lie back and listen. Someone is shuffling around in another room. A refrigerator door opens and closes.

I have woken up in an unfamiliar bed in a house belonging to people whose names I cannot even remember. A wave of apprehension led to my driving off the road. The peculiar little man all dressed in green walks towards me with a rope in his hand; it is fuzzy and disjointed, and I have no clear idea of how I came to be in this place.

I sit up and swing my legs out to put my feet on the floor. My suitcase sits by the end of the bed. I stand up, surprised to find myself stripped down to my underwear. I hope this is something I managed on my own.

Tiptoeing to the door, I make sure that it is tightly closed, then throw the suitcase up on the bed and open it. All my clothes have been washed, ironed, folded and neatly placed back into the case. Even the few things that Agnes brought along have been laundered and carefully replaced on one side of the suitcase. I lift a folded pair of clean, white panties to my face and inhale, but all I can smell is detergent.

I select what I want to wear and pull them out with my fingertips. It has been a while since I have seen clothes this clean and I feel filthy by comparison. I dress slowly, enjoying the unsullied material next to my skin. I tuck in my shirt and examine the room for some clue of where I am.

I hardly recognize myself in the mirror. Unshaven, long hair standing out haphazardly from my head, I look gaunt and weary and bent over. My face is tinged red from all the sun the day before. I try to smooth out my hair with my hands but don't have much success. I pull open the top drawer of the dresser, hoping to find a comb or a brush, but the drawer is empty except for a brown sheet of paper curling on the bottom.

"You moving around in there?" A woman inquires. I have a vision of her kind round face looking down at me, her pudgy hand stroking my forehead. I can't remember her name and I stand paralysed in the centre of the room, unable to answer.

"It's Marguerite, son. Everything all right?" Her voice is deep and resonant but gently reassuring.

"Yes, Marguerite." My own sounds broken and shaky. "Thanks for the clothes."

"Listen, William. Why don't you have a bath and shave and then I'll make you a nice lunch?"

I pick my watch up off the dresser, but it has stopped running. The hands indicate 9:15. I clear my throat. I want to get out of here and back on the road.

"Uh, thanks, Marguerite but..."

She pushes the door open. "No argument. You have a bath, you shave, you have something good to eat, and then you can do whatever you want."

Marguerite is a large, meaty woman with a red polka-dot kerchief tied around her head, a faint mustache and a very serious look. Even if she were only half her size, there would still be no denying her. She reaches out and grabs my arm above the elbow in the kind of grip my father used to put on me when I was twelve years old. I offer no resistance and she pulls me out of the room, down a narrow hallway and shoves me into a tiny bathroom with a sink, a toilet, and a stand-up shower.

"Now you scrape that hair off your face and I'll get your lunch ready." She pushes the door closed forcefully, and I obey.

An hour later I have enjoyed a good hot shower, shaved, consumed two large toasted western sandwiches and am on my third cup of coffee. In between huge bites, while Marguerite watches, I give her the brief history of my journey.

Pushing myself back from the table, I toy with the coffee cup, turning it slowly with one hand, and say, "That's my sad story."

"It must be very hard on your mother." The remark surprises me. I expected the sympathy would be for me.

"My mother?"

"Have you talked to her lately?"

"No..."

"So that's it. After all those years of feeding you and clothing you and caring for you, you cut her loose when she was all alone."

I am taken aback. I am the one who has suffered. Who's had the rug pulled out from under his feet.

"Look, no offense, but I don't think you really understand, Marguerite. I grew up being William Sawnet and that was all a lie. Suddenly I had no idea who I was or were I belonged or who my real parents were. I..."

Marguerite plants her flabby hands on the table and pulls her bulk up out of the simple wooden chair. "Oh I,I,I," she bellows as she turns and makes her way towards the coffee maker. "Jesus, Mary, and Joseph. That's all you ever hear from any man. William, if you had shown up here two summers ago, you couldna' had that nice hot shower you had this morning. That old bastard Adrian had me livin' twenty-some years in this shack without running water. Fine for him out working all day then comin' home and flopping his fat ass in the chair. I hauled the water and washed the clothes and cleaned the house and cooked the meals. Okay for that sonovabitch to run out the door and piss in the snow, but it's different for a woman, let me tell you." She is pointing right at me and her face is crimson. The tension goes out of her jabbing forefinger. "Listen, boy, you're not a name. You're whoever you are. You're whatever happens between who brought you into the world and who gets you through it."

Her voice softens a couple of more degrees. "You want to talk about lost? What about a woman who puts almost fifty years into loving and looking after a man and a child and then loses them both? What's left for her? That's not an easy place to start from."

I stare down into my empty coffee mug. What Marguerite said made me feel treacherous and insensitive. Despite this remorse, I can still only think of myself. I am unable to dredge up any pity for Mona.

Marguerite stands behind me, one hand on my shoulder as she leans over to refill my cup.

"You won't find it in an old cupboard or hidden under a stone, William. It's already there under your own skin."

I can only nod.

Marguerite sits back down heavily. "I'll tell you one thing though," she says, smiling, "there couldn't be all that much Indian in you or Adrian would have smelled it out. He doesn't think much of company in general, but he won't have any truck with Indians. One cheated him out of a wad of money one time, and money is his one true love."

I twist my head and look at her with incredulity. She holds her hands up in a gesture of surrender.

"I said to him many times, I says 'Old man, you've had the wool pulled over your eyes so many times I could cut you up for lamb chops, and ninety-nine point nine percent of the time it was by white men.' Of course he doesn't see it that way. It's a hate he grew up with and it ain't right. But it ain't uncommon, and it ain't likely to change neither. It's as much a part of you as the blood you're born with."

I have no words. Not on my tongue, not trapped in my throat, not even mixed in with the swirling miasma filling my brain. I can only shake my head and smile weakly. Marguerite turns her attention out through the window over the sink.

"Don't judge him too harshly. He's ignorant, but he's a good man and people around here know they can turn to him when they're in serious need."

Minutes stretch like elastic between us and the kitchen becomes a closed and solitary place that I have known all my life. The warped floor, with its cigarette burns and dust, the wallpaper decorated with sheaves of wheat, the chipped white enamel stove, the green refrigerator with its loud hum, the unpainted cupboard doors. It is as if I created it.

Adrian charges in from outside, the screen door slamming shut behind him. A fine coating of ice shatters and drops from everything.

"Jesus Christ, old man, do you have to let that goddamn door slam a hundred times a day? I almost pissed myself." Marguerite leaps from her chair like a boxer answering the bell for round two in a championship bout.

Adrian stops dead and snorts. "Go. To. HELL." The last syllable an absolute bellow. He holds up his thick hands for emphasis. They are coated with a thick yellowish mucus. "I got grease up to the eyebrows and you're worried about a little goddamn noise." He gestures for emphasis and thick gobs of lubricant fly off and smack wetly against the walls.

"Stop swinging your hands, you old bastard. I just cleaned these walls."

Stuck between two huge snarling attack dogs, I keep my head low and concentrate on the table top. I don't even flinch when a large clod of grease lands on my head. Adrian twists the taps angrily and plunges his hands under the faucet.

"A hundred fucking times I asked you for rags. Give me some rags out in the shop, I said."

Marguerite stands with her fists buried in the rolls of fat on her sides, her face red as a stoplight. "I put a stack of fucking rags in the fucking drawer last week." When one raised the level of cursing, the other matched it immediately.

"What goddamn drawer?" Adrian is backing down.

"The big drawer next to the arc welder," she has him on the ropes now.

He turns the taps off and flicks his hands into the sink. "Well why in the hell didn't you share that news flash?" Wiping his hands on his pant legs to dry them, he shoulders his way back outside. The screen door slams loudly behind him.

"That sorry sonovabitch," Marguerite hisses through clenched teeth.

Half an hour later, I make my way out that same door, suitcase in hand. Marguerite follows with a bag of sandwiches and cookies for me to take along. On the doorstep I survey the cluttered yard, an acre jam-packed with battered cars, old school buses, trailers, fuel drums and mysterious jumbles of machinery.

I look at Marguerite. "Do you guys have a junkyard business?"

She throws back her head and chortles heartily. "No. It's just Adrian's little hobby."

"Oh." I walk to my car and open the door, tossing the suitcase over the seat into the back. When I turn around to thank Marguerite for all her kindness, Adrian is standing there behind her, wiping his hands with a rag.

"I tuned the engine a little," he growls matter-of-factly. "Threw in some better spark plugs I had lying around and I had a couple of rims with better rubber on them so I put those on the back. Your old ones are in the trunk."

I peruse the new tires. They are shiny and black as though hardly used. "Thanks..." I start to say, and begin to reach out to shake his hand, but he has already turned and is shambling back towards his workshop.

Marguerite takes my outstretched hand and squeezes. "I don't know how to thank you," I say, dazed by their generosity. She waves it off, shrugging. I sit down behind the wheel and close the door. I turn the key and rev the engine a few times. Looking up at her warm corpulent face, I say, "Tell him it sounds great. I appreciate it."

She reaches in and runs her hand underneath my chin. Slowly, softly. "You have such a gentle face." It is almost a whisper. "Even when you looked like a wild man ranting on the side of the road I thought you looked like an angel."

I can't meet her eyes, and only mutter a small, strangled *Thank you.*

She straightens up and steps back from the window, "Don't get your shit in a knot. I'm not sweet on you or anything."

"Take care," I say. I put the car into gear and drive away. When I look back, she is in front of her house, her arm waving slowly over her head like an overly thick sapling swaying in a summer breeze.

I drive down the long curving driveway and turn onto the gravel road that leads out to the highway. The farther I drive away from the small farm the more my uneasiness grows. I am leaving a place of sanctuary and the fear that has followed me since I left Red Clay is closing in again. Stones thrown up by the spinning tires beat against the sides of the car. First one or two bounce dully off the lower fender and a few off the doors, then, as I pick up speed, the tempo increases. Louder, a steady drumming down the sides of the car, building to a crescendo. I step on the gas, in a hurry to get to the highway, and as I top a small rise I can see cars whizzing by on the pavement less than a kilometre away. The pounding increases, like something desperate to get in, clawing at the metal, beating wildly against the sides of the car. I fix on the highway, my hands gripping the steering wheel more and more tightly, and I see a large semi truck turn onto the gravel road and start towards me.

I pull over as far to my side of the road as I can and try not to focus on the massive diesel-powered bulk picking up speed and roaring my way. It belches black smoke through its stacks as the driver works the gears, accelerating. The grill is a gleaming shaft of silver but I refuse to be distracted. I want only to escape the rhythmic flogging of stones against my car. Even as we pass, I refuse to look into the thick patterned eyes of the headlights or glance at the painted logo on the trailer.

It spins lazily up into my narrow tunnel of vision, lop-sided and grey and turning over and over. It is hypnotic, everything slowed down, yet I am rivetted and unable to duck. Only at the last second, when my screaming brain finally makes it clear that an egg-sized rock is streaking towards my head, do I manage to throw my arm across my face.

It hits the corner of the windshield and a glistening spray of glass falls over me like brilliant confetti. My foot goes instinctively to the brake and the car slides to a stop at an angle in the middle of the road.

I sit in a stupor, enthralled by the crystalline grit in my lap, waiting to see how much pain there will be. There isn't any. Rough pebbles of glass fall from my hair and I stare at the windshield. The corner is filled with concentric fractures and at the centre of the bizarre etched flower of cracks and divots is a round hole. I push my finger into the hole and find a thin membrane of glass still intact. It gives with the pressure of my fingertip and bows out a little. I pull my hand back slowly, afraid to burst that last meagre layer. I look in the side mirror but the transport has not even slowed down, the driver no doubt oblivious to the fact that he very nearly ended my life. The rock has bounced off somewhere and is now lying anonymously with the other stones on the dirt road.

I sweep a little of the glass litter off the dash and from my clothes, my stomach turning over. It comes in a hot, profuse rush. I barely get the door open, leaning out as best I can, restrained by my seatbelt. I vomit forcefully onto the dusty road top, retching and convulsing as my body empties itself out. I am not to be allowed nourishment.

Finally, it is over. Pulling the back of my hand across my wet chin, I slam the door and continue on to the intersection with the eastbound half of a divided highway. Without having to think, I turn into the merge lane with the flow of traffic. East is, by coincidence, the direction I have been travelling, but I am past worrying about that. I have no sense of a destination and have surrendered to instinct and whatever vagaries chance offers on this passage. I think of Mona and there is a wave of guilt over the things that Marguerite said, but I am unsure of what Mona really means to me. I think of Agnes and feel much the same way. The difference is that when I think of Mona I am William Sawnet. When I think of Agnes I am Billy Childforever. It seems that whenever I try to be one, someone or something makes me feel I am really the other.

EIGHT

Henry remained reticent for the rest of the day. I worked hard, hoping to impress him because I couldn't escape the feeling that I had done something wrong. That I had something to make up for. I ran the saw till it sputtered to a stop, out of gas, then immediately started loading what I could into the trunk and back seat while Henry sharpened the blade, refilled the gas tank and topped off the chain oil. Then, without saying a word, I would pick up the refreshed saw and begin cutting again. By the end of the day we had already made three trips fully loaded and now the car was once again packed with wood wherever it could hold it. It was hard on the old thing, the springs flattened out and groaning over every bump in the rough road, and hard on us; every bounce seeming to jar up through our internal organs.

We grunted and gritted our teeth and I felt like a worn-out attachment to the frame as we made our way home. I found myself trembling uncontrollably from the constant strain and vibration of running the chainsaw. At first I thought I had been struck by some kind of nervous disorder. Henry, however, seemed to take no notice of my affliction, and I came to the realization that all I had really been struck with was physical labour.

We swung onto the main road which was wider and regularly graded, much smoother than the crude cow path we'd been on. The sun was hot and as we made this final run late in the afternoon, it angled directly through the windshield. I lowered the visor to block it out and with one hand on the steering wheel worked my t-shirt off over my head. Rolling the side window down I stuck my arm out into the breeze. The air was warm and the sun was soothing. The tires, rushing over the crushed stones, sounded like a whispered prayer. The trees were green and lush on both sides, swaying slightly, side to side, like happy spectators. The sky was blue, unblemished, deep and endless.

It was hypnotic. The unchanging road. The seamless sky. The green corridor blurring past on either side. For a moment it seemed as though the car wasn't moving at all, but just the world spinning under us, the universe turning overhead. We were the pivot point of everything. The dozing old man and his afflicted apprentice, hands gripping the wheel, arms quivering in ecstasy. I felt every molecule glow like a fanned ember, felt the sun seep into my flesh.

The bee came like a winged bullet out of the shadows and in through the open window. I saw it only as an orange smudge of movement a half-second before it exploded on my naked chest. Bee parts and pollen splattered up in sticky droplets along my neck and face. It took me a minute or two to piece together what had happened. I thought at first that someone had spit on me. My tongue touched a viscous globule that had come to rest on my lower lip and it tasted sweet. Then I plucked something from my cheek and discovered it to be a tiny translucent wing. I laughed out loud at this unexpected anointing and looked over at Henry, who was still snoozing, arms folded across his chest, head lolling.

There was a sudden fuss and turmoil in the immaculate sky and I watched, my chest burning slightly where the stinger had gone in, as several blackbirds flew screeching around a large crow that flapped heavily across the blue expanse. They circled and dove and the crow was a silent, morose shadow plodding along on his unwavering course. The blackbirds swarmed relentlessly, like leaves spinning in a dust devil, and the crow was the black eye of that furious storm of wings.

"Watch the road, William."

His voice startled me. "Did you see those..." I started, steering the car back into the proper lane.

"Watch where you're goin'." It sounded like an order.

While I unpacked the overloaded car and piled the wood under the shelter built in the back yard to keep the rain and snow off, Henry went inside to make supper. I flung the wood from the car vehemently and for the first time began to take notice of all the sawdust in the car and all the little tears and rips in the upholstery.

I was busy slamming blocks of wood into place in neat rows under the plywood lean-to when I looked up and saw Henry watching me. Our eyes met and without saying a word he turned and disappeared around the corner of the house. I interpreted that as the signal that supper was ready and left everything where it was and went in to eat.

Dinner was painful. We chewed and drank and swallowed at the same small table like newlyweds in the middle of a spat. Blank stares and hurt feelings and long reaches across the table. I finished the last mouthful of lukewarm coffee, tossing my head back and then banging the mug down on the simple wooden surface. I looked at Henry, an angry question on my lips, then sighed heavily and got up to go.

"You're angry," he said flatly, lighting his pipe.

I stopped without turning around. "No. You are angry."

He kind of chuckled, "I'm not angry. You're angry."

I turned around, teeth clenched tightly. "I'm... not... angry."

"I saw you. You were angry," he asserted, his arms crossed, talking around the pipe stem.

"You mean with the wood. I was..."

"It's no good to watch such birds, William. The old ones say that if you do, your soul might go with them. The birds'll take it from you and carry it away and you will go crazy without it. Even the geese when they fly south. You shouldn't look at them in the sky."

Henry puffed and studied the floor as he related this story to me, not once meeting my eyes. He always became shy talking about such things and I was never sure if he felt I might laugh, or if he was being respectful of my ignorance. It was something I noticed when we were cutting wood, as well. If I was not doing something correctly he would take the saw and show me the proper way. He would never say, "This is the way it should be done," or "That's wrong." All he ever said was something along the lines of: *This is the way I was taught.*

"I didn't know," I said, simply.

"I saw you angry before that. When I held the eagle feather in the smoke. I saw you leavin' and you were angry. Angry because I got no more to tell you about your mother."

I was taken aback. I remembered him on his haunches by the fire, the feather passing back and forth through the smoke, and the long-ago vision of his brother. "I don't get it. Is this like a... vision? Like ESP?" I snorted, not in derision, but because it was beyond the scope of my understanding.

"I saw you," he pointed at me with the stem of his pipe, becoming defensive.

I was baffled and amused by this impass. I began to get a sense of what I was up against. A different and divergent history extending back to an unfamiliar world. My hand went to the crucifix I carried in my pocket, the gold emblem of my mother that Henry had seemed to pull out of my own dream to give to me. I put my hand on his shoulder.

"Listen. Don't feel bad if you don't remember, Henry. It was a long time ago. It's okay. I've already learned more than I could have imagined. I'm not going anywhere yet." His eyes moistened and he put his hand on mine, holding it there on top of his shoulder.

"Henry, look," I said. "I got to meet you. You're like the grandfather I never had."

He bowed his head. "I want to help you, William."

I went outside to finish up. I watched the darkness approach through the trees as I stacked the firewood, while a dozen different thoughts played inside my head. I missed Agnes greatly, and yearned for her as I relived our night of lovemaking in the tepee over and over in my head. I tossed the remaining wood haphazardly under the shelter, swept out what debris I could from the car and ran into the house.

Henry was sitting by the woodstove, drinking tea.

"Henry," I could hardly contain myself. "Henry, teach me some words."

He looked at me, puzzled, "Words?"

I was excited. "Indian words. Cree words."

"Ahh," he said, nodding. "What words?"

"You know, like today. Bear, wolf, hello, goodbye." I hesitated, giving myself away. "Sweetheart."

"Ahh," he said. "Words."

I was blushing. "Well, I'd like to go over and visit Agnes tonight. I haven't seen her in a while."

"This is good. I thought we would take tomorrow off anyway. I'm too old to work so hard."

I met his eyes and once again we shared what was in my heart, though this time I knew it was written blatantly on my face for anyone to see.

I passed the laneway leading down to Agnes' grandmother's house twice. I would have passed it a third time except that he was suddenly standing there, rising up out of the tall, verdant weeds along the road. The wild man. Ditchhair. He stood at the end of the narrow, obscured drive like a sentry. I turned on my signal light to let him know of my intention to drive onto the hidden lane, but he didn't budge. I slowed to a crawl and started to turn off the main road. I drove up until the bumper was practically resting against his legs. He still would not move. I sat a while, clutching the wheel, the tattered figure with the dead eye stubbornly holding his ground, shadowy and macabre between the beams of my headlights.

I honked the horn as though he was a daydreaming pedestrian who simply hadn't noticed my approach. He didn't flinch. Not a muscle twitched. I rolled down the side window and stuck my head out.

"Hey," I said. I had decided to be tough but to keep my equanimity. "Hey, get out of the way. Can't you see I'm turning here?"

He turned towards me by degrees, bird-like, the mad eruption of hair haloing his head like strange plumage, ceremonial headdress for a dark and murderous ritual. He leaned forward, resting his palms on the hood of the car, the shadows swallowing his blasted features. "Got a cigarette?"

If that was what this was all about, I would gladly give him the whole pack. I searched for the little white package, trying to form a plan of action. I would toss the pack out the window off to one side, and when Ditchhair went to retrieve it I would step on the gas and disappear down the lane.

When I heard the passenger door swing open I realized I was not the only one plotting strategy. The overhead light came on and I watched the clouded marble of his dead eye as it came towards me. He sat down, leaning in close, the door still propped open, the stink of him filling the car.

He pointed to the dome light. "Most people 'round here break that." He poked at the opaque plastic cover with his finger.

"Why's that?" I asked, sounding too interested.

He jabbed the plastic light harder, his fingernail clicking loudly against the translucent cover. "That way you can open the door and roll beers out if the cops stop you." He prodded the interior light fiercely, rapidly. I put my hand on his, gently, to stop him. His good eye narrowed, taking me in. "I used to be a Special Constable, you know that."

"You told me," I said.

He reached down between his feet. "Hey, here's your smokes." He opened the pack and held it towards me. I extracted a cigarette and he did the same. Then he closed the package and slid it into the pocket of his grimy jacket. I ignored this, pulled my lighter out and lit up, then extended the thin yellow flame to him. He cupped his hand over mine, puffed once or twice, and exhaled blue smoke into my face. I blinked reflexively, twisting away. He reached across me, turned off the engine and snatched the keys out of the ignition.

"What are you doing?" I tried to remain calm. He pulled the door shut and seemed to grow huge in the sudden darkness. The door was pressed against my back and I reached behind myself with my left hand to try and locate the door handle.

"Put your lights out."

"What?"

"Put your lights out, man. You'll kill your battery."

I stared stupidly into the tunnel of light and leaves in front of the car. I tried to figure out how I had come to be trapped in my own car with a maniac. I pushed in the button for the lights and the shadows deepened. There was no reflected light now, no soft glow from the dashboard.

Ditchhair rattled the keys near my ear. I made a half-hearted grab for them. It was hopeless.

"Give me the keys, Ditchhair," I growled. He seemed less threatening in the dark.

"You call me Raymond," he growled back.

"Give me the keys, Raymond."

He started to roll his window down. "You ever see somebody witta pipe sticking through them. Waugh! That's ugly, I tell you. I useta patrol all up and down this road. Lookin' for crashes mostly. Call the mounties. Call the ambulance. Try 'n' help. But pretty much everythin' was an hour away. I sat with my cousin Norris when he had a pipe stickin' through him. Just fell asleep, drove off the road into this pile of pipe the oil guys left in the woods. Norris, he hit it pretty good. Smack!" Raymond drove his hands together for emphasis and I jumped, my head bouncing off the side window.

"Long pipe goes right through the front of the car, through my cousin, through the seat and into the back. I sat there over an hour with Norris. Could smell his guts and everythin'. He kept sayin', 'Take it out, Ray. It hurts, man. Take it out.'" He raised the pitch of his voice to imitate his dying cousin, like someone mocking a whining child. I winced because it seemed so cruel. "No way I could take that out. No way I could stop the bleedin'. Norris was dead a half hour 'fore the ambulance got there. The driver, he's mad because I didn't radio to tell him Norris died. He didn't like havin' to drive fast on that road for no good reason."

I didn't know what to say. I'd never seen anyone die. I'd never even seen a dead person outside a funeral home. I couldn't imagine sitting in a dark car, the way we were now, somewhere on this lonely stretch of forsaken gravel, watching the life bleed out of someone.

He snorted. "Kinda funny. I couldn't even get a blanket on him properly 'cause the pipe was in the way." He held the keys up in front of himself, next to the open window, and swung them back and forth on the fob.

"Raymond, come on, man. Give me the keys," I inched towards him, my right hand creeping along the back of the seat like a five-legged spider.

He twisted towards me and I froze. His voice was even and measured. "I seen a lot of people I know die on this road. Young guys, old women. Whole families. People burned. People with their heads ripped off. Drunks killin' each other. Killin' their families, their kids. I tried to stop the drinkin'. I tried." He flicked the keys out the window. I made a desperate dive to try and catch them and slammed hard into Raymond. The door wasn't properly latched and we both tumbled out into the long grass beside the lane.

He wrapped his arms around my head and squeezed me against his chest. His filthy shirt smelled of sweat and oil and road dust. I tried to drive my fists into his stomach but he held me too closely and my punches were ineffectual. I wanted to roll off to the side but he went with me and we pitched back and forth, finally coming to rest against the car, with me trapped underneath, panting and heaving, stuck together like lovers.

"Raymond. Get off of him. Now." It was Agnes. My angel. My lady of the reservation.

Ditchhair pushed himself off and stood teetering above me. We were bathed in light and an engine was running. I dusted myself off while Agnes watched. One of the aunts sat in an old pick-up, with a couple of kids beside her. Agnes had been driving.

"You saved me again," I said, smiling.

"What are you doing here?" She didn't sound happy.

She avoided my eyes. Still, she was beautiful, long hair pulled back in a ponytail, deep hazel eyes flashing with anger.

"I was coming to see you."

"Horny again?"

"No," I replied defensively, my voice rising, the "o" long and drawn out.

"Then move this piece of shit."

"Agnes," I reached for her but thought better of it when I saw her expression. "I can't," I told her, folding my arms across my chest. "Ditchhair threw the keys away."

"Where?" she sighed heavily and I pointed off to the right. We walked into the tall grass and kicked around with our feet.

"I been busy, Agnes."

She grunted derisively.

"Henry's had me working hard all week, cutting firewood for him."

"I know what you've been up to." She kept probing the ground.

"I've been hoping he could tell me something about my mother."

"That old man doesn't know anything about your mother." She bent suddenly and scooped the keys up off the ground. "Move it," she said tersely, and walked towards the truck.

I wanted to shout after her the word that Henry had taught me, but I was afraid to mangle it, twist it around my dull, lazy tongue and say something meaningless. Or worse, something insulting. I searched through my pockets for the small square of paper on which I had jotted down the syllables of my affection.

I pulled the crumpled note out of my pocket just as she started around the open driver's side door of the pick-up. She had one leg thrown up into the cab when I called it out.

"Nei che mei sim."

She stopped half in, half out of the cab. Everyone, her aunt, the kids, Agnes, was looking.

"What?" she said, struggling to hide her amusement.

I was filled with a horrible sense of apprehension. I was sure I was mispronouncing the entire phrase. I repeated it anyway. "Nei che mei sim," I said more quietly, crumpling the paper in my hand.

Auntie Eleanor, Wylie, and Rosemary were giggling, holding their hands lightly over their mouths. Agnes took quick, long steps towards me, pointing her finger at my heart.

"I'm not your sweetheart," she said emphatically, her eyes narrowing.

I leaned forward, whispering, "Well, I like you."

"You just want to get laid, Childforever."

I smiled when I heard the name and shrugged. "Well, what do you want, Fire-in-the-eyes? Let's talk about it."

She moved closer and poked at my chest again. "Fire-in-the-eyes? You've seen too many westerns, whiteboy. Oh, sorry. I keep forgetting," she leaned into me, her eyes wide with mock scorn, "you're one of us, now."

I stood toe to toe with her, refusing to be run off. Her face softened and the suspense broke.

The truck horn honked and we both turned to see Auntie Eleanor behind the wheel, smiling and waving for us to get out of the way.

Agnes laughed. "Guess you're drivin' me home."

"Great," I said, not even trying to hide my enthusiasm, and opening the passenger door for her. I ran around the car, jumped in, and backed out of the way. Aunt Eleanor pulled out and we waved maniacally to the kids. As soon as the taillights of the truck disappeared around the first curve I wheeled back into the lane and drove about a hundred feet.

"This isn't the way home," Agnes said with feigned innocence.

"Let's talk," I suggested, tuning in a slow, romantic song on the radio.

Agnes pulled her feet up under her on the seat. "Screw that," she said vaulting into the back seat. "Let's get naked."

It took me a few seconds to wedge myself out from under the steering wheel and pull myself over the back of the seat. I landed on her with a grunt and then slid off onto the floor. "Come here," she growled, deep and throaty as she grabbed my jacket and pulled me to her. My hand reached out and closed tightly on her breast. Her finger traced the inseam of my pants and closed over my crotch. A sweet, excruciating ache started under her grip and spread like electricity through every nerve. Then it was quick passionate kisses and panting and fingers releasing buttons as we undressed each other and ourselves and thrashed free of our clothes in the cramped imploding space.

It went on in its own time and space. It was graceful and elemental. Savage and transcendental. Afterwards I lay on top of her, still and reverent like someone waking from a powerful, intoxicating trance. I regained my awareness in degrees. The fragrance and texture of her hair against my face; the music of our ragged, forced breathing; her teeth nibbling my ear; her hands sliding along my back; her nipple melting in the palm of my hand.

Then she was pushing on my chest. "Get off."

I was perturbed over the broken spell. "What's wrong?" I pulled myself up clumsily, tangled in the tight space.

She laid her hand against my face and spoke softly, as though to a child. "Don't be angry. I'm afraid Ray will come back."

I watched, mollified, as she arched her back and slid her pants back up around her waist. Her shirt hung open, and I stared at her round firm breasts, her nipples, large and brown, stiffening in the chill again. I leaned in and took one between my lips, tracing it with my tongue. She cradled my head softly, ran her fingers through my hair.

Then she pulled my head away from her with both hands. I stared at her glistening erect nipple. She brought my face to hers. "I need a cigarette," she said.

I pulled my pants up and fastened them, then leaned into the front of the car and searched the dash. Then I remembered. "Ray's got my smokes," I told her.

"Where's my jacket?"

I pulled it from where it had been crammed under the back window and she extracted a slightly crumpled package. They were bent but unbroken and we both lit up.

"What's wrong with him?" I asked, exhaling a blue cloud of smoke.

"He's koo koosh."

"He's what?"

"Crazy. When an Indian person loses their," she searched for the right word, "... spirit." Her hands traced tight circles in the air trying to give the word the proper inflection. "When this happens they're said to be koo koosh."

"Just plain koo koo, I think."

"It's more than that, Childforever. Ray was a good man. A good constable. He wanted to make things better and he got tired of always picking up the pieces."

"And that drove him crazy?" I wasn't ready to allow him any measure of sympathy.

She exhaled noisily and shook her head. "He didn't go crazy, Billy. It wasn't like that. He was definitely stressed out. He wanted to enforce the dry reserve laws and keep booze out. He wanted to stop the bootleggers who drove in from town and sold on the reserve. He wanted Red Clay to be the way it was when we were growing up."

"So."

"So one night two men he knew came and told him some guys were bootlegging out of the trunk of their car. He follows them there and they end up in this abandoned sandpit back in the middle of nowhere. The ones who led him there block him in, and then two more guys get out of the bootlegger's car, haul Ray out on the ground and start beatin' on him with two-by-fours. They left him for dead. He had broken arms, broken legs, a cracked head," she touched each part as she said the words.

I saw him differently. Proud and neat in his uniform, then lying alone and broken on the ground. Betrayed.

"He would have died, but somebody phoned in an anonymous tip. Still, he was in the hospital a long time and when he got out he was never the same."

I perceived something more. "He loved you."

"We were going to get married."

We sat smoking while the radio faded in and out on the caprice of atmospheric skip, then landed solidly on an evangelist spewing fire and brimstone. "... No room on the starship to heaven for sinners and fornicators. You must forego the ways of the flesh, the temptations of the Jezebel, the loose women, the temptress in her red dress. I have a seat reserved for you. For you all. But." A short pause. "BUT." He was shouting. "You must give yourself to Jesus. You must be washed in the blood. Hallelujah. Hall... ah... alle..." The radio faltered, sputtered and hissed. There was unintelligible ranting and a static drum beat. Then music again. She began to straighten her clothes in the disconcerting quiet. Head down, she examined her pants and pulled her shirt out at the waist. She brushed vigorously at her clothes with the backs of her fingers, then reached out and pulled a large chunk of bark off my cheek. I squinted into the dark and saw that her long hair was full of sawdust and woodchips and other such detritus.

She went back to trying to slap the debris from her pants. "Shit," she said. "Are you running a sawmill in here or something?"

We looked at each other and laughed.

Except for directions, and there weren't many of those, the conversation was sparse on the way to Agnes' place. It wasn't unpleasant, though. It was as warm and gentle as the temperate summer night. We held hands and glanced at the stars and exchanged looks like high school lovers.

Her place was small. A trailer that I guessed had once served as a field office for a construction company or some other such outfit. It was rectangular and forlornly ordinary, standing in the middle of the big empty lot.

Agnes turned her hands palms up in an abbreviated flourish. "It ain't much, but it's home."

We got out of the car. I slammed my door closed. "It's nice," I said inanely.

She shook her head as she walked towards the little place. "Always the gentleman. Just like a whiteman, Childforever. Never say what you mean."

I was behind her, staring at her ass. "I mean it. It's really, really nice." I was becoming aroused again, my voice dripping with lechery.

She paused with her hand on the doorknob and made her eyebrows bounce a la Groucho Marx, "Come on in."

"Jesus. What is that?" The smell assaulted us the minute the door was pushed open. "Is that gas?"

Agnes flicked the light on. For a second I was caught up in the surprise that she had electricity. She crouched down beside a young boy on the floor. Deja vu. It was the same kid I'd seen lying on the floor at Henry's place. The very one Agnes had scooped up in front of the Red Clay Cafe during the cloudburst.

"Hey, that's the kid..." I exclaimed.

"He's my brother," Agnes snapped. She snatched a plastic milk bag off the floor and threw it up to me. "Get rid of this."

I was hurt by her commanding tone and I moved slowly towards the door, opening the bag. The petroleum smell rushed out, settled in the pit of my stomach. Inside the bag were a couple of rags saturated with gasoline.

"Throw it out," she was practically screaming.

I flung the bag out the open door. "Jesus, Agnes," I yelled at her. "I didn't give him the fucking stuff."

She knelt, cradling her brother's head. His eyelids flickered in small seizures and he moaned. Agnes' face was twisted in a mix of anger and alarm. "Maybe you better go," she hissed at me. Her brother began to vomit and choke, his body jerking. She turned his head and jammed her fingers into his mouth to help clear everything out.

"I want to help," I said quietly.

She ignored me, whispering soft soothing things into her brother's ear.

I sat down on a blue wooden chair near the open door. The sudden violent change of mood, the rigid snap of tension that had come out of nowhere, the cloying odour of gas, and the spreading ooze regurgitated out of her brother started the room spinning. Beads of perspiration materialized on my forehead and I slid out of my jacket.

I stared at the slow flow of puke dribbling from the corner of the boy's mouth, viscous and yellow, stretching like an elongated slug across Agnes' knee and onto the floor. A wretched, cursive alphabet for long, dead nights in a place with nothing to offer.

My own bile began to rise and I looked around the trailer to keep my eyes occupied and averted from the wretched scene.

It was an efficient place. I was sitting on a wooden folding chair against one end. The open door was on the right side and about four feet down the wall. Next to me, on the left, was an old, battered, drop-leaf table, one leaf folded down and pressed against the end wall. On the other side of the table, directly across from me, was another folding chair. Down the left side of the trailer, across from the open door, was a row of coat hooks holding various articles of clothing. A single bed extended down into the far corner. Over the bed was a crude shelf of books. In the corner opposite the bed was a small heater, the same kind Henry had in his shack. Against the right wall near the woodstove sat a small half-fridge, and next to that a narrow counter that held a hot plate and a blue water jug with a plastic tap. Underneath the counter were a few shelves cluttered with pots and pans and tinned goods.

Agnes was wetting a cloth from the jug and the boy was sitting up with his head resting on his knees. She gently pulled his head back so she could wipe his face.

"How's he doing?" I asked feeling forgotten and inept.

She shrugged, ministering to her brother.

I was perturbed by this lack of attention. Frustrated again by an erratic shift of events. I could never predict what would happen here. I'd arrived less than two weeks before and already I'd been in two fights, had my car vandalized, done more physical labour than I had done in the last ten years, eaten the flesh of animals I'd previously only seen in zoos, and made love in a tepee.

"You know, Agnes," I said, rubbing my hands together, possessed by an abrupt twinge of meanness, "I saw this kid about a week ago passed out at Henry's. It was glue he was sniffing that time. The kid's not gonna have a decent brain cell left by the time he's..."

She whirled around, teeth flashing. "His name is Joseph. Thanks for your compassion." I was astonished by the hatred contorting her face. I stood and stormed out the open door.

I was still sitting on the hood of my car when she reached out fifteen minutes later to close the door.

"Hi," she said quietly, her eyes moist, her face seraphic in the moonlight. "I thought you were gone."

I studied her eyes, something dropping inside me, a space opening under my ribs and filling with the colour of her face, the shape of her lips, the way the light fell across her cheeks. I eased off the car. "My keys are in my jacket and I was too embarrassed to go back in."

She laughed. A short, plosive bark cut off by something else, strangled somewhere deep in her lungs. The next second she was in my arms, weeping, sobbing, clutching at my shirt. I held her close, my eyes filling with tears. In the night sky, the stars spun out their patterns over our heads, telling their ancient stories. Her body melted into mine and the earth clutched at our feet. I closed my eyes and the roots of great trees erupted out of the ground, entwining around us, pulling away our clothes as we sank to the earth. The tall grass folded under us, into a bed that was warm, fragrant and lush.

We sat at the table drinking tea by candlelight while Joseph slept in the neat single bed, snoring like an old drunk. We held hands, talking in hushed tones and picking at the debris in our hair and on our clothes. We both looked as though we had been dragged through the bush by our feet. We had sawdust, bark, dry grass, leaves and dirt clinging to us like decorations.

I took a sip of tea. "Do you think we'll ever make love in a bed?"

She raised her eyebrows, "Are you complaining?"

I shook my head. "Nooo, ma'am."

Joseph choked and made a gargling sound in his throat, then flipped over to face the wall. He looked small and faraway, curled under the blankets at the far end of the room.

I looked down at the table. "Why does he do it?"

"He's a kid. He's lonely and bored, he has nothing to look forward to..." her mouth was open, her shoulders trembling slightly, as if touched by a sudden chilling breeze. There seemed to be more she wanted to say, but couldn't put into words.

"Where are your parents?" I asked.

"Dead." She still stared off into the middle space, into the flickering shadows beyond our little table. Her eyes were flat and fixed. "Their place used to be right here. Actually my stepfather and mother lived here. My dad shot himself years and years ago. Before Joseph."

"So he's your half-brother."

She looked at me with her moribund gaze, the reply emotionless and practised. "Yes, he's my half-brother. The place burned down and they died. Joseph was okay because he had been hiding underneath the house."

I interrupted again, bewildered. "Under the house?"

Agnes glanced at her brother sleeping fitfully at the other end of the trailer. "Yeah, he used to do that when Charlie came home drunk. Otherwise Charlie would beat on him and..."

"Beat on him?" I was in a different world.

She turned to me, offering the kind of sympathy reserved for idiots and other innocents. "Are you deaf?" she asked gently.

I felt foolish and naive. "No, but so much misfortune crammed into one family. It's..." I was at a loss.

"There are a lot of families here, Childforever, that could tell you the same kind of story. Charlie beat everybody. He stabbed my mother once, even threatened her with a gun. I was away at school then, but Joseph told me about it. My aunts would find him sometimes sleeping under the house. He wouldn't leave, though. Even in the winter he stayed to make sure Mom was all right. Once when I came home to visit he was being treated for frostbite..." She started to cry. No sobbing or gasping. No trembling, just tears running from her eyes, large drops beading in the corners then stretched by gravity across her cheeks. I reached out and laid my hand against her face and wiped one away with my thumb. She held my hand there with hers for a second, then pushed it away. "I don't want to talk any more," she said. "Maybe it would be better if you left. I'm not going to be very good company and I have Joseph to look after."

"Okay," I said. "Hey, did I ever tell you about my friend Maurice?"

She gave me an exasperated look. "You've never told me much about anyone."

"Things always seemed to happen to Maurice. Through no fault of his own. Things just happened."

She sat back heavily in her chair. "What's your point?"

I ignored her and carried on with the story. "Once, when we were about seven or eight, Maurice and I were playing at this schoolyard park. We were really into the game, being superheroes or something, running up the slides, jumping off the merry-go-round, duking it out with bad guys. We were lying over the swings on our stomachs and pretending to fly when Maurice suddenly comes to a dead stop, dragging his feet in the loose sand. 'Oh man, I gotta crap,' he says. I don't know if it was from the swing pushing on his stomach or something he ate or if he'd just waited too damn long. But it was serious. I mean, pulling at your pants, taking short little steps on your toes serious."

She was leaning forward, drawn into my prosaic drama.

"He was looking around desperately for something to shit behind. I was appalled that he would even consider such a thing, my tightass, excuse the pun, upbringing, I guess. Anyway, I told him we'd make a run for my house. It seemed like the only sensible thing to do. In my mind he could only relieve himself in the proper, sanitary confines of an actual bathroom and nowhere else.

"Off we went across the green yards, taking every short cut I could remember. I ran ahead shouting encouragement. I ran beside him urging him to hold on. 'You can make it,' I kept shouting. He could only nod. His face was red, his knees were locked together, one hand clenched over the seat of his pants. It seemed like something from one of those western matinees that were popular back then. Only I wasn't helping my wounded partner struggle through the desert. I was trying to get Maurice to a respectable bathroom.

"It was a nice day, bright and warm. Everything peaceful. Music was playing somewhere as I vaulted up onto the back porch of my house. The door was locked. I pounded on it desperately, calling for my mother. It seemed to take hours before she was there, working the lock and swinging the door open. She'd been napping and she was very put out. 'What is the problem?' she yelled at me. I started to tell her, I had just opened my mouth to speak, when I heard a little voice behind me. 'Never mind.' It was Maurice. I turned around and he was looking down at his feet. My mother and I saw it at the same time, a moist, brown turd leaning against the instep of his running shoe. Mona gasped and as she did another turd rolled free of his pant leg and across our back step. A peaceful look came over Maurice's face. Suddenly it all seemed perfect. The green lawn behind us, the quiet music, the crap nestled against the white hightop. Like it was meant to be. Like that's just the way it is."

She looked at me, into my eyes. "How do you mean?" she asked.

I shrugged. "Despite the best intentions..." I paused, "... shit happens."

She held my gaze, the preposterous statement turning in the air between us. It was an inadequate gift, but it was all I had to offer. I tensed, afraid that it wouldn't be enough. Then she fell back into her chair, laughing over my ridiculous parable. We laughed together for a long time.

When we woke in the morning after that first night, stretched out like corpses on the plywood floor, Joseph was gone. We pulled ourselves off the unforgiving wood like a couple of geriatric cases, stiff and sore and bent with the arthritis of too little sleep on too hard a surface. My mouth felt as if it was full of straw, and my pants literally were— with straw, leaves, bits of wood and whatever else had crawled in during our furious lovemaking the night before. Agnes stood up, brushing at her clothes, and fidgeting in odd little tremors.

"I can't stand this," she declared. I was about to say something amusing when she snatched up my hand and pulled me after her, bursting through the door and vaulting from the top step. I could barely keep my balance behind her. We hit the ground running, heading across the wide lot, across the road and into a stand of trees.

"Where..." I had to duck a low hanging branch. "Agnes..." I stumbled over a root. She had a death grip on my hand as we raced along the narrow path, dodging stumps and leaping deadfalls. My heart was pounding, my head spinning. I was about to dig in my heels and demand to know what was going on when we burst onto a narrow stretch of gravelly beach beside a small, placid lake.

She immediately began stripping off her clothes and dropping them into a little pile at her feet. I followed suit, my head swivelling around self-consciously to see if anyone was watching.

"Are you crazy?" I asked.

"Crazy Indian," she hooted, dropping her panties onto the heap of clothes. Then, with a long wild whoop that echoed across the still surface and sent two ducks plunging up into the sky, she turned and dove into the water. I dropped my bristling underwear and quickly followed, swimming out behind her to deeper waters.

The bottom dropped away suddenly and she turned to face me, treading water. In the dark water, I was startled by my white flashing feet, kicking below me. In my haste to follow her I'd forgotten to take my socks off.

I threw back my head and howled with the elemental joy, over my surprise at what William Sawnet had done. I felt Agnes' hand on my shoulder and whirled around ready for whatever came next. Eager to be reckless.

"D'you bring the soap?" she said.

For the next two days Agnes and I hardly left the trailer. We lounged around her snug and windowless place, reading, drinking coffee and tea, playing cards and making love. Twice we collapsed the folding metal bed underneath us. We survived on canned soup and cigarettes and went out for short walks and skinny dips to rinse the funkiness from our bodies. I think that what kept it cosy and not claustrophobic was the amount of time we were naked. Lust does not know too small a place. I didn't want sunshine or stars or blue skies, only the tender, brown universe of her body.

The only blot came late Sunday afternoon. She took me out for a long, after-dinner walk. Not knowing where we were going, I walked along happily beside her, hands in my pockets. We strolled along the dirt road, talking idly, when she stopped abruptly and told me she had to go back to work the next morning.

I felt myself pouting automatically, like a twelve-year-old.

"Work?" I whined. "Where?" terrified that she was going back to the city.

"It's only up the road a bit. I started last Tuesday. The Ministry of

Natural Resources has a greenhouse there and they hired a few women from the reserve to transplant seedlings. That's where I went the other morning, after the night at ko koom's. I told you before I left. Don't you remember?"

"No. You have to make sure I'm really awake. Morning is not my best time."

"Where did you think I was?"

I shrugged. "I don't know. I thought you ran out on me." I played at mock indignation. "Used me like a cheap piece of meat and cast me aside."

She chuckled. "You're a funny man, Childforever. Auntie thinks you have a nice, uh, body." She was kicking faintly at a furrow of gravel built up along the edge of the road. "So that's where I was, at work. I'm trying to save money."

"Why?" I threw my arms up in exasperation. Why this sudden need for money? Weren't we happy? Couldn't it wait a month or two? It was beyond my understanding.

Agnes pointed over my shoulder, off into the space behind me. I swivelled around.

Across a field of tall, withered grass that stood in clumps among shards of broken glass and discarded metal and the bloated bodies of plastic bags and chunks of broken concrete, was a faded grey quonset hut, its double doors pock-marked with holes and footprints, every visible window smashed or boarded over. Three metal chairs lay out front on their backs like strange dead animals.

I looked back at her. "I don't understand."

"I want to see the old community centre turned into a place for kids. A drop-in centre, maybe. Maybe even a daycare if they'll let me, I don't know. Pool tables, pinball, an outside rink."

I stood looking at the wrecked building. "What happened to it?"

She took a couple of steps towards the dilapidated structure. "Like you said, Childforever. Shit happens. Things have been going downhill for a long time." She let out a fleeting, despondent chuckle. "Since Columbus. It got a lot worse here when they found oil on reserve land and everybody in the settlement got money. The oil companies built the road for their trucks. Believe it or not, there was no road to town when I was a kid. You had to fly out or in. Then men got work and made more money. Bootleggers were everywhere and everyone started drinking. Dances turned into brawls. People started going to town more. Everybody wanted to party. I don't know, you know. Its not that simple and it is. "

"How can you live like this?" I asked sadly.

"What choice do I have? This is who I am. These are my people."

"We could go somewhere. Go back east."

"Will we take Joseph? And his friends? I can't leave here. I don't want to leave here. Ko koom, my aunts. I tried once and it's no good. It only makes for more ghosts."

I was behind her now, staring at the ruined building. It seemed impossible to me. "It'll take a lot of money."

"I know," she said. "I'm not going to finance it all on my own, but I want things to be different and I'm not going to wait for the government to tell me it's okay. A year or so ago you wouldn't have liked me, William. I was somebody else. Now I want to be somebody people will take seriously."

"Then what?"

"Then I'll go back to school, finish my degree. Try and get on the band council or at least put pressure on them. I want the bootleggers out. I want children to learn their traditions. Their language."

I wanted to say something encouraging and enthusiastic but my sense of logic and probability wouldn't let me. Nice dream, my brain was saying. "I didn't know you were so political," I muttered stupidly.

Agnes glanced up at me. "Yeah, right," she said sardonically. "Don't you get it? We let ourselves be pulled apart. Look at you, Billy. They took our children. Sent them away to school or put them up for adoption.

Killed their sense of pride and heritage, tried to break all the connections. Now we have to pull ourselves back together. We have to..."

"Hey, Aggie. What are you doing with the whiteman?" This was shouted in such a good-natured way that I found myself smiling broadly. Then it sunk in that I was the "whiteman."

They came around from behind the old community centre, swaggering and kicking at lumps of garbage. Four young men in t-shirts and jeans who clumped together as they drew closer to us.

Agnes stood with her hands on her hips. "You the one gave Joseph gas to sniff, Kah kah ge ow."

The one who had shouted stopped dead. His face was a deep coffee brown, much darker than the others. "No one calls me that any more, Agnes." His tone and his eyes were dangerous.

"Everybody calls you that, Kah kah ge ow," she was unflinching, defiant. I was looking at the others as benignly as a rabbit. Their faces were hard, their eyes flint.

The one she called Kah kah ge ow took a menacing step, his finger stabbing into the air between them. "I'll kick your ass, woman. You think you're better than everybody? Like Raymond? We got enough do-gooders and troublemakers around here."

Agnes took a step to meet him, hands still on her hips, the young man's finger almost pressing into her throat. "You do that," she paused for emphasis, "Kah kah ge ow, and half the people on the rez will line up to kick yours. And that includes your own mother." One of the other young men snickered but the belligerent one shut him down with a quick, glacial look. Then he turned his attention my way and the others moved to encircle me. I was obviously the easier target.

"You fuckin' this shei kag, Aggie?" he asked with disdain.

"Yes, I am," she answered coolly, "and which one of these pretty fellows are you jumpin'?"

A deep shadow fell across his face, the veins in his dark neck dancing, his knuckles whitening. I considered hitting him, positive that it was the only way I would get in one good blow, but my hands remained at my sides, distant and disconnected. Incapable of inflicting any injury. Agnes' pugnacious defiance had me sweating, my mind buzzing. I wanted to be protective but I could not think with the same agility and nerve as she did in these situations.

Kah kah ge ow turned completely around, exhaled harshly between his tight lips, and strode off down the road without a word. He was losing face rapidly, and unable to use his fists, had no way to fight back. His cronies shoved me aside, one cuffing the back of my head, and hurried after him.

We watched them saunter away, kicking up clouds of dust and pitching rocks at a skulking mongrel that tried to sneak by on the opposite side of the gravel road. The dog yelped, tail between its legs, as a stone glanced from its hip. It ran a few quick steps, then returned to its slow easy pace. Once the young men passed they lost interest and the dog didn't even look back. It was a measured dose of cruelty and all the players knew their parts. The mutt glanced our way nervously to see if we were bending to pick up some projectile as it ambled by.

"Why do they call him that?"

"Kah kah ge ow? It means crow." She shrugged, still watching the young men as they moved away. "It's because his skin is so dark. He was always teased about it. Always getting into fights. Now he's the leader. The wildest. Most people tease him behind his back these days." There seemed to be something wistful, like regret, in her voice.

"What did he call me then?" I asked.

"A skunk."

I put my arm around her. Her shoulders were tight and hard, her arms folded across her chest. "Nice guys." I was trying to make light of it. To ease the tension.

"How do you think they get treated, Childforever, every time they go to town?" she snapped. "Ever since the day they were born?"

She spun out from under my arm and began walking briskly back towards home. We had quietly declared the trailer to be neutral ground. It had become a sanctuary, our own private reservation.

She sat drowsily beside me Monday morning as I drove up the long undulating stretch of gravel to where she was working. I squinted against the sun hanging low and dispirited, barely above the tree-tops. It had an outlandish appearance. The sun from another season, confused and nostalgic, drifting by to touch the earth as though it were a dusty memento.

Agnes yawned widely and it reminded me of an image from our freshly dead weekend. I had awakened alone in bed, and looking up caught her yawning like a cat. She was at the table smoking, the cigarette held loosely, wrist bent, elbow resting next to the chipped ashtray. She sat completely naked on the blue, ramshackle chair, its legs ⸏ ⸏ed with thick strands of twisted wire. Her hair was smooth and black as a ⸏ ⸏ven's wing and her head was wreathed in a cobalt veil of smoke. Her long cinnamon legs were crossed and the curve of her hip was lustrous, touched by a scintilla of morning sunlight angling through the small window in the door. It was a moment of uncomplicated beauty like I'd never known and I gawked till she sensed me.

"What?" she asked turning, sloe-eyed and ethereal.

"Nothing," I mumbled, because in the dazed centre of that moment I was without foundation, my tedious history falling away with each wondrous second.

When I stumbled into Henry's he was just clearing away his breakfast dishes. The place smelled of coffee and fried meat and pipe smoke and my stomach growled noisily. I was ravenous. Henry took one look at me and laughed.

"William, your eyes look like two piss-holes in a snow bank. Sit down and I'll make you some breakfast."

I dropped into the chair, eyeing Henry's bed. He brought me a cup of coffee and shook his head.

"I don't think I'll take you in the bush today, William. Probably cut your arm off with a saw or drop a tree on me or somethin'."

I mumbled a flimsy argument which he easily ignored. "Besides, Danny Elkhorn is gonna take me to town." I nodded and slurped coffee and cast fond looks at his simple cot. His hand came to rest on my shoulder. "You get some sleep and then maybe you could go out back and split some of that wood for me, eh?" When he said the word sleep I almost wept.

Later, while I sat eating the eggs and ham he'd fried up and he sat across from me watching and waiting for his ride, I asked about my mother again.

"Do you remember if she was nice, Henry?"

"Yeah, pretty nice. It was a long time ago. Not as nice or pretty as that Agnes, though," he winked.

"Why did she go down south?"

He shuffled in the chair and seemed uncomfortable with my questions. "I don't know. It happens all the time. Young people go away. Young girls get tired of this place. Maybe she wanted a job, some money. Ever since the road went in men come and work around here and meet girls in Grande Level in the hotel, say certain things. Then one day they're gone, back to their homes. Sometimes a girl will follow after the man. Sometimes the man will take her away. Then things happen and the girls are alone, takin' care of themselves."

He stopped and lit his pipe, eyes lost in the middle distance, his face grim. I swallowed the last of my breakfast. I wanted details. Another talisman besides the crucifix I kept in my pocket. A picture postcard from the past. *Hi. Things are great. Weather's fine. Wish you were here. Love, Mom.*

I moved out of Henry's the next Wednesday; I was spending all my nights with Agnes anyway. Still, it felt like a betrayal, standing on his forlorn front step clutching my few possessions and stuttering out reassurances. Henry seemed to have been expecting it. Another exit in a long line of desertions.

"Henry," I kept saying, "Henry, I'll still be here to help you every day. First I'll drive Agnes to work and then I'll be straight over."

"That's okay, William," he said, the smouldering pipe clenched in his teeth, slapping me on the back. "We got lots of wood cut."

"Yeah, but I'll be over to split it and pile it and we'll cut more. You'll have enough for two years." I was walking backwards across the rough yard towards my derelict car.

"That's okay, William. We got lots of wood cut," he said again, soothingly. "Danny'll help me."

The name Danny Elkhorn had become like a knife in my ribs over those last couple of weeks. 'Danny will take me to town,' or 'Don't worry, I'll get Danny to help.' Most of the time Danny was like a ghost and I never saw him. I would drive over from Agnes' place and find a fresh stack of split wood waiting to be piled. Only once did I walk into Henry's and find Danny there. They both looked at me and then went back to talking in Cree. I felt left out, with no hope of competing.

I wanted to be there for Henry, but the pull towards Agnes was stronger. With her I forgot why I was in Red Clay. I was just there. I was Childforever. With Henry there were too many unanswered questions, so many things I should have been doing. Maybe the idea of real answers frightened me all along. Maybe I had a sense that if I knew the truth then I couldn't stay.

He waved as if I were boarding an airplane then stepped inside and closed the door to the little white shack with its peeling red trim and feather of smoke lifting straight into the air. It looked too small for habitation, a scale replica in a model display. Even the twisted tree in the front yard didn't look real. I remembered the first night there. Not so long before and yet distant, distant the way an old posting was when you stepped into the new house, its rooms cramped by the boxes that held your life. Painted red arrows everywhere, pointing, *This side up*. Distant the way Wilfred was when the air force sent him away on course, sometimes for months, his civilian shoes waiting in the front hall, the car gone from the driveway. The street empty and grey all the way to the horizon.

I shoved my things into the back seat, then paused for a minute, looking out over the motley settlement of disparate buildings. Log cabins, shacks, mobile homes, shiny bungalows with aluminum siding and sheets hung in the windows in place of draperies.

A huge flock of birds flew past overhead, starlings, I think. Take it, I thought. Take my soul away with you. Shredded in your smooth beaks. Hollow me out, here and now, and let me start again.

A pick-up passed by on the road, dull brown and spotted with rust and rough lesions, its tailgate missing. A man stared out of the passenger-side window, his face stern and hostile. I saw the thin mustache, the clump of dark hair on his chin, the camouflage hunting cap pulled down low over a dour face. Our eyes locked as the truck passed, his head turning to stretch out the inimical look as long as possible, the middle finger of his right hand held against the glass. Malice settled over everything. Over the intent dogs watching me from the end of their chains, over the decaying metal littering the side of the road, over the quiet homes with their closed doors.

I had a hard time shaking the feeling that I had worn out my welcome, if I'd ever had one to wear out in the first place. Even at Agnes' I felt out of place. I tried to read a few of her books but I couldn't get comfortable. I felt trapped, the trailer somehow smaller when she wasn't there. Mainly because without her there, I felt uneasy about going outside.

That night I dreamed of her again. The dream began the same way. Woman and child in the pleasant back yard, the sombre, staunch house in the background, the warm shadows of people moving behind the bright windows.

Husha. She is singing. *Husha, husha.* Then things began to shift. The spinning began to accelerate and it was me, now. It wasn't the boy. I looked up, the world whirling past, and saw Agnes' face. She was holding Henry's hand, he was holding mine. We spun faster and faster and the grip on my hand tightened and it wasn't Henry any more. It was Ditchhair. I couldn't think of his proper name because in the dream he looked beyond any human reference. Agnes looked at him with love. *No. No,* I shouted. *Husha, husha,* she said, and the whirling increased, the blue sky becoming a grey smear over our heads, the grass reeling away into blackness.

Agnes started to lift from us, her white dress like a flag, the gold chain holding the cross twisting around her throat. Our hands began to slip apart till only our fingertips were touching. Then she was gone, turning head over heels, swallowed by the swirling sky. We were falling, Ditchhair holding me close, my arms pinned to my sides, twirling down in some force other than gravity. I don't know how long. When we stopped he was lying on top of me, his dead fish's eye inches from my face.

I woke, clutching the mattress with both hands, sweating profusely. Agnes was shaking me. I stared up at her, gasping, unable to speak. There was a look of real fright on her face.

"Jesus! This bed isn't big enough for that kind of crap, Billy."

I sat up and held her close. "I had the dream. The one about my mother only it was different. Awful."

She held me as I trembled and my heart pounded in my chest, my eyes searching the dark trailer. It was the night spilling in, creeping in through every crack and crevice, seeping under the door. Out from under the lids of our sleeping eyes. I had a sense of something lurking, something listening in the resonant dark. A branch snapped off in the distance and there was a tap on the flat tin roof. Then another. Then two more. It was pouring rain.

It was still raining in the morning. We had opened the door and were preparing to make a dash for the car when Auntie Eleanor pulled up, rolled down her window and shouted that she had had a phone call and work was cancelled for the day. We waved and she drove off, bouncing and splashing down the rutted road.

We crawled back into bed for a while, made love, read to each other, shared cigarettes and took turns putting the kettle on for tea.

"Do you think you would ever leave here?" I asked as I waited for the water to boil.

"Maybe. Someday. I don't know. Why?"

I watched the steam building as it billowed out through the whistle-hole. "I don't feel welcome here, that's all."

"Would I be greeted with open arms by everyone in your home town?"

I shrugged. "Sure. Why not?" The kettle started its thin low whistle.

She lay back on the bed and threw her arms up over her head. "Childforever," she sighed. She propped herself up on her elbow in one quick smooth motion. The kettle blew more forcefully and as I reached for it she said, "I know. I could say my mother was really a whitewoman and I was adopted by some Indians..."

I snatched the kettle up as it began to screech and spit water onto the glowing burner. "Funny. Ha. Ha."

She swung out of bed and put her arms around me from behind. "That's the way it is here. If you lived here all your life and died of old age, people would say, 'You goin' to the new guy's funeral?'"

"You can't save all of them, Agnes." It was the wrong thing to say.

She pushed away from me and I had to fight to keep my balance. My hand tipped over the teacup I had just filled and scalding water poured onto the floor around my feet. I danced away towards the far end of the trailer, alternately lifting each foot and rubbing at the burning skin.

She was sitting with her legs tucked underneath her on the end of the bed, pointing her finger and ignoring my naked contortions.

"I'm not trying to save anybody, you little shit. Are you really that naive, Childforever, or did I put some kind of curse on you?" She turned her finger towards herself, poking it forcefully against her chest. "I live here. I belong here. I want to make things better, yes. But I'm not trying to save anybody. I'm not some do-good social-fucking-worker."

"Sorry." It was the first time I really felt naked in front of her. "Sorry," I repeated.

"Forget it," she said tersely. She snatched up the paperback we had been reading and flopped back on the bed.

I stared at her lean, naked brown body and felt the outside world melting away.

"Look," I said tenderly. "Why don't we get away from here for a while? I'll pick you up after work on Friday and we'll go into town and get a motel room. Shower, TV, pizza. A bed big enough for two people."

She brightened and let the book fall at her side. "That sounds great."

I thought so, too, but then, I still had much to learn.

Coyote found two stones in his pit and he began to fool with them. He smacked them together the way he had seen the Ei lei lo do. Chips began to fly from the frail rock and worked it into an edge. Soon he stopped to admire his handiwork in the moonlight, and as he ran his thumb along the crude blade a strange thing happened. The darkness had grown thicker around him and sounds were difficult to make out and indistinct in his puny human ears. He sniffed the air but could only smell the most obvious scents; so much seemed to be missing that it frightened him. He peered into the night and strained to hear more but this only increased his anxiety. He snatched up a stick and used some of the smaller roots lying around to fasten the stone to one end. He lay back, clutching the axe to his chest. Maybe it was just the fasting, he thought. It was an alien emotion, this fear, and he was fascinated by it, awed by its power. He refused to let it drive him from the shape of a human. He looked up, puzzled by the light of the distant stars, and drifted off to sleep.

It slithers like a flat black snake across the white enamel of the table top and ripples over the edge. I push the chair back as fast as I can but some of the hot liquid still manages to find its way into my right shoe. I stand, lifting that foot gingerly and wiggling it around as if trying to shake loose a small dog.

"Oh, shit," the waitress says. "Shit, I'm sorry." She has a cascade of red hair around her head, her arms milky white. She is holding the coffee pot off at an angle from her body and is busily wiping up the spilled mess with a clutch of napkins she seems to produce magically.

I study the outline of her brassiere, easily visible through the white uniform. Her vigorous movements cause her large breasts to sway and the hard nodes of her nipples to appear. I forget about my scalded foot and wet sock. "Now I know why refills are free," I say smiling.

She chuckles and lets her head drop, her hair bouncing. Her face is fine-boned and freckled, her lips full, her hair like flame around her head. Like a fever. Like a wound. "Care for that refill now?" she asks.

"Sure," I reply reaching out to right the cup in its wet saucer. She reaches also and our hands brush. We both linger on the contact and her perfume fills my nostrils, makes my teeth ache. Heat creeps under my skin, rising like mercury behind my eyes, over my sweating forehead, into the pockets of my cheeks until I feel my face will spontaneously combust and my mouth fill with dry ashes.

"Thanks," I mutter and sit down clumsily.

"Anything else?" she asks, her blue eyes wide and soft.

I am feeble, paralysed. "No. No thanks."

She turns away.

"Where am I?"

She is amused by this. "You don't know where you are?"

I shrug and the heat returns to my face. "I kinda lost track."

"Damn. You better lay off the bennies, trucker. You're about a mile west of Granite Bay..." she pauses to see if a light has come on behind my eyes or not. "... Ontario..." Pause. "... Canada..." She's making circles with her free hand, trying to encourage some acknowledgement from me. They are just names to me. I have no sense of being anywhere.

"Hey, Mona. How about servin' some of the other customers?" a gruff voice yells. I can see a table of three men holding their ceramic cups in the air. They are all bearded and bulging at the waist. A trio of black baseball caps sits on the table in front of them. It is startling to hear my mother's name. My eyes trace the curve of her body up onto the generous swelling of her chest. A black name-tag is perched over her heart. *Mona,* it reads.

She pivots and starts towards the gruff men. "I knew I was in Ontario," I shout after her for some reason. She looks at me over her shoulder and the truck drivers regard me with distaste.

I watch Mona idly as I sip my coffee, the way she moves in her virginal uniform, the offering of black liquid desire sloshing in its neat bulb. She dances, carafe held out to the right, from table to table, giving each patron the same sincere interest. Glancing here and there, nodding at lifted cups, smiling over remarks made across the room, all winks and pursed lips and tossed hair. The semaphore of waitresses that lets you know they know that you are watching.

The warm, bitter drink plummets straight through to my groin as Mona bends to fill a cup in one far corner. Her foot lifts ever so slightly, the toe of her loafer pointed delicately. She pirouettes away neatly just as the man seated on the outside lifts his hand, mumbling some feeble distraction into his beard, hoping to lull her with a dull worn joke as he tries to trace the arctic drift of her hip. She turns from the embrace in a slow pyrex arc and in one movement is filling another cup at another table. Bending deeply, her pretty face descending into the haze of cigarette smoke and double entendre. It is a dance filled with the music of heavy-duty ceramic ware and kitchen heat. Watching Mona gives me a moment of powerful loneliness. I think of Agnes, softly invoke her name. It makes me laugh out loud.

I want to laugh every time I try to spit out those dry lifeless syllables. Flaccid as a punctured balloon. They have nothing to do with the woman I knew.

One of the men at the table across the way is sending me hard looks.

My private amusement upsets him even more. His friend on the other side has taken hold of his arm, trying to mollify him. The man's mouth is set, his lips pulled off to one side as he talks to the peacemaker. Spit launches out of his seething mouth so that he reminds me of a snarling dog. His eyes flash from me to his friend who is holding his elbow. The man in the middle sits there grinning and watching his buddies argue over me.

The angry one stands abruptly, jerking his sleeve free of the other's grip, and then sits back down.

"Jake. Jake, come on," his friends say to him in unison.

Jake leans towards them, his huge hands splayed out on the table. He talks in a harsh, fanged whisper, loud enough for me to hear. "Listen, I don't like that mutt. I don't like the way he's lookin' at Mona."

I look down into my coffee cup. I don't understand why I invite this hostility everywhere I go now, as if I'm marked.

"Look at him, Frank. That guy's a mess. His hair. His clothes. No decent trucker looks like that. There's somethin' screwy about that clown. I can smell it."

"It's true," the man in the middle says, as though confirming some bit of common knowledge. "Jake can tell. Jake's got a talent for sniffing out weirdos and wagon-burners."

The one with the bald head runs a hand over his naked scalp. "Jesus," he says in a sigh, exasperated.

"Hey, I'm tellin' ya, Frank. That's some kinda troublemaker. We should be kickin' his ass outta here."

I look over at the one called Jake. My eyes focus for a second or so on two drops of brownish coffee that have fallen from his beard onto his down vest. His nose is bulbous and bent and he has the eyes of a pig. I can't imagine that Mona has anything to do with him. In a way, I feel sorry for him in his pathetic, imaginary romance.

He fixes me with a stare meant to intimidate, but I don't care enough to be intimidated. He straightens up and pulls his sweatshirt back down over the hairy seam of his belly. It's a gesture that shrinks him. I down what's left of my coffee and stand up.

"Hey, buddy, you some sorta hippie throwback or somethin'?"

"No," I say flatly, without emotion.

"Hey, Jake," his buddy offers, "maybe he's one of those terrorists."

Jake looks at me, utterly serious. "You an Arab? Is that it?"

The entire restaurant is watching now. "Yeah, right," I answer.

Fat Jake is determined and he feels the audience in the truck stop watching him. Even Mona is frozen in place. "Well, what are you? There's something peculiar about you. I'm sure of that. You from off the reservation?"

The question sears into me. I hear it in a dozen different voices. I could declare myself now. Stand up and shout it into the intent faces of all these docile patrons gleaning a morning's entertainment from Jake's crude taunting.

"I'm just passing through," I tell him.

"Get off it, Jake," his friend at the table says. He gives me a sympathetic look. "Sorry, pal. Ignore this guy. He just came in off a long haul and he hasn't re-socialized yet."

"Screw you," Jake says to his friend. He looks at me with his cold, piggy eyes. He won't let go of the bone he's sunk his teeth into. "There's somethin' about that guy."

"Fuck you, fatso," I blurt out through a tight smile.

He makes a show of trying to get up, but it doesn't take much for his friends to hold him back. He is afraid of me, and it has all been bluff and bluster. I toss a generous tip onto the table and leave.

All the way to the car, though, I hear the pig man asking, 'What are you?' I didn't owe him an answer, but my silence feels like a betrayal.

Sitting in the car, looking back through the dark glass into the restaurant, I can see the spectral form of Mona moving from table to table, indistinct and wavering like something swimming far below the water's surface. I remember her tossing her head back and laughing over the things

I said, but I'm not even a memory for her, only a flash out of her daily routine, like a hundred other lonely travellers. I visualize the black name-tag, the white letters perched on her ample breast.

I'm out of the car again, keys in hand, walking to the phone booth perched by itself in a corner of the parking lot. Even as I hear the operator saying, "Collect call from William Sawnet. Will you except the charges?" I have no idea what I'm going to tell her.

There is a moment's hesitation that fills me with dread. Then she says quietly, "Yes."

"Hi," I offer.

"Hello, William. How are you?"

She is keeping her distance. She wants me to know she is still hurt.

"I'm fine, Mona. How are you?"

"I'm keeping busy, William. Did you find out about your mother?" Her voice turns to ice over the word *mother*.

"No." There is only the sound of our breathing. "I didn't get very far with that. I'm not much of an investigative reporter."

"I always liked what you wrote, William." A peace offering.

"I know, Mom." It is there on my lips before I can think about it. "I was wrong. The things I said..."

"Where are you, dear?"

"Granite Bay, I think it's called," I answer, reading the cover of the phone directory, thankful for the small talk.

"Granite Bay? You're kidding. When we first moved from out west we stayed there with your grandparents for a while."

"What!"

"For a year while your father was on the DEW line. His parents had a big house there."

"How come we never went to visit?"

"About a year after we left, your grandfather died and Granny went to live in B.C. with Uncle Fred and Aunt Theresa. She died five years later. We never did get out to see her." There was sadness in her voice. "She was a good woman."

"Do you remember the address?" I am curious to see this place.

"222 Fourth Street. Those were happy times, William. We were so glad to have you. So glad," she says wistfully.

I can hear the emotion in her voice and I don't know how to answer it. A space, an emptiness opens up in me. A rift that begins in the pit of my stomach and stretches up along my spine like a cat sharpening its claws, turning me inside out by slow degrees. I cling to the black handset and study the solid rectangular bulk of the pay phone and its strange icons and simple, carefully worded instructions for long-distance communication. I hang dangling on the end of nine hundred miles of wire and cable and electronic effort and cannot manage a syllable.

"William?" her voice, reaching.

"I'm here." Words that are meaningless to me.

"It was wrong. What we did was wrong."

"Mom..." Her words hurtle towards me. Over that incredible distance. Huge and dark. It can't be stopped. "Mom. Don't..."

"Even then we knew it was wrong. It seemed too pat. Too easy. We even timed everything with the transfer. I felt like a thief in the night." Her voice breaks and it is like fragments of glass. "Holding you. Your father driving non-stop that first night. But you were so beautiful. I only had to look at you and it gave me strength. I'd never done anything wrong in my life, but we'd tried for so long to have children."

She pauses and I listen to the quiet tremolo of her breathing as she steadies herself. "Miscarriage after miscarriage. Wilfred was so disappointed. Heartbroken. And the doctors would say to try again. Keep trying, they would say. But it's not that easy, William. To have death slip inside you like that time after time. A part of me died with each one, with each..."

A long silence. Feeble amenities tumbling in my brain, faltering in my throat, language lost among overcharged nerve endings. I want to find a phrase that can rescue us both from the past.

"I used to dream about them, you know. Horrible dreams. White, white, white little babies. Pale and bloodless. They had no faces. Just blank circles of flesh. I remember waking in terror once and shaking your father. 'How will I feed them?' I was screaming. 'How will they breathe?' I was hysterical. And I was never the type to lose my composure. I thought women who had nervous breakdowns were just silly or weak but I was slipping. Wilfred wasn't much help. He didn't know what to say. It ended up in a fight and he went to sleep on the couch. He didn't know how to deal with such things, but it hurt him deeply and he knew I was becoming very depressed. So when this opportunity presented itself, he decided to grease the wheels."

Grease the wheels. What an odd phrase. Nonsensical.

"I never knew the details. I never wanted to know. I believed what he told me and said what he wanted me to say. I wanted a baby so badly and we were convinced it was the best thing for you."

I swallow hard. "Was my mother...Was she really Indian?"

Mona has become solid again. "Oh, yes. I'm sure that much is true. Wilfred worried that someone would notice. That the Indian blood would show through."

Silence and even the air is numb around me. The sky has taken on the appearance of a painting.

"William."

"Yes."

"Do you think they're together now?"

"Who?"

"Your father and all our dead babies. Do you think they are together now?"

"Yes. Yes, Mona, they must be." I hung up the phone without saying goodbye.

NINE

I was twenty minutes early picking Agnes up at work that Friday, enthusiastic about being in a place with a real bed and television and a shower. Fantasies about the upcoming weekend ran through my head on fast-forward.

The tree nursery was at the end of a short, gravel road, distinguished by being well-maintained, flat and level and wide enough for two full lanes. The compound consisted of three large greenhouses, a shed for tools and equipment, a smaller shed for the generator and pump and a little trailer embarrassingly similar to the one Agnes called home, only this one had running water.

In front of the greenhouses were rows and rows of what looked like plastic ice-cube trays. Some of the squares had healthy seedlings sprouting from them and some held only barren dirt or the curled brown remains of the beginnings of trees. Apparently some problem in the greenhouse earlier in the spring had killed off about a quarter of the crop. The Ministry had hired a dozen women from the reserve to transplant live growth into the dead spots on other trays so that each completed tray was full of green, living seedlings. Empty trays were cleaned and put aside for the next crop.

As I drove in, Agnes gave me a quick wave, her fingertips black with soil. It was simple piecework and they were being paid by the seedling. As I parked in front of the office building the door opened and Tim, the maintenance man, stepped out. It was his responsibility to keep the place in order as well as supervising the women. He lived there full time, to keep the pumps and generator running and to discourage vandalism.

He was older than me, in his early forties, and surprisingly gentle and soft-spoken. Despite this, he was possessed of a quiet, unshakeable self-confidence. I had only spoken to him briefly a few times, yet I developed a sense of real friendship and warmth towards him, and our conversations were usually interesting and substantial. He was of a good size, and if he didn't smile he could look imposing. His long, dirty blond hair was pulled back tightly in a ponytail and he wore a bushy beard. He opened the passenger side door and got in beside me.

"So how's things on the reserve?" he asked affably.

"Pretty good. Course, we keep pretty much to ourselves. Agnes and me. How's things here at Fort Apache?" Everybody knew that was the pet name the Ministry guys had given this place and that Tim lived out in the trailer mainly to cut down on late-night visits. There were powerful spotlights everywhere and Tim had been hired because of his size and burly looks. Given his gentle nature this was an inside joke between us.

"Really quiet since the women started working here." He paused to collect his thoughts. He paused this way often, contemplative, his hand pulling at his beard. "It was never really all that bad, anyway. The first few weeks. Kids. Teenagers, I guess, would come around two a.m. or so and bounce rocks off the trailer. That was a little disturbing." He gave me a quick sideways glance, full of wry humour. "The first night. The first night I heard this BANG, BANG, BANG." He smacked his fist into the palm of his other hand for emphasis. "I wasn't sleeping, I was still up reading and getting to know the place. But, nonetheless." He guffawed loudly and I chuckled beside him. "So I went charging outside with the shotgun they gave me and flipped right off the top step. It was a good thing I hadn't bothered to load the gun." Tim lifted his hands palms up and shrugged his shoulders to express his bemusement. "I mean, like I'm gonna shoot somebody over a few shrubs. It just seemed so natural to grab the gun. I must admit, that kind of disturbed me. I mean, I never did like guns. Not at all. Yet, at the first sign of trouble, there I am, snatching one up and charging outside. I think," his speaking was punctuated with another long, thoughtful pause, "maybe it was all the stories I heard before I came out here. It really played on my mind. Anyway, I heard them laughing in the bushes so I knew what the game was. Since that time I just stay in the trailer and ignore 'em."

The most amusing thing to me in the whole story wasn't Tim being frightened or how he ended up on his ass in front of the trailer; the thing that was most comical was that he had snatched up the shotgun.

"You spent time on other reserves?" I asked him.

His hands were on the dash. One finger had made a trail in the dust. "I was a teacher, way back when. When I went to school, if you agreed to work up north they gave you a break on your government loans. I worked in two different places. The last one was a bad place. Really isolated with nothing goin' for it. There was a lot of drinking. I ended up walking off the place."

I could see the hurt in his face. "How come?"

"Well, it's tough," he snorted. "Really, really demanding to go into a classroom every day and see the kind of lives the kids lead, the abuse and neglect and... if you care about kids. It wasn't every kid, but it was going on way too much. There were suicides and knifings and that kind of shit but the last straw was this twelve year old girl, a student, who offered me a blow job for a buck after class one day. Everything imploded and I walked out down the road and caught a ride to town."

"Jesus," was all I could say. I had not a shred of doubt that he was telling the truth.

"Yeah," he said earnestly, stroking his beard again. "They oughtta just shut down places like Red Clay. Bulldoze them."

I almost started to laugh, then I realized he was serious. "What?"

"Don't get me wrong. I'm not bigoted. I think it would be best for them." He paused and turned to look out the side window at the women working a few metres away.

"Them?" I repeated.

He slowly turned back to face me and our eyes locked. I wanted some indication that he wasn't serious. His eyes hardened and a tremor ran through his features, revealing the depth of his pity. "The old ways are dead for them, you have to face that. They're a part of history and this isolated self-destruction is painful."

A thin, clean mantle of pretense had shattered and dropped away. We sat silently, disappointment churning in my stomach like foul medicine, his wisdom and complacency going bad right in front of me. He searched my face.

"I think you're misunderstanding me, Will. The change has already happened. It's a fact." He was searching for some way to win me over. To convince me. "Like those stories where the character is dead but doesn't realize it yet and can't figure out what's wrong." Tim's hands were working the air in front of him. Grasping for a firm hold. He nodded towards the women. "You think Agnes should be here, replanting fuckin' little trees at a few cents a piece? No. But where should she be? Drunk at home in a house the government built? Living in the bush and talking to the animals? One with nature. That's mythological bullshit and you know it."

He was angry. Frustrated even though I had hardly said a word. Something was burning away under my skin, like a fever peaking. A poison I hadn't even realized was there, working its way to the surface and evaporating. I couldn't argue with him, pointless as it would have been, not because I thought he had a point, but because he was wrong.

He threw his hands in the air. "All you hear now is native this, First Nations that. Tell it like it is and you're a racist. Like you and this find-your-roots crap. You're just trying to make a buck. Sell a few books to politically correct suckers. You're about as Indian as I am."

I regretted now that I had told him about seeking my mother and finding Henry and falling in love with Agnes. I was ashamed of my plans to write a book. It was cheap and exploitative and he recognized it. I couldn't comprehend why he had become so vehement and felt he needed to attack me personally. "That's not true," I said. It was weak and unconvincing.

"Yeah? Why didn't you get in touch with any of the government agencies or some adoption group or something?"

I shrugged. Exposed and hurt by his true feelings. I tried to explain, even though I knew he wouldn't understand. "I didn't want to go through government agencies. I had the information my adoptive mother had given me. My biological mother is supposedly dead."

"Ah, bullshit. You didn't want to know the truth. It might fuck up the story."

Tim got out and slammed the door. How could I have been so wrong? He had seemed so intelligent to me. Open and sensitive. Even in the few short conversations we'd had when I came to pick up Agnes I had felt there was some connection between us. Now it had changed in a matter of minutes. I should have been enraged by the things he said, but instead there was something more akin to sadness, a melancholy that seemed to push the marrow from my bones.

Tim bellowed, "Quitting time," and I flinched. I looked towards the greenhouses and Agnes waved me over, smiling. Most of the women stood and stretched or arched their backs and waited by their line of trays for Tim to come and tally them up. I got out of the car reluctantly and started towards them, avoiding Tim's eyes. I didn't want another confrontation.

I felt distracted even as I embraced Agnes and we kissed. We stood holding hands while the day's work was totalled up and he handed out pay envelopes.

"So this is your away meis tei koshoow, Agnes."

We both turned towards the husky gravel-edged voice and I could see by the sour expression on Agnes' face that she already knew who had spoken.

"He ain't white, Dolores."

Dolores stood with her hands on her hips. She was dark and lean, what some would call good looking, but not pretty. There was an edge to her, a hardness in her mouth, and dull acceptance in her eyes.

"He looks white to me. White as a fish belly." The other women laughed. Dolores said something in Cree and the women tittered even more. She bent her knees off to one side as she stooped to pick her purse up off the ground, moving slowly and leaning towards me so that I could see down the low-cut tank-top to the brown swelling of her generous breasts, the dark hint of her aureola. There was an earthiness about her, a wild, voluptuous knowledge she sent out in telepathic waves. I was still disturbed by the altercation with Tim and didn't even realize I was staring into the soft deep shadow of her cleavage, the perfect mysterious curves of her ample body. She stood up, looking into my eyes, and caught me.

"Just another whiteman who likes dark meat, I think," she said as she placed a cigarette between her full lips. My gaze dropped to the ground.

"His mother was Cree," Agnes took a step forward.

Dolores' eyes went wide and she raised her eyebrows. "Oh. Where does she live?"

"We don't know..." There was another convulsive burst of hilarity from everyone. Agnes kicked over a tray of freshly replanted seedlings. "She's dead," she spat the words out, more to shut everybody up than anything else.

Dolores flicked her cigarette. "What's her name? Was she from here? She got family in Red Clay?"

"Elsie White..." I started to answer. Agnes cut in front of me.

"None of your fuckin' business, Dolores." She spun me around and we headed for the car as Tim ran up and handed Agnes her pay.

Dolores stood with the entire group behind her. "You better have some proof, Agnes. The band won't let him live here. You better take your whiteman and go live somewhere else."

Agnes didn't answer. She walked quickly to the car, pulling me along, and then shoved me towards the driver's side before getting in and slamming her door. Dolores was still watching us, the little group milling about in the background, collecting their things. She gave me a goodbye wave as I got into the car.

"What's wrong?"

Agnes glared out the passenger window. "Are we going to town or what?"

There seemed to be enmity everywhere. The horizon turned black with it. My mouth filled with acrimony and I rolled down the window to spit the bitterness out onto the ground. Huge dark waves washed over me and filled the car with a hostile, overwhelming presence of contempt and self-loathing. I started the engine and slammed the shift into reverse. I backed up and then smacked it into drive, spinning the tires and throwing gravel as I drove down the narrow lane leading to the main stretch of road, barely slowing down as the car lurched out onto it.

We fishtailed across the loose road top and swerved over to the opposite side, the back end swinging around again, the rear wheels spinning millimetres from the ditch. I cranked the wheel and the car skidded back to the right, jerking back and forth a few times before straightening out. I pushed the gas pedal to the floor and by the time we passed Red Clay we were flying, pulling a huge tail of dust and bouncing like a carnival ride. As we zoomed past the entrance to the cafe I thought I saw a ragged, twisted figure rising up out of the ditch, one eye gleaming red and malevolent, but when I looked in the mirror there was only the grey spectre of the plume we were churning up off the dusty road.

"William, if you think you can scare me on this road, you really are stupid." She sat with her arms folded across her chest, her seat belt undone, staring out the side window.

I ignored her. I didn't care if she called me William or Mr. Sawnet or Whiteman. My anger seethed, a hot brutal rage in the pit of my stomach. It fed on the noise of the gravel bouncing off the undercarriage, on the black, gnarled, knocked-over trees with their groping roots, on the huge froth of dirt choking out the sky behind us.

We came to a series of steep hills that rose and fell like humps on the back of some prehistoric beast. Flying up the initial slope felt like a ramp, so that Agnes looked out the windshield and put her hands on the dash to brace herself. We crested the top and the wheels left the road and I imagined us driving out over the sky, the rooster tail breaking off behind us and sagging like an amputated limb to the ground. Endless miles of green forest stretched in every direction, and the occasional dark blotch of a small lake, the lost thread of a meandering river. We rose up and over it all and I saw it as it had been for thousands of years, green and grey and shadowed. Tangled and endless. Full of spirits. Manitous. The ones that had risen out of the untouched earth, out of lakes that had known only the sun. Manitous that had assembled themselves from fallen pieces of the sky on mornings that were pure and white with frost. Friendly sprites that had formed from columns of morning fog that twisted together in the sky, or fish that had grown so gargantuan in their diminutive lakes that they were forced to swim into the air. Demons that pulled themselves from lightning-blasted trees, or out of the thick ice that moaned and trembled on clear moon-filled nights.

The car hit the road with a cracked metallic grunt and I had to fight with the steering wheel to keep from driving off into the bush flashing by us in a blur. We raced up the next incline but this time didn't leave the ground. We roared over the crest and surprised three huge ravens pecking viciously at an unrecognizable lump of fur and ripped flesh. Two hopped over to the edge of the road and flapped off into the trees, but the third beat his wings and headed off at an angle for the other side. I saw every detail as the hood of the car caught him in the middle of his inky back and his wings spread, swallowing the horizon. Frantically, I hit the brakes, looking deep into the cold pit of his eye as he bent backwards over the front of the car, then slid up the hood and smacked hard into the windshield before bouncing up over the roof.

The car slid to a stop and we both sat staring while the dust cleared. A small black feather, stuck to the windshield, shook in the breeze, and the wet crunch of the bird hitting the glass echoed in my head. In the mirror I saw a formless lump of night-dark plumage heaped in the centre of our lane.

I opened the door and got out. Agnes remained motionless in her seat. I walked back to where the dead bird lay with its wings bent and broken, splayed on the ground like a discarded cape, its taloned feet loosely curled. The eyes were shut tight and gave me the impression of someone hoping it would all just go away. Of course, the raven was very dead. I picked it up by one wing and it hung heavy and broken, twisting slightly back and forth. I carried it to the side of the road and laid it gently in the ditch.

I got back in the car and fumbled, unable to think of what I was supposed to do.

"You happy now?" her voice was empty.

"No," I said.

It began to rain. I put the car into gear and started to drive. The rain came down heavily and when I turned the windshield wipers on the one on the passenger side went for about three beats before the top half simply flew off, the bottom stub scraping against the glass. I turned them off, stopped the car and went back to locate the missing piece. It was easy enough to find, but there was no way to reattach it. I had to take a couple of band-aids out of the glove compartment to wrap around the metal end of what was left so it wouldn't scratch up the windshield. When I got back into the car I was soaking wet and at the very end of my patience.

"What am I doing here?" I muttered.

Agnes turned to me, her eyes flashing. "Why don't you just go home, then?"

I clutched the steering wheel and tried to rip it loose, rocking violently back and forth in my seat. "What the hell is your problem?"

"You like Dolores, whiteboy? You like that?"

"What the hell are you talking about?"

"I saw you staring at her. You like those big dark tits? You can have them. Everybody else has."

"Oh, for Christ's sakes," I pulled savagely at the wheel. "She practically shoved them in my face. What am I supposed to do?"

"Go home. Go back to your mother. Back to your big white world." She burst into tears.

The rain drummed on the roof and Agnes sobbed. A huge brown

four-door went past the other way, honking its horn joyfully and throwing mud up on my windshield.

I couldn't take the crying. "Agnes," I said gently. "What is it?"

"Can't you see everything is against us? It's always this way for me. Everything I try turns to shit. I try to go to school, live off the reserve, but I get lonely and start drinking, and while I'm away people die. I can't turn my back on my family, but I can't help them."

"I'll help you." Her crying was wretched. Coming from deep inside, shaking her and chilling her. I was ready to start weeping myself.

"They won't let you stay, Childforever. Don't you see that? You'll have to prove your status. Prove where you're from."

I didn't want it to be true. I didn't want official paperwork. I only wanted to know as much as I knew then. In that moment I only wanted the world inside the bubble of the car, Agnes, and the mythology of my lost mother and my secret name. Childforever. And ever and ever.

Coyote didn't wake until the bear was almost on top of him, the great black snout snuffling over his naked human skin. His eyes, blinking open against the dark, at first could not even make out the shape of the huge head hovering over him. Then he caught the glimmer of the feral eyes and the glint of long white fangs as the beast snarled. When he realized it was Ma-Kwa, Coyote scrambled to the end of his pit. The bear pulled himself up onto his hind legs and roared so deeply and loudly that even the moon overhead trembled.

Coyote jumped to his feet and swung his stone axe. He felt it smack against the ribs of Ma-Kwa, the concussion reverberating up through his arms. He swung again, ducking under the bear's forepaws, and the sound of the giant ribs cracking with the force of the stone filled him with strength. The bear moaned and dropped to all fours, air exploding out through his nostrils. Coyote raised the axe high above his head, the chiselled edge cutting through a shaft of moonlight, poised against the sky like a fist. Then with all his might, with power beyond any human's, he brought it down on the huge hairy head. The skull split like a ripe nut and the bear dropped at his feet.

It is easy enough to find 222 Fourth Street but I am surprised at how long the trip into Granite Bay takes. Everything changes once you have a destination. The road begins to work against you, and time lays out the minutes like someone playing cards. A slow, indulgent, studied game of solitaire.

You kind of ease into Granite Bay. A few houses are interspersed between the rock cuts, one or two small dairy operations, the railway curving out of the bush and running parallel with the highway, a large brown sign announcing the turn off to the mill. Then, coming around a slow downhill curve, a big truck stop appears with sheltered pumps and a sign promising showers and home-cooked meals. After that the houses are tucked in close together along the highway and there are three gas stations, then side-streets appear and schools and churches, until, coming over a low hill, you see the first stoplight and there on the corner, a convenience store with huge red prices plastered in the windows. Then two blocks of shops and banks and chain stores, and before you know it you are on your way out of town again.

I drive right through the first time, into the mirror image of my entering the little town. Out past the drugstore on the other side, looking at the two-storey stucco places and the white bungalows built when the railroad and the lumber mill meant prosperity, the side-streets growing shorter as I go. I turn around at the second gas station and head back in, paying more attention this time to the street signs. I am on Main and all the cross streets are named after trees. At Pine I can see I am getting close to the downtown core again. On the left is a single row of houses, and flashing off in the background are the railroad tracks. I turn right, and cross Second a block later. Two streets and then right again.

The houses here are larger and farther apart. I drive along watching the house numbers on the even side of the street, one- eighty-two, one-eighty-six, one-ninety, intersection. Two-ten before I can read another address. I study the yards, the front porches, the laundry hanging in the back yards, and wait for some glimmer of recognition. Two-fourteen and I almost drive through a stop sign. Not that it would have mattered. Things are dead quiet. An unnatural stillness. Even the sky seems frozen. There is no sound. A waiting, as though the entire world is infected with my anticipation. Two-eighteen, the car is barely crawling along, and I stay fixed on two-eighteen for a long time till I am directly in front of the next house. I look to it slowly, tunnel vision on the house numbers, big brass numerals with curving flourishes set inches apart, each one a little lower than the one before. A descending gaudy triad. I was a child here. This is a location from beyond memory, the deepest part of my past, which I have the ability to revisit.

I was here. I walked on this street, through this yard, into that doorway. I was still somebody else when I was here, fresh from another existence. Still clinging to memories of people for whom I can no longer even find any shadow of a trace. When I was here, perhaps I still knew my mother's smell, still could recall the sound of her voice and the places where I had played and known sleep.

I allow my vision to widen and let my mind take in all that is there. It is the house of my dream. It is the yard in which I saw myself as the child with his golden gift.

For a moment there is confusion as I stare at the comfortable grey house. How could Elsie have been here when I was adopted out west? How could we have played in this yard? Realization hits me. It wasn't Elsie. It was Mona, playing with the child for whom she had waited so long, the child she had thought she would never have. She is the one twirling me around and around. She is the one who started my world spinning. The one singing to me. And yet it is not Mona I see in the dream. It is someone darker. Someone younger. Somehow, the Other, it seems, has pushed her way into my memory. She has pulled herself out of whatever darkness she now lies in and slipped into a long-ago summer day. She has come to me from the unknown beginning of my life and brought me this dreaming.

It all begins to crumble around me. I have no idea of who I am, who

I am supposed to be. I am turning alone in the darkness and everything is falling down around me. *Husha. Husha.* One father unknown, the other gone without ever revealing himself. *Husha. Husha.* One mother becoming less and less tangible, her last shadow burning away in the green, green yard. The other, betrayed and alone. *Hush.*

TEN

It was a grim trip into town for Agnes and me. The cool rain fell, making the road slick. Agnes' side of the windshield was covered in mud. Two or three times I stopped and got out and scraped the glass clean with my hand, but then we'd hit a pothole or a truck would fly past in the opposite direction and deliver a fresh coating of greasy dirt. The wiper on my side would clear its half and Agnes would be looking at the underside of muck again. She finally just sat back and closed her eyes. From time to time a tear would run out from under her long dark lashes and trace the high brown curve of her cheek. Each tear dropped inside me, falling deep into the sour emptiness of my stomach, the secret erosion growing deeper and deeper.

The town looked miserable under the drizzle. Mud-caked cars and trucks were parked everywhere, passing each other in the wide streets. There were no people on the sidewalks and everything looked anemic and remote. We pulled into the parking lot of a dull motel, its red neon sign pale and sickly against the leaden, sombre sky. It was called The Twin Pines, but the only trees I could see were two obscure triangular shapes on the painted billboard, advertising accommodations and room rates.

I went in and got us a room, the desk clerk peering past me, as I filled in the paperwork, at Agnes sitting in the car with her dark glasses on. He handed me the key with a knowing, mechanical smile and he held onto the long plastic wedge for a second. We stood there joined in this odd handshake over the narrow formica counter, me holding the key and him holding the oversized plastic fob.

His smile broadened coldly. "I don't want any trouble tonight, okay, guy?"

I jerked the key out of his fingers and left.

It was the standard motel room. Bathroom to the left, just inside the door, and divided in two. First a small room with a sink and large mirror, then a second door separating that from the toilet and shower. On the right, a closet with hangers that couldn't be removed, then a short hallway that opened up into the room proper. A bureau with a mirror, round table with two chairs under the square window, and in the centre, a double bed with a lamp on either side.

Over the bed was a framed print of a prairie scene. Tall wind-blown grass, an old granary leaning in the background, broken wagon wheel in the foreground. There was an air-conditioner jammed through the wall, a telephone by the bed, and a television with a built-in am/fm radio perched next to the bureau. All the basic amenities of civilization.

I closed the door and Agnes ran and threw herself onto the bed. She rebounded once, her sunglasses bouncing up onto her forehead then settling on the end of her nose. She slapped her hands down on the comforter.

"Nice and firm," she said approvingly, looking at me over the tops of her displaced shades.

Her mood was improving. We were sealed away in our own cozy world, ensconced in our private delitescence. I studied her as she lay on the bed, jeans jacket spread out under her like denim wings, the strands of long dark hair that fell across her face, the movement of her breasts as her chest rose and fell, her cowboy boots as she clicked the toes together.

I went and stood at her feet. I tugged at the right boot, working it free of her foot, sliding it slowly out of the long shaft. I dropped it to the carpet and then rolled the white sock down, off her ankle, past her heel, the arch of her foot, her small toes. I caressed the naked foot gently. Tenderly. Gripping the toes together in my hand, running my fingers up and under the sole of her foot, holding it in the palm of my hand. I released it, let it dangle warm and brown over the edge of the bed. I pulled off the other boot, looking up the long inseam of her tight pants, losing my composure. I tugged the other sock free by its tapered end. It resisted till it passed the heel and then my hand flew back and smacked the television console.

I caressed each foot. One after the other, with both hands, squeezing and kneading, then both at the same time, gently moving them farther apart, away from each other. I cupped the heel of her right foot and lifted it, kissed it tenderly on the arch. I cupped the heel of the left, lifted it a little higher, kissed the bottom, just behind the toes.

I recalled the first time I had seen her feet, bare and dark against the white flank of the horse, wet and splattered with mud as she rode past me in the gravel parking lot and pulled Joseph up behind her. It was something I hadn't thought of for a while, my strange dream of death and the white stallion, Agnes drenched and shimmering, her heels kicking the horse for speed.

I ran my hands up the outside of her pants, and began creeping slowly up between her legs. Suddenly her right foot came up against my chest and shoved. I flew backwards, bounced off the TV and fell in a heap on the floor at the foot of the bed.

She sat up abruptly, the sunglasses tumbling over her face to end up hanging under her chin.

"You get the suitcases out of the car and I'll run a bath." She swung her legs off the bed and ran into the bathroom, slamming the door.

I pulled myself from the floor and stood, getting my bearings. I was still in a state of extreme arousal and I don't think my body knew what the hell was going on. A bath sounded nice. I grabbed the key off the bureau and went out to the car to get the suitcases.

The rain had stopped and the sun was out, bright and harsh, as though the time was wrong. I had thought it was much later, a different part of the day. It was as though I had walked out into an alternate, elongated allotment of sunlight. I grabbed the bags and hurried back inside.

The water was running but the bathroom door was locked.

"Hey."

"Go away."

"Don't you want me to wash your back?"

"No."

"What's going on?" I stood looking at myself in the chrome-edged mirror over the sink, anxious. The mood of our get-away weekend had been swinging back and forth like a berserk pendulum.

"I want to have a nice quiet bath. Go get some food."

"What?" The water had stopped and my shouting seemed foolish.

"Go get some hamburgers. Or K-fry."

I began to feel sullen. I didn't want to venture out into the uncharitable daylight. I didn't want to be on those petty, saturnine streets or in the morose stores, among the dour, hostile citizens.

"Maybe they have room service?" I said.

She laughed and I could hear her body sliding in the hot soapy water.

"Let me in," I pleaded.

"GO."

It wasn't as bad as I had assumed it would be and I soon regretted having slammed the door so hard when I left. The sunlight was brutal, the town was lacklustre and geometric, and some guy in a cowboy hat honked and gave me the finger in the mirror for pausing too long at a yield sign. But other than that, it wasn't all that unappealing.

I was the only customer at the chicken place and the young woman behind the cash register was pretty and very friendly. When she said, "Have a nice day," as I was leaving, it sounded sincere.

I had gotten away so easily picking up the food that I decided to stop at the liquor store.

Agnes was still in the bathroom when I got back, but she was out of the tub and in the first room now. I could hear her brushing her teeth at the sink.

"Supper's here," I called cheerfully.

No answer. I felt a certain trepidation. She was probably put out over me leaving in such a huff.

I put the large brown bag of steaming chicken parts and french fries down on the inadequate round table and sat on the bed.

"Smells delicious," I said in a sing-song voice, trying to sound relaxed and remorseful at the same time.

The door opened slowly and her arm reached out around the corner, her hand slapping at the wall. She found the light switch and clicked it off. She came out of the bathroom naked, soft sunlight filtering in through the closed curtains. She stepped into the light slowly and it played up along her long brown legs, glistened on the dark thatch, gleamed on the curve of her hip. She stood in front of me, her hair wet ebony, her body shadows and silk. I fell to my knees in front of her.

The chicken was cold by the time we got to it. We sat cross-legged and nude on the bed, tearing meat from the bones with our teeth and staring into the hunger in each other's eyes. I pointed at her with a gnawed drumstick and said, "You are incredible. I've never known anyone like you."

Agnes held up her hand and forced herself to swallow a large chunk of breast meat. "Please," she managed to mumble, then paused to clear her throat. She licked her lips. "Please don't compare me to any white girls."

I got up from the bed, stretched, and walked over to the big brown bag sitting on the table. I pulled out a grease-stained box. "You want any fries?" I asked earnestly.

She grimaced. "Cold fries? You must be kidding."

I shrugged. "You could hold the box between your legs. That should heat them up."

"You pig!" she shrieked and threw what was left of her piece of chicken at me. It bounced off my chest and fell into the bag.

"Hey." I wiped bits of seasoning off my chest. "The manager said he didn't want any trouble."

"Is that what he said to you? What a shithead."

I waved both hands at her to say forget it. "You want to watch TV?"

I turned the set on and we cleared the bed off and snuggled together to watch. Ten minutes into some inane sitcom, I couldn't keep my hands off her. She pushed me away. "Go have a shower. I haven't watched TV in a long time." She picked the remote up off the bed and flicked through the stations while I watched the coloured light from the screen silhouette her body in flashes. A mundane, everyday activity, a sweet, lyrical vision. She settled on a movie and I forced myself to go and shower.

Once I got in, it was long and glorious. I had taken two or three perfunctory showers at Aunt Eleanor's place but they had been quick and nasty affairs. They were on a well so it was necessary to be as expedient as possible. Get in, get wet, turn off the water, soap up, turn on the water and rinse off. It was an artless metal cubicle with a meagre dribble of water. The sides clanged and boomed as you moved around or bumped them with an elbow or knee. If someone absent-mindedly turned on a tap, then the shower slowed to an absolute trickle. When the tap was turned off again the shower head spurted forth, either scalding hot or ice cold. It was best just to get out altogether and wait to re-adjust the water.

The shower in the motel was total indulgence. I kept the water as hot as I could tolerate and it came out in such a forceful torrent that I thought it would tear the skin off my back. I let it pour over me, standing under it, the water drumming against the back of my neck, sluicing over my head so abundantly that I couldn't open my eyes, beating me into submission, making me dizzy with its power and heat, a mini-bar of soap melting away to nothing in my hand.

When I finally managed to pull myself from the muggy grotto and dry off, I found Agnes settled on the bed, still watching the movie. She had on one of my t-shirts and a pair of white panties that glowed against her tan flesh. She was eating a piece of chicken, staring at the screen in the semi-dark.

"Now I feel human again," I said jokingly. Agnes turned and I was shocked by the wounded look on her face, as though I had spit on her.

"What does that mean? Were you starting to feel like too much of an Indian? Did you wash the stink off?"

I let my hands drop. "Come on, Agnes. I didn't mean anything by it. It's just an expression."

She sat watching the television as if I wasn't in the room.

"You enjoyed your bath, didn't you?" I asked.

She wouldn't look at me. "It's just sometimes... it seems there is so much against us. People are starting to say things. Even my aunts. People are complaining about us living together on the reserve." She ran a curled finger under her eye, wiping away a tear.

"Fuck 'em." I tried to sound cavalier.

She smiled weakly. "It's easy for you, Childforever. You can always leave. A lot of people on the rez already don't like me. They say I'm a shit disturber. Why do you think I haven't been picked for a new house yet? It's been almost five years since the fire, but each time the allotments come up the Band Council manages to find others more needy. They're polite and very proper about it, but everyone knows they think I'm trouble. Don't make waves, Agnes, everyone says. Don't make waves."

"We'll work it out," I said, trying to sound reassuring, but I felt a sense of foreboding. We had sprinted away from the world for a few weeks and lost ourselves. Now I could feel it reeling us back in.

Agnes looked at me indulgently. "Childforever," she said, shaking her head.

There was an awkward stretch of silence so I busied myself back in the bathroom and she watched her movie. She called out something but I couldn't hear over the noise from the exhaust fan and running water. I stopped brushing my teeth. "What?" I hollered, turning the tap off. She yelled something again but I still couldn't make it out. I walked into the room, "Huh?"

"Did you get anything to drink?" she asked without looking away from the drama.

"Yeah," I said, looking around for the paper bag from the liquor store. "I have to turn the light on."

"Okay. Hurry up. This guy's getting ready to kill his wife."

I flicked the switch for the main overhead light. The bag was in the alcove next to the entrance. I pulled the cellophane-wrapped box out and held it up. It had an open front, and inside, behind the plastic membrane, were two bottles of pink champagne and two champagne flutes set in styrofoam. A petite pink ribbon was tied around the neck of each bottle. "Ta da," I said.

She looked over, puzzled, then her face fell and became hard.

"What the fuck is that?"

The light suddenly seemed very severe, the room bleak. I was only wearing a towel. "It's the Romantic Weekend for Two set. I got it for us."

She turned back to the television set and pulled the comforter up over herself. "You know I don't drink." It was a flat, cold statement of fact, practised.

I smiled weakly and clutched at the towel as it began to slip. "Champagne isn't drinking." My expression was so expansive that my cheeks began to ache. "It's an elixir of love filled with magic bubbles."

She looked at me with raised eyebrows, her face softening.

"It's an aphrodisiac." I made my eyebrows jump lasciviously and let the towel drop. The corners of her mouth began to turn up. I flicked the light off and stood in the glow of the cathode-ray tube and said in my cheesiest commercial voice, "It cleans. It whitens. It's a gift from Gitchie Manitou."

She couldn't keep from giggling.

Agnes agreed to have one drink so I got her to open the package while I slipped on a pair of jogging pants and a t-shirt.

"What lovely glasses," she said, tearing away the cellophane. She tossed me one. It was plastic with a detachable base.

"Nothin' but the best for you, sweetheart."

She handed me one of the bottles. I tore away the foil, twisted the wire seal off and worked my thumbs under the plastic cork. I gave the bottle a quick shake as the stopper began to work free and it exploded with a loud pop, bouncing off the ceiling, ricocheting off the wall, and rolling under the bureau somewhere, while we cringed. I filled her glass with churning white foam and she had to drink swiftly to keep it from overflowing.

Coyote leapt from his place in the ground and began to dance. He swung his axe and whooped to taunt the spirit of the slain animal. He liked the feeling of sweat and blood on his naked human skin, the pounding of his human heart. He whirled and kicked and stomped the earth with his feet. Then something caught his eye and he stopped dead. Frozen in place.

The bulk of the great bear had begun to move. It shifted, without making a sound, the horrible wound in its skull leaking blood and brains. It rose up, forepaws and head drooping, mouth slack. It rose until even the back paws lifted from the ground. The bear hung, suspended before him, and Coyote retreated in astonishment until his back rested against Grandfather Oak. Suddenly the hide of the beast dropped away like a discarded garment and it was the Binay-Sih before him. The giant wings spread and the bird screamed out, "Why, Coyote? Why?" But before he could answer a bolt of lightning exploded from Thunderbird's belly and burned through Coyote's chest. He felt the pain of it ignite every cell of his being and he collapsed, changing back to his true form. The bolt had even struck the tree behind him, blasting into the core of the ancient oak, setting it on fire. Something rumbled deep down in the earth and flames licked up the massive trunk.

Coyote could say nothing. He had never known such fear or hurt. Binay-Sih stared at him with terrible red eyes. Lightning seared the night and thunder punished the air. *"You never listen, Coyote. You never took your proper place among us. Ma-Kwa came to give you strength, to guide you onto the proper path. We are all going away, Coyote. All but you. I have taken a piece of your heart, Foolish One. You can never alter your shape again and you can never leave this world. A change is coming and things may never be the same. No matter where you travel, the new world will find you. And even though some may remember your name, you will always be alone."*

Then he was gone. Coyote stood for a while as the old tree burned like a great torch. Burned so brightly it chased away the night. When the flames finally began to die and the darkness started to slink back over the land, Coyote felt the loneliness seep into his bones.

I drive away from Granite Bay in a daze, glancing again and again into the mirror as I retrace the short stretch back to the main highway. Even my eyes are becoming less distinct now. A few days ago they belonged to William Sawnet, perhaps because from a distance I thought I recognized him, but now, as I draw closer to the place he called home, he is beginning to blur. Everything has changed. Mona was forgiving and conciliatory on the phone but even that is different now. I realize how much I have betrayed her. She was the one all along in my sacred dream. She was my talisman of the past.

It occurs to me that she must have felt very lost in those days, living with in-laws, with her husband away, and left to look after a baby that had been acquired under shady circumstances. Maybe that is my true inheritance. This rootlessness, this gypsy poison in the blood. The nomadic current that closes behind itself like a river and wipes away all traces. The schizophrenic metamorphosis that forces you to be different people in different places.

And Childforever, what of him? Is he dead? Murdered by circumstance, stillborn all those years ago, or kidnapped and murdered? Nothing I have believed has been true. I can't remember back to the truth. Everyone has offered me nothing but lies.

It is late in the day. The sun flashes through the tree-tops and long shadows darken the pavement. I move from shadow to light to shadow in the unrepentant glare of the plummeting, naked sun, the brief, portentous twilight where the earth holds up its vegetative hand or the highway squeezes into a high rockcut.

Then, in the middle of nowhere, he is there, standing at the edge of the road. Barely visible against the turbid green background flashing past behind him. The silhouette is unmistakeable. Plical hair like a twisted headdress, the ragged, tattered clothes, the look of the milky dead eye, as I drive past.

I pounce on the brake, driving it to the floor, and wrench the wheel over too quickly onto the unpaved shoulder. The wheels slide, cutting into the loose stones, and the back end of the car starts to come around. I see the verdigris smear of the tree-line scrolling past at high speed, then a violent jolt, the wheels catching, the car teetering up on the crest of sudden inertia, surrendering as it begins to roll over the steep incline.

I'm not sure how many times it rolls, though I don't lose consciousness. The side window shatters as my head slams against it, and for the blink of an eye I am moving inside a kaleidoscope. Minute jagged prisms of glass float all around me, bright and dazzling. There is the green of the ditch, the blue sky, the tan interior of the car, all tumbling around me in a ball. Then a sudden explosion of colour behind my eyes, and everything stops.

I sit for a while, listening to my own breathing. My head aches. I put my hand up against the pain and there is a lump and a spot of blood, but not much really. A high-pitched humming fills my ears and then is gone. The car has landed on its wheels. I kick open the door and climb out. It is sitting at the bottom of the incline as though I'd parked it there on purpose. If you didn't notice the dents or the shattered window you'd never suppose it had been in an accident. From the road, through the line of thin trees and tall shrubs, it would be hard to spot at all.

I struggle up out of the ditch and stand there stupidly, trying to think of what should be done. A truck roars by and at the last minute I raise my hand weakly and wave. The airhorn sounds to return the salute and it echoes as the rig disappears over the hill.

A raven flies across the highway, skimming the dull pavement, and lands in the uppermost branch of a tall, dead tree that stands ashen and bone dry. The kind Henry and I had looked for during our wood–gathering expeditions. The raven caws its naked, mocking sound. It calls again and again until it sounds like a name.

I walk back down the embankment past the car. There is no traffic either way, not even the sound of any approaching. I look to the spot where I witnessed the spectre of Ditchhair. I am thinking of him, of how we are alike. I am lost because of the places I have left and he is floundering because a place has left him. I drift in a daze, bewildered by the dreaming that has grown steadily stronger since that first night at Mona's. Now it is overtaking my waking life the way a more violent darkness has swallowed Raymond and made him into Ditchhair, a caricature of his own pain. His own broken identity.

The raven is watching me and in return I study it. There is a persistent ache radiating from deep inside my brain. I close my eyes, press my palms against my temples. I want to squeeze the dreaming out of my head as though it were a pustulant infection. When I look at the bird again, I almost lose my balance.

Its eye. Clouded and indistinct. The barbed pulsing swells inside my skull. I squint in concentration. The raven is the highest shadow in a world of shadows. I move closer and the raven flies a little way into the trees. It barks again, short and abrasive. Tormenting. I move into the bush after it.

Rage fills my veins, infecting every corpuscle with its fever. Ever since that first night when I began to think of finding my past, things have been distorted. The dreaming flowed into my head like run–off from the murky history I wanted to share. Perhaps it is the taint of my own intentions. Perhaps it is something in me, an irresistible gullibilty that invites people to invent the things they think I want to hear. I want to have control again. I want to push away the dreams and hallucinations and deceptions. I want to forget about spirits and manitous and traditions.

The black bird seems to be the malevolent embodiment of all my confusion. It flutters back into the trees and laughs, raucous and chiding.

I pick up a couple of good-sized stones from the ground and tramp deeper into the woods towards where I last saw the raven. The bird is no doubt some trick of my own confused mind but I am determined to find out. Perhaps I am only dreaming.

The bird caws the secret name again. Calling me. Mocking me. I plunge deeper, in through the trees.

Quite suddenly I recall a name Henry taught me in one of his stories. Ashi kah kah gih, the evil raven, the one they call the bird of death. Is he calling to me? Somewhere in the heart of these woods I wonder if he sits and calls my name, gloating over all he has destroyed, and I burn with the need to spill his blood. I want to pull the pain out of my head, knock him from his high perch and wring his scrawny feathered neck. I hate him with a deep, combustible hate that flares under my skin and convulses through me in waves. It is soothing.

The trees pull at me like beggars and the undergrowth grapples my legs and snares my feet. Spider webs fall across my face like filaments of hair, and small grey branches poke and claw, scratching my cheeks. Sweat runs in my eyes so that I stumble drunkenly through the spaces between trees.

There is no path. No blaze marking the way. I follow my bristling wrath and blunder against the thick growth, propelled along the path of least resistance. The raven caws and flits ahead of me, a scornful shadow above. I throw one of the stones, but it only bounces harmlessly off a branch and clatters to the ground. The trees and the shrubs seem to be handing me along like a sun-stroked spectator in a crowd. I see only a vision of green and the black intermittent stain of the spiteful bird. The veined leaves are a series of veils before my eyes, the leaf-strewn ground barely visible under my feet. I careen hard against one trunk and then another as slender limbs whip across my face and jab at my eyes. Suddenly all the anger is gone, and I am deflated and powerless at the centre of a great verdant conspiracy.

I stumble forward and back and to the side, caught up in underbrush and dead branches. Tripped and held up and speared and blinded, as the shadows grow deep and bottomless around me. I put my hand on a dead stick jutting up from a decaying trunk and it snaps off so that I tumble over the mossy log and roll down a slight incline into a small wet clearing.

I look up to the shattered grey geometry of the sky. Up through the splayed tangle of branches. The forest spins around and around, the tree-tops whirling under the distant sky. I close my eyes and hear my mother's voice. She is singing, *Husha, husha.* I know the voice. It is Mona, singing to her adopted son, and it saddens me to think that that singing may be the only music of my childhood. It could be that my real mother never sang to me or never really cared. I'll never know. It was all lost to me the moment I was born, the moment I was conceived, maybe the moment my mother was conceived. Maybe even before. Back to the second the first whiteman set foot on this continent. The first crack in this shattered history. I'm just a fleck of dust from an exploded world, thrown too far from the centre to have any meaningful shape or history. I open my eyes and she is there above me in that fabled back yard. Only this time it is Agnes that I see.

It is a hot summer day, full of sweat and glistening skin and humming insects. She skips around me, her face young and even more beautiful than I remember. Full of light. Her brown eyes deep and dancing, her hair alive and willful, flicking onto her face, her cheeks and forehead covered with a moist sheen.

Husha.

Husha.

She is holding the hand of a child and they both circle me as I lie on my back. They are laughing as they look down on me and dance around and around, singing to me as I become the mulberry bush, the centre of the song, the very axis on which the blue universe rotates above us in cloudless joy. Her sweet face is a brown sun smiling down on us both.

She comes to the boy's favourite part and the two of them fall beside me, the gold crucifix jumping against her white blouse on its glimmering chain. I reach for it but she tickles me and I curl into a ball and giggle uncontrollably, my eyes pinched shut, my face buried in her hair, her perfume warm and fragrant all around me. "Say you love me, Childforever," she whispers. "Say you love me."

I say it and open my eyes and she is gone. Only ashi kah kah gih is there now, in a tree on the edge of the clearing, barely visible in the growing dusk. Watching me, head tilting side to side, its long black beak glistening with plastic hardness. It lifts its pointed face and caws loudly to the tree-tops, its stentorian voice a sharp-cornered chant in the green hush of the woods.

The raven calls again, spitting my name from its dry throat. I open my eyes and watch it hop down to the ground, its head angling left and right mechanically. It spreads its wings and propels violently forward, the last rays of the sun glinting on its curved black beak as I stare, frozen in terror. It has become huge, transforming even as I am looking into the milky dead eye. Growing, changing, more and more man-like until it is Ditchhair hurtling towards me, his hands raised to strike. I scream and close my eyes, throwing my arms across my face.

Nothing happens. I open my eyes again, arms still raised protectively. He is gone. The forest is silent. Ominous and dark. I attempt to get my bearings but nothing makes any sense. I mumble a little prayer of protection. It seems incoherent at first, but familiar. "Naga. Waya. Beekum." What was it? "Naga waya beekum." Something Henry had taught me? "Naga waya beekum." The fear begins to fester and bloat inside me. "Naga waya beekum. Naga waya beekum." The cabalistic words, the sound of my fractured voice compounding the terror. "Nagawayabeekum. Nagawayabeekum." Then I realize where they came from. They were my words. "Naga." Words I invented years ago. "Waya." They have no power. "Beekum." They belong to the foolish dialect of the Mohican Blood Brothers.

In a panic, laughing like a maniac at my own absurdity, I jump to my feet and run.

I don't get more than a dozen or so steps into the thick, tangled woods before I fall again, crashing hard among the brittle branches and undergrowth. I pull myself up, anxiety rising, the darkness pouring in like water among the trees, an inky flood drowning everything, erasing the world. I plunge on, bouncing off dark, indistinct trees, branches pulling at my clothes and hair, tangling around my feet to be dragged along behind for a few clumsy steps. I stumble and pitch forward, hands clawing at the earth, scuttling through the night on all fours. Then, upright again, a large spider web breaks across my face and hundreds of tiny, hairy legs are scurrying across my skin. I brush spasmodically at my head and shoulders.

A pine bough rakes my face as I charge on, my arms jerking up before I crash headlong into the butt of an upended tree, ploughing heavily into the cluster of roots, like a moth smashed by an open hand. Momentum causes me to career off to one side, landing hard on an old, punky stump which gives way under my weight and shatters into hundreds of wet, mouldy pieces. I roll into the jumbled mess of fallen limbs, dead leaves, dirt, and scurrying insects.

It seems best to stay down this time, on my back, right arm across my eyes, breathing. I fight the rising hysteria by hiding from it. By not looking into the darkness. I think only of what I should be doing. Stay put if you're lost, they tell you. But the night and the woods won't let you be. The mosquitoes find me and begin buzzing in my ears and sucking blood from every exposed centimetre of skin.

I slap at them without opening my eyes, my hands flailing. Some I catch in the act of siphoning blood and pinch between my fingers till they pop. They are around me in a cloud. Undeniable. I kill them in handfuls, but it hardly deters them. I swat and swing and slap myself like a petulant child in a tantrum. Finally I must open my eyes.

It is dark but I can still see, somewhat. There is the sound of a truck on the highway but it seems a long way off, cloaked in the night, hidden under the dark shroud that has risen out of the woods and covered everything. It becomes quiet again. Something is moving through the brush not too far away and I resist the urge to slap, listening intently. Then I feel the prick of a mosquito sliding his proboscis under the skin of my forehead. I swing hard and fast and the palm of my hand smacks loudly. There is a second of absolute silence and then whatever it was scampers away through the trees.

I listen. Frogs chirping, the buzz of insects, a light breeze moving the leaves. Water running. I stand and move slowly towards the whisper of a little stream. My hands circle my face like addled white birds.

The ground is soft under my feet and I sink down a few inches into the swampy ground. Water seeps into my shoes. Each step produces a loud wet sucking sound and the rich odour of mud fills my nostrils. I'm not sure where the inspiration comes from, but I bend down and work my fingers into the mud and rub it over my exposed face, coating the skin with the moist, fetid muck, grimacing as I spread it over the swollen abrasion on my forehead. It stinks but it feels good and cool as it dries on my skin, and it discourages the mosquitoes.

After a few more slow halting steps, the earth pulling at my feet, I step into the cool stream, cup my hand and scoop water up to my lips. I hold it in my mouth a second before swallowing. There is no bad taste and it soothes my parched throat.

Ankle-deep in the shallow brook, the hysteria that gripped me drops away. The bugs are only a minor nuisance. The mud hardens on my face. I smell the swamp, listen to the trees sway in the night, their shadowy forms quivering as the moon rises above them.

I put my hands into the pockets of my jacket and my cigarettes are there. I take the pack out, slide it open and it is a relief to find my disposable lighter tucked inside. I walk out of the swamp the way I came in. I am unsure of how big it is or how deep the creek gets. Once I'm on dry ground, I begin to pick up any dead limbs I stumble across.

Odd how exhilarating it is to be relying so much on my other senses, to be accomplishing the things I want to do by touch and smell and hearing. By intuition, even. To turn this way or feel around here simply because it seems right. Without all the distraction from my eyes I can hear some dim and distant portion of my brain shouting advice, like someone far below calling out directions to a stranded climber.

I drag my bundle of twigs and dry branches under the canopy of a tall pine. Near the trunk I can actually stand without touching the lowest branches. I use a section of rotten log lying on the ground as a reflector for the heat, and sweep away the loose litter and pine needles. Using whatever bits of tissue and paper I find in my pockets for tinder, I build a tepee of twigs for a campfire. As I light one corner of the crumpled paper I can see it is a receipt from the Grande Level liquor store. It flares up, hot and brief, then crumbles into ash as the wood takes light around it.

I have a nice blaze going. Henry would be proud.

ELEVEN

I woke up naked, staring at a vapid, pale blue nothingness. I closed my eyes and opened them slowly, thinking that there must be something wrong with my vision. I saw the same featureless wall. I started to sit up and suddenly there was perspective and my heart started to beat again. I was lying in the bathtub facing the back wall.

I rolled over gingerly and light poured in from the outside room. I struggled to stand but a wave of nausea washed over me. Something sharp bounced chaotically inside my head. I sat back down on the cool porcelain and let my head flop over to rest on the edge of the tub. The tiny room spun and bile rose up out of my sour stomach so that my cheeks bulged, but I managed to fight it off. My mouth tasted like an ashtray and I felt weak and empty as though the marrow had been scraped out of my bones.

Without getting up, I scooted forward and turned on the taps. The cold water crept up over my feet, between my legs, and gripped my testicles. I trembled violently but this was better than standing. I cupped my hand under the running water and pulled it into my mouth, swirled it around, spat it out. I could feel my teeth again and my dehydrated tongue began to swell and blossom. I rinsed and drank over and over as I adjusted the water. Finally I pushed back the plastic wedge that turned on the shower and opened my mouth to the warm rain.

After a few minutes I was able to stand, leaning against the wall with the shower streaming down my back. The night before started to come back to me, Agnes resisting the champagne. After I had cajoled her into two plastic glasses full, she changed. We drained the bottles in no time. Giddy and playful, I tried to get her into bed, but she pushed me away.

"I'm gonna phone a friend."

"What?" I said. I was lying on the bed, sullen at being rebuffed.

"I'm gonna phone a friend," she repeated, at the phone, dialling already.

"This is our weekend alone," I complained.

She turned shakily, waving me off. The champagne had quite an effect on her. "Don't get your shit in a knot. I'm calling a bootlegger. If I'm goin' off the wagon, I'm goin' all the... Hey. Hi, Roy. You still bootleggin'? Yeah. Great. It's Agnes. It is not bullshit. I'm at The Twin Pines. A friend. You got any whisky? Cool. A forty. How much? Holy shit." She laughed deep and full, and rolled her eyes at me. I remained serious, pouting.

"You could do better for a friend though, right?" She tipped her chin up. "How much money you got?"

"Lots," I replied. I had never bothered opening an account and I still carried my bundle around rolled up and tucked in the zippered pocket of my shaving kit.

They finally negotiated a price and Roy was at the door in less than ten minutes. We barely had time to get dressed. Agnes answered the knock and Roy barged in, seizing her and lifting her off the floor in a big bear hug.

Roy was massive. His bulk towered over Agnes and filled up the entranceway. He had long reddish brown hair, a bushy beard and a gold cross dangling on a chain from his left ear. He was wearing a short leather jacket that bunched at his shoulders, and there was no hope of him ever doing it up. His belly protruded, squeezing out between his sweatshirt and wide leather belt. He released Agnes and gripped her shoulders in his huge thick-fingered hands.

"How ya been, squaw-woman? I ain't seen ya since we did that weekend trip to Calgary on my scooter."

Agnes was laughing. I was jealous. Not just over the way he was touching her, or the idea of them spending a weekend together. I knew I could never get away with calling her something like squaw-woman.

They reminisced while I sat at the table, smoking a cigarette. The champagne was looking more and more like a bad idea. I was rolling my half-finished smoke back and forth in one of the glass grooves of the ashtray, intent on the ember and grey flakes of ash, when I heard Agnes mention my name. Roy was coming towards me, gargantuan and all in black except for the huge silver belt buckle with a Harley-Davidson logo.

I jumped up, taking an involuntary step backwards. Roy slammed a bottle of whisky down on the table and thrust his hand out at me. I tried to shake it in the conventional manner but he gripped me by the thumb, wrapping his huge sausage-like digits around the back of my hand. I attempted to follow suit but my fingers were lost in his grip. He shook my whole arm right up to the shoulder blade and smacked my biceps with his other hand.

"How's it hangin', man?" he said earnestly.

"Fine," I answered feebly.

Agnes got three glasses, still in their white protective bags, and sat on the bed. Roy sat in the chair next to her. I was stuck on the other side of the table.

Roy pulled a glass out of its paper sleeve and handed it to Agnes, then got one for himself. I took the glass that was left. He broke the seal on the liquor, then snapped his fingers. The cap spun off the neck of the bottle, hit the table and whirled onto the floor.

"Hey, man. We need some ice." Roy was looking at me with his intense blue eyes.

"Sure. Why don't I get some?" I said, smiling in an exaggerated way. Roy didn't make any move to get up. I had to walk across the bed to get out of the corner.

"Thanks," Agnes said as I put on my shoes. She didn't look at me.

As I reached the door Roy spoke up. "They don't got an ice machine here, guy. You gotta go to the convenience store on the corner."

"Thanks," I said, and went out.

The freezer at the convenience place was broken but they told me I could probably get some ice at the garage up the street. I thought about going back and saying they had none but I figured Roy would only tell me about the garage, too. I looked at the car parked in the lot but decided to walk the couple of blocks.

When I returned with the bag of ice, Agnes was sitting at the table alone. She had a glass of whisky in her hand. Roy's glass was smashed in the corner.

"Where were you?" she demanded, slurring her words.

"I had to go to the garage for this shit," I retorted. "Where's Roy?"

"I threw him out. He always was an asshole."

"You okay?"

"Yeah."

"You went with that goon?" I asked incredulously, dropping a couple of ice cubes in her glass and sitting in Roy's vacated chair.

Her head snapped up, her eyes flashing. "Don't start. You don't... start."

"All right," I shouted. I poured myself a drink, and things went downhill from there.

I turned off the shower and stepped out. The towels were all over the floor. I found one that was only slightly damp and sat on the toilet to dry myself. Still dripping, I walked out past the big mirror. Leaning against the wall, I made my way to the main room.

An ashtray was upside down in the middle of the carpet. Clothes and blankets were scattered everywhere. Agnes was lying nude, face down on the bed, her features hidden by the tangled black mass of her hair. The whisky bottle stood empty on the table. Looking at it I could taste the raw liquor again and felt my gorge rising. I draped my arm across my stomach. The ice bag lay in a pool of water next to the table, a few distorted cubes huddled together inside.

I looked at Agnes on the bed and had flashes of memory. Clumsy, brutal, sex, more of a belligerent contest than anything to do with love. No ending or beginning. No climax. Just bodies smashing together until we fell apart, exhausted. Before that, shouting and pushing, the phone ringing, the manager at the door. I think I gave him fifty dollars. I remember stumbling around the room in my underwear, searching, tossing things here and there while he fumed and muttered in the doorway. Agnes hiding under the blankets as the red-faced manager snatched the bills from my hand.

The phone rang. I picked it up only to stop the clamour.

"One hour. I want you out." The sound of the handset slamming down in my ear.

Agnes moaned and lifted her head as though it was a great weight.

Her hair stood out in long confused tangles, matted with unknown substances.

I sat down on the bed next to her and rubbed her back. "We have to get going, baby," I said.

She tensed, and then sprang up, pushing me aside. She raced to the bathroom but only made it as far as the sink before she puked violently. I sat on the bed, wondering if I should go to her or if she'd only be angry and embarrassed. She retched horribly, sputtering and gasping and heaving into the sink again. I heard the water running and her wet coughing. I started to take her a glass and then the door slammed, sounding like a gunshot, sounding final.

I began to gather up the clothes and clean up as much as I could, my stomach gurgling and threatening. I turned on the radio hoping the music would be a distraction, and collected some clean clothes to put on. I had dumped out the suitcase in my drunken searching. Anxiety took hold of me and I snatched up the shaving kit and tore it open. My roll of bills was still inside. Some spark of self-preservation had remained alive and I had looked after the money. I also found a flat, yellow tin of aspirin tucked away in a small pocket. I took two, swallowing them without water, and put the container down on the bureau for Agnes.

She emerged from the bathroom after about twenty minutes, having taken a shower, with one towel wrapped around her body and another around her head, her long hair tucked up inside. I had folded all her clothes, stuck them into one side of the suitcase and left the suitcase open on top of the bed. When she came out I was down on my hands and knees, using one of my t-shirts to soak up the water from the melted ice.

"There are some aspirins on the bureau." I spoke pleasantly.

She ignored me, yanking articles of clothing from the suitcase with exaggerated force. She turned, grabbed up the painkillers and walked briskly back into the bathroom to get dressed.

Once the door banged shut again I found myself feeling extremely exasperated by her anger. I continued straightening up in a fit of pique, mumbling and cursing under my breath, and slamming things into place, driving bits of paper and broken glass into the wastebasket with all the force I could muster. I turned the radio up and bounced around the room, grumbling loudly and tidying in a frenzy. By the time she came charging out of the bathroom, the room was almost in better shape than when we had checked in.

"I hope you're happy," she was pointing at me with her hairbrush, gripping it so tightly her arm trembled.

"What do you mean?" I shot back indignantly. "It was your idea to phone up good ol' Roy. I didn't..."

She took a step towards me, the brush jabbing like a knife, her face twisted. "You don't get it, do you? Do you know how long it took me to get off booze? Do you know what my life was like? I've been fighting for a dry reserve. For substance abuse counselling. For a real community centre. This will be all over town. Roy'll be tellin' everyone 'The old Aggie is back.'" She held her hands up, spread wide apart to frame an imaginary marquee. "The Return of Squaw-woman." Agnes looked at me, her hazel eyes like cold, distant planets. "Thanks. Thanks a lot."

I was struck numb. Mute. Paralysed. She was right. I shouldn't have pushed her into drinking. I didn't know, I wanted to say, I was ignorant, I was unknowing. Unenlightened. Backward. Blind. I was foolish and immature. I was Childforever.

She stood, tears rolling down her cheeks, her arms fallen to her sides, a broken look in her face, in the way she stood. It pierced me, ran through my heart and my spine, through all the days I'd spent since leaving home.

"Agnes..." I said, not knowing what I was going to say. Not knowing how to fix things. "Agnes..."

"Shut up."

"But."

"Shut up."

At first I thought she wasn't even going to give me a chance. Then I realized she was trying to listen to the news report on the radio.

We said nothing to each other on the way over to the hospital. The newscast had said something about a tragedy on the Red Clay Reserve and the problems of gas sniffing and substance abuse. The reporter went on, each word coming more slowly than the one before, falling out of the electric mystery behind the radio like stones dropping into a deep well. The silence. The dark. Splash. The silence. The dark. Splash. In carefully measured tones, a female voice informed us that six youths had been taken to hospital and there were unconfirmed reports of deaths. They promised more news as it became available.

We stared in disbelief at the black eye of the television, listening to the music pouring from the same speaker that had an instant before held us palsied in the cold grip of promised death. Then we were scrambling towards the car.

Coyote wandered. For a long time, everything seemed the same. Nothing was changed, except that much of his medicine was gone and he wanted to believe that what happened had been nothing more than a very bad dream. Some shaman taking revenge, perhaps. After all, he had many enemies. But he was never able to find Grandfather Oak, or any trace of where the great tree had stood. And then the manitous began to leave and the land changed. Coyote followed them towards the setting sun but they had no time for him or his pranks. No one laughed any more and soon they were all gone, back beyond the sky.

Coyote travels still. Nose to the ground. Seeking his old friends or the lost part of himself that keeps him here, even though he knows it burned away with Grandfather Oak. He hopes that there might be some mercy hidden for him somewhere. He is left between two worlds. Remembering the sweetness of the old, but not a part of the new.

Coyote travels still.

Once I have a good fire going it is much easier to search around my makeshift campsite for firewood. There is no shortage of dead limbs and fallen trees and I soon have enough wood to last a few hours.

I sit down in front of the flames exhausted, light a cigarette and stretch out on my side, propping myself up on one arm. I begin to think about Henry and the cook fires he made in the woods. There was still a lot of work to be done before winter. I try to imagine that tiny plywood shack of his on a frigid January night. How cold it would be. I suppose it's something he's used to, but imagining that place in the frozen heart of the season of snow, it is easy to understand why he did what he did.

I take another cigarette out of the pack, break the filter off, tear the paper away and roll the tobacco into a ball in my hand. I think of all that Henry taught me as I drop the tobacco into the fire. While it burns I say a little prayer for him. A prayer that doesn't really call on any deity but only speaks to the sky and the wind. The stars wink in black space overhead and I repeat Henry's name in my head over and over like a chant.

Then I begin to speak in a language of my own, only a few words, over and over. The sound of them makes me smile. Musical syllables that spill from my lips. I watch the trees sway in the darkness and I fill the spaces in between with my invocation, my charm of protection for an old man, alone and far away. Words from an imaginary tongue made up by children. The language of a lost tribe of little boys from a long dead summer. Why not? All words are illusions. Their meaning is in our heads and in our history.

I throw a few bigger chunks into the flames, then settle onto my back. The branches of the tree mask the sky directly overhead so that only an occasional star shows through. I think I see a dark shape hopping about in the shadows above my head, then my eyes grow heavy. I close them and lie quietly on the spinning earth while the night sings. I surrender myself to the realm of moss and fern and fungus and the adhesive passage of snails. I am filled with the need to stretch out on the forest floor among the leaves and twigs and dust from the bones of countless scattered lives. I wait for the insects to gnaw away my clothes, for the mammoth roots of the ancient tree to part the ground beneath me, for its pine boughs to drop and scour the taint from my pale flesh. I want snakish subterranean arms to lower me into the soil and for the earth to pump her own blood into my veins and for my skin to darken with her love.

I drift into sleep, then wake suddenly, my eyes open and aware. The fire is only embers and an occasional finger of flame that flares up and dances, then falls again like some afflicted sleeper. I reach for a few smaller branches to throw on when I notice eyes watching me through the smoke. Canine eyes. I stare, motionless, trying to make out the shape and size of the body behind them.

It is a coyote. She takes a few steps forward. I have the distinct impression that it is female, but in the settled darkness over the flickering fire there is really no way to tell. She comes stealthily closer, long snout held down, the sheen of her wet nose brushing the earth, slowly, a single tensed step at a time, one paw always held in the air. Slowly, around the fire, our eyes locking. She is huge. Long legs, lean body, tail down behind her. She sniffs my feet. I can hear my scent being sucked in through her sensitive nostrils, feel the light touch of her nose as she moves along my body, whiskers brushing the back of my hand.

We are face to face. I look down the long perspective of her snout to the triangular head, the feral glimmering of her eyes. We stare deeply into each other and a melancholy chill shivers through my body. A rich, resigned loneliness. A sad acceptance. I hold my breath, marvelling at her beauty even as she turns abruptly and leaps the fire in a single flowing motion and disappears among the shadowed trees like a ghost. As though she had fallen apart into her billion separate molecules and floated away through the air.

I exhale and close my eyes to try and lock in the vision that I have been given. I see Coyote through the smoke. Sleek and still. Simply Coyote. Always Coyote. She moves through the impetuous night without stumbling or faltering, following the scent of her ancestors. She knows the secret name of the wind and the moon and the trees. She listens to their lessons. Coyote doesn't know self-doubt, doesn't wonder about direction. No future, no past, no mistaken identity. She lives on the peak of the electric moment and knows only the time that sparks along her synapses. The world turns and the seasons themselves whisper into her velvet ears, anoint her with blessings while the songs of the first Coyote resonate through her bones. She is never more, never less, than Coyote.

The vision begins to fade and shift. The eyes change. The fur darkens and shimmers. The shape softens and becomes less angular, until I can see Agnes watching me through the grey curtain of smoke. Agnes watching me with the eyes of the night.

TWELVE

The hospital looked too big for the town. Three storeys of brick and rectangular glass, square and squat and mean. Back in Red Clay, when Agnes and I used to listen to the radio, we heard the occasional announcement concerning this place, a perfunctory notice giving someone's name, usually someone from the reserve, reporting that they had been released from hospital. Agnes had explained to me that people often didn't have phone service nor the resources to stay in town or get in to the hospital every day. It was sensible, I suppose, but it always seemed cold to me. Merciless. I imagined the person, frail and alone in the lobby, while their name went out over the airwaves in the hope that someone who knew them would hear and come.

There were two RCMP cruisers in the parking lot. Side by side, they seemed overly official with their markings and numbers and two-tone paint jobs. I followed Agnes, trying to keep up as she ran in through the double doors and down the hallways. Corner after corner, then the long corridors past room after room. I felt dizzy and disoriented.

First we went to Emergency, but they directed us upstairs. Agnes trembled in the elevator, her face blank under her dark glasses. I glanced at her from time to time and stayed in the opposite corner, clinging to the silver railings for support.

As soon as the doors opened we knew it was very bad. The hall was lined with people from the reserve, some sitting, some leaning against the walls. Two police officers stood in the middle of it all, tall and dark like giant crows, their beaked caps held under their arms as they talked to a doctor and scribbled notes.

We stepped off the elevator and the hallway seemed to pulse more brightly. The fluorescent lights grew more intense, the pale walls shifting to curtains of pure light. I pinched my thumb and forefinger into my eyes till I was squeezing the bridge of my nose.

Agnes moved stiffly beside me, very straight, the way kids move when they're trading punches, pounding each other's shoulders to see who will flinch first. Someone called her name in a kind of cry. A plea. Agnes' Aunt Eleanor was floating towards us out of the iridescent haze. Tears were streaming down her face and her eyes were rimmed with red. She clutched a big wad of kleenex in her right hand and her purse bounced noisily against her ample hip. Agnes didn't raise her arms or open her mouth or relax. She stood her ground, waiting for the blow.

"Agnes. It's bad." Aunt Eleanor had Agnes by the elbows and was shaking her as she spoke, her fat purse caught on her wrist, swinging back and forth. "They're dead, Agnes. Them crazy kids broke into the school. They drank photocopy fluid or somethin'."

"Who?" Agnes said.

"Why would they do that, Aggie? Why would they drink that stuff?" Aunt Eleanor was staring into the black reflective pools of Agnes' sunglasses, alternating from one to the other, looking for the human eyes behind them.

"Who?"

Aunt Eleanor looked around for help, and a few of the other women stood up from their chairs and pulled away from the gleaming walls. They shuffled towards us down the hall.

"Who?"

Eleanor turned back to Agnes. "Ray and Tony Bad Eagle." Agnes took a sharp sudden breath. "Martin First Rider. Ramona Dancer." Agnes took a half step backwards. The women who had gathered around began to moan and weep with the sound of the names.

"Jamie, the one they call Big Mouth."

Agnes teetered, her arm reaching out for support. "Jamie..." she repeated.

Somehow I knew what was coming, in the way Agnes saw it coming. Out of the glaring white chemical mystery behind the double doors, like a bolt screaming down the pristine corridor. Flashing past the white walls and the people gathered in their little clutches of sorrow, straight into her forehead, knocking her back, drilling into her brain, her sunglasses flying from her face, her eyes rolling back into her head.

"Your son, Joseph, Aggie. Your sweet boy."

She fell and the women caught her and they collapsed together and wailed over her. Cried out in their pain and in hers. Her mouth working but unable to utter any sound.

I heard the words and it was as if the light or some other force propelled me back into the elevator. Spun me around. The floor dropped beneath me and I fell to one knee, everything spinning around me. The doors chimed and opened. I stumbled out. Weaved erratically through the geometric halls till I found an exit. The sky was grey and the wind blew in gusts, rattling the tree branches. I thought of Paguck in the story Henry had told me that first night. The Bone Man, caught in a tree, his skeleton flopping and clattering among the limbs. Sorrow and Death snagged on its battered rib cage, waving like tattered white flags.

I sat in the car outside the hospital, my head reeling. I kept seeing Joseph curled in Agnes's bed and wondered why it hadn't clicked that he was her son. There was no reason it should have, but in situations like that you always feel as though you were a bit slow. I wondered if Joseph had known or if he died believing his mother was his sister. I couldn't believe a thing like that would be kept a secret in a small place like Red Clay. She must have had him when she was very young.

I thought of Jamie, too, passed out on Henry's floor, killing himself by degrees with whatever he could get his hands on. Kids that never had a chance. There was so much I didn't understand, it filled my head with a thick and heavy presence. Even living there with Henry and with Agnes I had been outside of it all.

I puzzled over the same questions. Turning the names of the dead over and over in my head. Trying to recall something I might have seen in their young faces that led to all of this pain. People came and went, in and out of the double doors. They stood around out front, smoking and shaking their heads. I sat and waited, re-living the last twenty-four hours again and again.

I wasn't aware of Agnes until the car door opened. She got in on the passenger side looking tired and wrung out.

"Hi," I said.

"Hi," she said, expressionless, staring out through the windshield, me watching her as she watched the parking lot, waving a couple of times to others walking past, looking as beaten and weary as she.

"I didn't think I could ever leave. They let me see him. It was as though he were only..." she wept, choking.

"Do you want to go home?" I asked.

She shook her head, "No. Not now. Not yet. I have to come in tomorrow to make arrangements. It might be a while. They have to do autopsies and toxicology tests in Edmonton." Her throat caught and her voice came out high and strained. "I can't stand to be around everyone right now. I'm sorry." She fell over against my shoulder and I held her in my arms. "I'm sorry," she said again.

She wept, then stopped abruptly, as though suddenly running out of tears. She pulled herself away from me and sat against the door looking out the side window.

"Look," I said. "You don't want to go back, we'll find a room and stay in town. First let's get something to eat. Okay?"

"Okay," she agreed. "Go to the China Garden so we can get a booth."

Quite a few people from Red Clay were already there. Agnes walked past them swiftly, nodding her head at those she knew, and swung into a booth, sliding across the seat until she was tight against the wall. I sat across from her.

"I just want coffee," she said, putting her dark glasses on again. The right lens had a deep scratch across one corner. I ordered the number two special and two coffees.

We avoided each other. I was filled with an awful foreboding and I was nervously trying to find some way to comfort Agnes and draw us back together.

"I guess Joseph and I had something in common," I said. I don't know why. The thought occurred to me and without considering I'd let it slip from my lips. She tensed as though an electric shock had gone through her.

"What do you mean?" there was a tremolo of anger in her voice.

"Nothing, Agnes. I just meant... You know..." I tried to smile but couldn't.

"You think I'm like your mother? You think I'm some drunk who deserted her child?" Her voice grew loud and her hands began to shake uncontrollably.

"No," I stammered, trying desperately to think of some way to take it back.

"Was your mother raped by her stepfather? Was she beaten? Did her entire family burn to death while she was away, trying to make a better life for herself?" The vehemence rose in her, slithering along the muscles in her throat, up over her face, so that every nerve ending twitched and jumped. Her eyes flared with irrepressible fury, her body trembled, and her hands gripped the edge of the table. There was a loud snap as the tip of one long fingernail broke away and tumbled through the air. "You don't know anything about me, Childforever. You don't know anything about your mother."

I reached for her hand but she pulled it away. "Agnes," I pleaded. "I'm sorry."

She calmed instantly. An unnatural shift. The tension dropped away from her and it was like an exorcism. Something possessed her, rippled along her vertebrae, coiled under her skin, then it was gone. She snatched up her bag and slid out of the booth. "I'm going to the bathroom." She turned and started for the ladies' room. She leaned into an empty booth and picked up something from among the dirty dishes, then she walked briskly to the sign indicating the washrooms.

She was gone a long time. The waitress brought my combination plate but I couldn't eat. I pushed the food away and was about to go and see if Agnes was still in the bathroom when she came out. She had her dark glasses off and her hands were shoved into her jacket pockets. She had long arcs painted over her eyes in eyebrow pencil, a thick dark line that ran from one cheekbone up over one eyebrow across her forehead, over the other eyebrow, curled around the corner of her eye and down to her other cheekbone.

She sat down heavily across from me. The place seemed deadly still.

"Agnes. What are you doing?"

"You really don't understand, do you?"

"Agnes. You're not thinking straight right now." I was desperate, reaching out to her across the table. I couldn't help staring at the dense, ominous line around her eyes. It looked primitive and fierce, a rash hieroglyph of impending disaster.

"Crazy Indian. Is that it, Childforever? Maybe the firewater is still in my head." Her eyes were blazing, her body taut, her arms held tightly against her sides, hands hidden under the table. She leaned towards me. "You don't drive onto a reserve and become an Indian, William Sawnet. It isn't a club you can join. Did you think I was part of the initiation? Part of the membership requirements?" Her hands flew up by her head, in mock quotation marks, the left sleeve soaked in blood, viscous red drops splattering onto the table top. "Did you ever, A, sleep with an Indian, or B, live with an old Indian and do charity work? Is there Indian blood running through your veins?" She pointed at me with her right hand, the wounded left going back under the table. "Let me guess. Your mother was an Indian princess, right?"

I grabbed her right wrist and held her close to the table, then reached across and pulled her left hand up to where I could see it. Agnes didn't resist. Her arm flopped onto the arborite surface like a dead fish. It was bloody to the elbow. A wad of toilet paper had been wrapped around the wrist. It was saturated and darkly stained with blood. I tore it away and a puddle began to form on the table and run around the cups and under the plates. Blood oozed steadily from a ragged gash in her wrist. She jerked her arm back.

"I felt like bleeding. Did you ever just feel like bleeding?"

She began to pull napkins from the bright silver container and wrap them around her wrist. Numb, I saw my own distorted, horrified reflection on the side of the dispenser.

"Agnes, what are you doing?" It was like a dream. The noise of the restaurant. The crimson blots staining the table. The serpentine mandala on her sagging face.

There were only a few napkins left. "Shit." She looked around the busy dining room. "Waitress," she yelled. "Waitress, we need more napkins." She turned to me. "I should have been there, you know. Every time I leave that goddamn place somebody gets killed. I should've been there right from the start for Joseph. Not off gettin' drunk. You want to know something funny?" She reached across the table with surprising speed and dexterity and ripped the chain from my neck, her broken nail digging a ragged furrow along my collarbone. "This crucifix that Henry gave you? They handed those out at every confirmation." She looked at me with disgust. "Everybody has one from the old days. Henry never knew your mother. He's just a lonely old man who needed someone to cut his wood. Did you really think the first reserve you drove onto you'd find a relation? Your mother could have been from anywhere. She was probably Métis or a halfbreed herself. Don't you know in the city we're all ignorant wagon burners from up north? Don't you know that back then they'd use any excuse to take a native kid away? Any way to fill an adoption? Hell, kids were sent all over North America. A fair-skin like you would have been a hot item. It's all been lies, Childforever. All our lives it's all been lies." She twisted around again like someone drugged, fighting to hold onto awareness. "Waitress! Fuck."

I tried to grab her arm again, my sleeve smearing through the blood congealing on the table. She pulled away and the crucifix flew across the dining room and clattered along the polished floor. A void opened under my feet and I was sliding in. "Agnes," I said. "You need help."

She laughed hysterically as the waitress appeared to see what the problem was. She took one look at the blood dripping from the table and screamed. "Mr. Lem," she called out. "Mr. Lem." Immediately people swivelled around on their stools and stood up in their booths. The manager came flying out of nowhere, surveyed the situation, and began shouting. "Restaurant close now. Everybody go. Restaurant close now."

There was stunned silence. People milled around, trying to see what was going on. The waitress and the manager stood staring at us. Agnes stared back.

"Could I get some more napkins, please?" she held up her bloody arm for emphasis and the waitress fainted. There were gasps and cries of surprise from all over the room.

The manager glared, stone-faced. I stood up and reached over the back of the booth and asked to borrow the napkin dispenser from the table behind us. One of the older men from the reserve, there with his family, looked at me with his mouth gaping and then handed me the silver box. I gave it to Agnes.

The manager was going from table to table, ushering people out, escorting them to the door. "You go now. Never mind bill. Restaurant close. You go now." He kept saying it over and over like a litany of protection. I think he was worried a full-scale riot was about to break out.

Agnes was trembling and refused to meet my eyes. "Agnes, let me take you to the hospital."

"I don't want you to take me anywhere." Her voice was cold and distant.

Mr. Lem was locking the door. We were the only ones left besides staff. Mr. Lem signalled to them as though calling his team in for a huddle, and they all gathered around the front of our booth.

"You go now. I called police."

Agnes folded her arms on the table, her slit wrist freshly wrapped in napkins, and rested her head on top of them.

I stood again. "Call a fuckin' ambulance," I screamed. A frenzy was building inside me over my own helplessness. Things had gone so bad.

Mr. Lem tugged on my sleeve as though I was somehow contaminated. "You go now." I knocked his hand away and several kitchen workers surged toward me. They grabbed my arms and pulled me out of the booth. I resisted and someone clouted me in the ear.

"Agnes!" I called out, my voice breaking, but she didn't move or answer. "Agnes, please." I fell to my knees and was kicked in the stomach.

Agnes raised her head, slowly, with great effort. "Just go, Childforever. Leave me alone."

I couldn't resist any more. They dragged me to the door. The front window was crowded with dark faces peering in between cupped hands. Angry young men were rattling the door from the outside. Mr. Lem pulled me in front of the door and a current of fury could be seen rippling through the crowd outside. He waved his hand and as if by magic they ebbed away. He turned the lock, opened up just enough, and pushed me outside. A mob was congregating in a semi-circle around me. Someone pushed through and stood directly in front of me. It was Danny Elkhorn.

"Danny..." I didn't know where to start. He cut me off.

"What's goin' on?" he asked, without taking his eyes off me. "This guy stabbed Agnes," a voice called out.

Danny gripped me by the lapels. "I knew you were nothin' but trouble, you bastard." He swung hard and I fell back against the door of the Chinese place. The crowd rushed forward and was on me.

The cops questioned me in Emergency, shaking their heads and muttering private jokes through the whole thing. They had arrived in time to save me from a real beating. The mob had been convinced that I had stabbed her and would probably have beaten me to a bloody pulp if they'd had the time to get organized. As it was, most of the blows had landed on my back and legs when I'd sprawled among them and then instinctively curled up.

I wouldn't tell the police who had delivered the first punch, and once they had established that I hadn't knifed Agnes, there were no charges to be laid anywhere. The cops sighed and lectured and then shambled away. I found out from a nurse that Agnes was all right, sedated and sleeping. She'd cut herself with a steak knife and though it was a nasty gash, it had never been life threatening. There would probably be a psychological evaluation done. No. Agnes definitely didn't want to see me.

I walked out of the hospital for the second time that day. It was dark. I began to walk towards downtown, to where my car was parked near the restaurant. I turned and looked at all the lighted windows of the three-storey building. I thought of Agnes in her drugged sleep somewhere in there, the body of her son lying in a dark vault a few floors below.

Maybe that was all she wanted, to be close to him that night in whatever way she could. Maybe I had to be pushed out of the way.

I walked slowly through the quiet residential streets, hands in my pockets, my body stiffening, my bruised face pulsing, the tears coming like condensation out of the evening air, filling my eyes and rolling down over my aching cheeks. Even the mediocre houses with their soft yellow lights seemed hostile. I was the alien. The outsider. I wanted to be somewhere else. I didn't know where. Somewhere familiar, warm and accepting. Somewhere far away. I didn't want to see Henry or Agnes again. I didn't want to travel that rough brutal road to Red Clay. My time there was a jumbled haphazard mystery. A collection of jigsaw pieces from several different puzzles stirred in the same box. A universe of creatures and beings I could never understand. A conundrum of assorted buildings and sorrows I would never get to know. A territory between the oblique landscape of trees for which I had no map or compass. A broken and hidden history. A legacy of lies and mistrust I knew nothing about. Different stars burned inside their blood. They knew different names for the wind and the increments of the turning earth which had formed from the dust of their ancestors.

The night became too immense. A huge shadow on the face of the moon. It filled me with a pulsing, urgent terror. I wanted to leave the recent past where it was, unseen and forgotten under the ancient dark. I wanted to scrape the memory of it from my skin, purge the taste of it from my tongue. Some seed of it was uncoiling under my flesh and taking root at the back of my brain. I started running. Something separate in the darkness began to pursue me. I could hear it giving chase and I was too afraid to turn around and look. Too afraid to face whatever it was that had pulled itself out of the darkness, levered itself out of the black confusion in my brain. I had the feeling it was something I knew, something I had just now recognized but didn't have the courage to stop and find out. I ran. Heart pounding like a drum, I ran all the way to the car.

The night has overtaken me. Where I am now isn't important.

I wake by the dead fire and I can find no evidence of Coyote having been there. The sun is high and the entire world is green around me. I rub my face and smile; the dried mud caked there crumbles away under my fingers like the remains of an old discarded skin.

I wander back to the creek and walk in, up to my knees. The cold grip of the water on my calves feels good. Vital, somehow. I bend and splash it up over my face and around the back of my neck, washing away the wet earth that has protected me. I can hear the traffic whizzing by on the highway. It is another language, crude and guttural. I follow the sound out of the woods, weaving back and forth through the trees until I emerge only thirty metres up the highway from my car.

It looks forlorn and deserted, ridiculous, sitting driverless and half-hidden in the ditch. I turn my back to it. It is a useless part of the places I've been.

I thought I'd arrived somewhere. I'd settled on a time and a place and a name and I'd pulled in all the round white stones we give purpose to and use to build walls around ourselves. Then a stone had rolled free and everything started to crumble. An avalanche caved in around me. Still, I tried to be places. Here, I was one person. There, I was someone else. In between I was no one.

I cross the highway. I am clean and fresh. I am thinking of her, of how we were our own little tribe. Of how much she means to me. It had nothing to do with my broken past. With the entombed memory of my mother. With all that has been lost or stolen from me. From us. We all must deal separately with our own blood. With the chemistry of our own lives. Even Agnes, living in the womb of her people, failed to see this. Maybe now she will. Maybe we will gather stones together.

All I have is the unknown, the unknown past and the unknowable future, and it is okay. This is what I have been running from all along, clinging to the fragments of what I believed to be true. No one had lied to me. Not Henry or

Agnes or even Mona. They simply hadn't interfered with the lies I was telling myself.

I turn to face the oncoming traffic and raise my thumb. Extend it to the west. Towards Agnes. Towards where I want to be, what I want to be my best chance. I have been to this place on the circle before, but I have learned much since then. I will travel the full circle back and find Agnes again.

This is my journey.

Where I am now isn't important.